The Advocate's Geocache

Teresa Burrell

Silent Thunder Publishing
San Diego

THE ADVOCATE'S GEOCACHE
Copyright 2015 by
Teresa Burrell

All rights reserved.
Cover Art by Zack Settle
Edited by Marilee Wood

Library of Congress Number: 2015906117
ISBN: 978-1-938680-16-8

Silent Thunder Publishing
San Diego

Dedication

This one is just for you, Marilee Wood,
my editor, my friend.

Acknowledgements

I want to thank the following people for providing me with much-needed information to make my facts and descriptions ring true:

Attorney Bob Pullman
Chris Broesel
Shane Klakken
Philip Fleischman, MD

Thanks to my Beta Reader team who is so good at finding errors and making me look good.

Linda Athridge-Langille
Vickie Barrier
Marilyn Burgner
Teresa Higgins
Lily Qualls Morales
Rodger Peabody
Colleen Scott
Heather Siani
Jodi Thomas
Nikki Tomlin
Brad Williams
Stephen Connell

A special thanks goes to **Charles and Shellie Settle** for taking me geocaching and inspiring me to write a novel about it.

And to **Ron and Kim Vincent** for helping me develop this twisted idea for a plot.

THE ADVOCATE SERIES

THE ADVOCATE
(Book 1)

THE ADVOCATE'S BETRAYAL
(Book 2)

THE ADVOCATE'S CONVICTION
(Book 3)

THE ADVOCATE'S DILEMMA
(Book 4)

THE ADVOCATE'S EX PARTE
(Book 5)

THE ADVOCATE'S FELONY
(Book 6)

THE ADVOCATE'S GEOCACHE
(Book 7)

Chapter 1

"**I** found it," Attorney Sabre Brown called out with the excitement of a child. Sabre stood, looking up into a tree, about two miles off of I-15 near Escondido, California.

Sabre's private investigator, JP Torn, meandered toward her, less than enthused about the process. He passed a man in a baseball cap who was walking in his direction. "Hello," JP said.

"Hello," the man said without raising his head.

JP had yet to understand Sabre's interest in geocaching, but agreed to accompany her this one time. He didn't understand the fun in looking up GPS coordinates online and then chasing them down only to find some little container with a trinket in it. Maybe he would have enjoyed it when he was nine or ten years old, but he would be fifty soon. He'd rather be at the shooting range or home watching a football game, but Sabre loved geocaching. To her, it was a treasure hunt and a good distraction from her juvenile court practice. And last weekend, Sabre had sat through an entire afternoon of football with him in spite of her lack of interest in the sport. It seemed only fair that he put some effort into sharing her interests.

JP reached the spot where Sabre was standing. He couldn't hold back a smile when he saw the look on Sabre's face. He loved her passion about everything she did in life. And she looked so beautiful. Her light brown hair lay in a French braid that stopped about six inches below the nape of her neck. It took all his self-control to keep from leaning down and kissing that gorgeous neck.

"Look, it's right there." She pointed up into a tree.

"Where? I don't see it." JP pushed his black cowboy hat back on his head as he looked up into the tree.

"Right there between those branches." She pointed to a grayish-brown tube nearly the same color as the bark of the eucalyptus tree. It was crammed in a pocket where a branch extended out from the tree.

Before JP could find the exact spot where the treasure was planted, Sabre grabbed hold of a branch, swung her leg up and over it, boosted herself up, and stood on the branch. From there she could reach the cylinder.

"Where did you learn to climb like that?"

"My brother, Ron, and his friends used to hide from me when we were kids. We had a huge oak tree in the backyard, where he built a fort. He didn't make stairs for it because he thought that would keep me out."

"Apparently it didn't work."

"It did for a while, but then I learned to climb the tree and sneak up there when he wasn't around and mess with his stuff."

JP shook his head. "Some things never change."

"What do you mean?"

"You still hang in there like a hair in a biscuit."

Sabre smiled at his remark, pried the treasure box loose, and sat down on the branch. Her legs swung slightly as she popped the plastic end off the cardboard cylinder. A rolled-up sheet of paper with blue trim was tucked inside of the tube. She attempted to remove it, but it caught on the edge. Sabre moistened her fingertip, reached inside, and twisted the paper around so it would tighten into a smaller roll. Then she pulled it out and unrolled it, but as she read the document her face drained of all color.

"Sabre, what is it?"

She peered down at JP with a curious look. "It's a death certificate. That's creepy."

JP reached his arms up toward her. "Come on down."

Sabre leaned forward into his arms and JP lowered her. He could feel her slender body quiver as he planted her feet on the ground. He kept his arm around her as she looked again at the paper.

"It looks official and like an original, not a copy," Sabre said.

"Why would someone put a death certificate in a geocache?" JP asked. "Is that normal?"

"No, this is really strange."

JP saw the look of concern on Sabre's face and said, "Maybe someone thought it would be a good way to honor their loved one. I find it pretty bizarre, but people do strange things when they're grieving. What's the name of the deceased?"

"It's for a man named Monroe. There's no last name, or maybe that's the last name and there's no first name."

"It sounds like it's somebody's idea of a sick joke— probably an April Fools' Day joke. That was only a couple of days ago." JP shrugged. "When did he die?"

Sabre glanced back at the document. She looked up. Her eyebrows furrowed. "He hasn't yet. The date of death is April fourteenth, one week from today. And the cause of death is 'Murder by Poison.'"

Chapter 2

Deputy Sheriff Ernest Madrigal led Sabre and JP into his office. They sat down, and Ernie put on a pair of latex gloves. Sabre handed him a plastic bag with the cylinder.

"I hope I haven't contaminated the evidence too badly. JP never touched it, and as soon as we realized it had a future date on it, I stopped handling it. I did take a photo of it before I put it back inside the tube."

"It's probably just a prank, but we'll check it out." Ernie looked at JP. "Explain to me how this geocaching thing works."

"This was my first time," JP said. "Sabre can tell you."

"It's like a modern-day treasure hunt. There's a site online where you can go and see where the caches are hidden. You sign in, enter the zip code for the area you want to go to, and a map comes up with all the spots where caches are hidden. You can click on one, and it will give you GPS coordinates. Then you drive to the spot and try to find it."

"And the cache is in plain sight?"

"It's usually hidden, like behind a rock or something."

"And then you get to keep whatever is inside?"

"Not exactly. You have some choices. You can just sign the log and leave, or you can take something from the box. If you do, you're supposed to leave something of equal value."

"Where's the log for this one?"

"There wasn't one," Sabre said.

"That's interesting." Ernie rubbed his goatee. "Is there always a log?"

"Every cache I've ever seen had one. That's part of the game. But in all fairness, I haven't been at this very long."

"Does either of you happen to know the person on the certificate? Anyone with the first or last name of Monroe?"

"No," Sabre and JP both responded at the same time.

"I'm guessing he doesn't exist," Madrigal said, as he removed the tube from the baggie, opened it, and looked inside. He slid the paper out, peeked inside for the log, and then tapped the open end of the tube on his desk. Finding the tube empty, he placed it back inside the bag and then unrolled the certificate.

"You can tell it hasn't been in there very long," JP said, "because the tube opens up so easily."

"That's what I was thinking," Madrigal said. "The certificate's a good counterfeit right down to the county seal. You can do just about anything on the computer these days, but that seal bothers me."

"It could be a real death certificate, and just the date and name were altered," JP said.

"Regardless," Sabre said, "the cause of death is suspicious: 'Murder by Poison.' And did you see the line under the cause of death?"

Ernie looked at the death certificate again. "It says, 'As a consequence of ingesting Prozac.'" He furrowed his brow. "What does that even mean?"

"That sounds more like an overdose than poison," Sabre said. "But I guess that line could've been altered too."

"I appreciate your looking into this, Ernie," JP said to his friend of more than twenty-five years. He and Ernie had met in the Sheriff's Academy and then worked together on the force for several years. They remained close friends, even after JP left the department and became a private investigator. Ernie continued to help JP whenever he needed it. He was JP's go-to guy when he needed something on one of his own cases.

"I can't really do much at this point," Ernie said. "As far as I can tell, no crime has been committed, at least not yet, but I'll check the document for prints and run the name through the database—although with just one name, that's really a waste of time. I'll tag it and keep the chain of evidence, just in case. In the meantime, if you're curious enough, you can check to see if you can find any Monroes with a death certificate on file at the clerk's office."

"I'll do that," JP said, and then inquired about Ernie's family.

"All is good," Ernie said. "I miss my son, but he's loving college life and had a great football season. He wants to play baseball too, but I think it's just too much. My daughter is a junior this year, and she's a pistol." He shook his head. "Boys are a lot easier to raise than girls. I worry about her all the time."

"Tell Nancy hello for me," JP said. "The four of us need to get together soon."

Ernie looked from Sabre to JP. "Are you two finally a couple?"

"Yes," JP muttered, as he stood to leave.

"'Bout time."

***

JP and Sabre pulled up to Sabre's condo. She would've jumped out and gone in by herself, but JP always insisted on walking her to her door. He said his mother taught him better manners than that. It took all her effort to get him to stop opening the car door for her. She had let him know, in no uncertain terms, that she was perfectly capable of opening her own door, but that never stopped him.

He walked her to the door of her condo, kissed her, and said, "I'll pick you up at seven."

"See you then," Sabre said and went inside. It was approximately three o'clock in the afternoon, so JP hadn't gone inside to check her house. If they came home late and he wasn't spending the night, he would take a quick look around the house to make sure no one was lurking there and nothing looked suspicious. Sabre appreciated his concern to protect her, especially after the stalker and the last boyfriend she'd had, but it was taking some time getting used to it.

Sabre had been practicing law for just over seven years. Recently her friend Jennifer Ross had introduced her to geocaching, and up until today, it had been a nice distraction from her work. This latest adventure, however, didn't feel much different than working a case. It was probably nothing, but she knew JP wouldn't let it go without a preliminary investigation, just in case it somehow put her in danger. And she kind of liked the idea of solving the mystery.

Sabre had several hours before she needed to start getting ready for her date. That gave her plenty of time to prepare her cases for court on Monday. She had several new cases with which she had to familiarize herself. She sat down at her desk, picked up the first file, and began to read her own notes: *Baby Girl Lewis born positive tox. Mother a hooker. Baby removed at hospital. Mother showed up for only one hearing so far.* Sabre surmised that the mother only came then because she was in custody in Las Colinas Detention Facility, and her attorney had her produced for the hearing. She likely only showed up then because it meant a few hours away from jail, but it was just enough to contest the allegations and prolong the process, thereby keeping the baby from a permanent placement.

The second file was the McFerran case. Twice she had been to see the McFerran children, and she had an appointment to see them again tomorrow. The two older boys—Conway Twitty McFerran and Trace Adkins McFerran—were in a foster home in Lakeside. The three girls—Dolly Parton McFerran, Reba McEntire McFerran, and Taylor Swift McFerran—were in another home in the neighboring town of El Cajon. Sabre had fought to keep them living as closely together as she could so they could continue to have contact with one another.

The mother, Brandy McFerran, was born and raised in Nashville and was a big country music fan. She fancied herself to be a "singer who never got a break." Brandy never married because she was always "pursuing her career," but she found herself pregnant at fifteen, at seventeen, and again at eighteen—all by different fathers and all of whom were abusive. Two years later, she gave birth to Reba and then Taylor, who shared the same father. When the youngest, Taylor, was four years old, Brandy and the children moved to California so she could become a film star. After a couple of unsuccessful years in Hollywood, she moved to San Diego with a new and abusive, live-in boyfriend.

But neither domestic violence nor abuse were the basis for the petition, in spite of all the years they occurred in that household. Instead, it was neglect, and it was difficult to pinpoint. But the squalor in which they were living was undeniable. There were no broken bones or bruises, and there was no malnutrition that could be empirically tested or examined and submitted to the court. However, when Sabre spoke with her clients, the children, she knew they could not return to that environment and live healthy lives without some major changes on behalf of the parent.

The mother was contesting the allegations, and her attorney, Bob Clark, who was Sabre's best friend, had more jurisdictional wins than anyone on the San Diego Superior Court, Juvenile Division dependency panel. Sabre knew this case wasn't going to be easy, even though these children had suffered years of neglect at the hands of their mother. Sabre was strategizing when the phone rang and interrupted her thoughts.

"Hi, Jenn."

"How was your geocaching adventure with JP this morning?"

Her friend and jogging partner, Jennifer Ross, was a real estate agent who had recently helped her with an investigation, and in doing so developed a taste for sleuthing. She was also the one who had introduced this new geocaching hobby to Sabre. They had been out a couple times a month since Sabre's induction into this new world of treasure hunting. Sabre loved puzzles, decoding things, and solving mysteries, and this was a fun way to do all of that. Besides, at the end of the hunt, there was a little surprise in the container— if you were lucky enough to find it. Today was more than she had bargained for. She explained to Jennifer what she had encountered.

"Cool! That's freaky but cool. I want to see it."

"A little too freaky. We took it to a friend of JP's who is a deputy sheriff. He's going to run it for prints to see if he can get any information on the 'soon-to-be-dead' guy. The sheriff thinks it's just a hoax, but just in case it isn't, he wanted to keep the evidence."

"Dang."

"I took some photos of the death certificate. I can text you those."

"Good. What can I do to help figure out who this 'soon-to-be-dead' guy is?"

"JP and the cops are looking into it. There's nothing for us to do."

"Okay, but can you go geocaching tomorrow morning for a few hours? I haven't been out in weeks, and since your trip today was interrupted, you should go with me."

"I have to go see some minors on a case tomorrow at nine, but I can go after that. How about one o'clock?"

"That would be great."

"Where do you want to go?" Sabre asked.

"It's your turn to pick."

"Okay, I'll go online and get some coordinates. I'll text you where we should meet, and you can pick some coordinates near there too."

"And JP won't mind if you go without him?"

"Are you kidding me? He was very gracious, but I think he hated every minute of it. We're going to dinner tonight, but he's not staying because he has to drive to Newport Beach first thing in the morning for a case. He'll be gone most of the day."

"See you tomorrow," Jennifer said. "By the way, did you read the log in the cache?"

"There wasn't one."

"What about the online log?"

"I forgot about that. Let me check." Sabre hit the speaker button on her cell phone and laid it on her desk. She opened up the geocache site on her computer and attempted to find the cache she had been to that morning. She typed in the number assigned to the site and the geocache popped up. "This is strange."

"What is it?"

"This isn't the same cache."

"Did you put in the wrong number?"

Sabre double-checked the geocache code. "No, it's right, but it's not the same geocache."

"Let me check," Jennifer said. "What's the number?"

"GC93682."

Sabre tried it one more time. "This one is a plastic container, not a tube."

"Didn't you know that when you were looking for the cache?"

"I don't remember. We had several caches we were looking for, and I didn't pay that much attention to what they were supposed to look like."

"This cache says it contains dice, paper money, colored chalk, tattoos, and a small puzzle. That's a far cry from what you found."

"That's for sure."

"Maybe you found the wrong cache," Jennifer said.

"Or maybe it wasn't a cache at all." Sabre sighed. "But why would someone stick a death certificate in a tube and put it in a tree?"

Chapter 3

Sabre drove onto the long dirt driveway that led to the house where the McFerran boys were temporarily detained. The spacious, ranch-style home was situated on three acres of land. A white fence in need of repair formed an empty horse corral. Off to the right was a barn adjacent to another fenced area that contained eight pigs.

Sabre spotted Conway leaning on the pigpen, talking to the animals. The tall, lanky teenager stopped talking when she walked up.

"Good morning," Sabre said.

"Mornin'," he said, without turning toward her.

Sabre looked at the pigs that were chomping and slurping at the trough. "Did you just feed them?"

"Yes. It was Trace's turn, but I let him sleep in a little."

"That was nice of you."

Conway shrugged. "I like the pigs. Our neighbor, old man Gerstner, had one in Tennessee. A potbelly. It lived in the house with him. We kinda grew up together—me and the pig. We played together all the time. The pig even let me ride him around the house."

"Does your friend still have him?"

"No, when Mr. Pig got older, he got kinda mean. He never hurt me, but he started biting the other kids. Trace has a scar on his leg from where he took a bite. At first he just bit kids, but the older he got, the meaner he got, and he started biting adults too, mostly strangers that came to the house. One day the local sheriff came by, and Mr. Pig grabbed his pant leg and yanked on it. The sheriff was kicking and scrambling to get away, but Mr. Pig held on tight, pulling him clear across the room and nearly knocking him down. That was pretty much the end of Mr. Pig."

Sabre chuckled at the thought. After a brief silence, Sabre asked, "Did you see your sisters yesterday?"

"Yes."

"How did the visit go?"

"Good. I wish they could live here with us. I worry about Taylor. She doesn't seem to be eating right."

"Why do you think that?"

"She looks thinner, and Reba says she doesn't eat much. And who's helping Dolly with her homework? Reba tries, but sometimes she doesn't know how to do it either. And I don't think Dolly is getting to go to church as much as she'd like. That's real important to her."

"I'm going to see them when I leave here, and I'll check on everything, Conway, but for now you need to try to quit worrying and take care of yourself." She smiled at him, but he didn't reciprocate. "How's school?"

"It's alright."

"I understand you made Honor Roll last year. Does school come easy for you?"

"Pretty much." He shrugged again. "Do you know when we'll be going back home?"

"I don't know. The judge will make that decision when we go to trial."

For the first time, he took his eyes off the pigs and turned toward Sabre. "Can you ask him to send me home? My mom needs me."

"What makes you think she needs your help?"

"She told me when I saw her yesterday. She said she's lonely without us. She kept crying."

Sabre's face turned red with frustration at this boy's mother for putting more pressure and responsibility on his shoulders. She knew from the records that Conway had been the "man of the house" since he was a small child.

"I'm sorry, Conway, but we'll have to wait and see. Your mom needs to get that house cleaned up, and there are some programs she has to attend."

"I could clean the house, and I could make sure she went to those programs if I was there."

"I know you could, but she needs to try and do these on her own."

"Can you get me my bike so I can ride it to work? My boss said I could have my job back if I can get there."

"Where were you working?"

"At the dairy here in Lakeside." He nodded his head to the right in the direction of the dairy.

"Couldn't you take the bus?"

"No, the bus doesn't go there, and I rode my bike before. It's only about three miles from here. It was twice that far from home, and I was doing that for nearly a year. I could walk it, but it takes so long and I have to go there pretty early in the morning."

"Let me see what I can do," Sabre said. "Is Trace still in bed?"

"No, I woke him up and told him to get up and take a shower before you got here."

"Thanks. Do you have any other questions before I go see Trace?"

Conway shook his head, and Sabre walked toward the house. The foster mother, Mary Peabody, greeted her at the door and took her to the bedroom Conway and Trace shared.

Trace was standing in front of a computer, deep into a game of *Call of Duty* when Sabre walked into the room.

"I have to limit the time on the computer and the

Xbox, or Trace would stay on it twenty-four seven." She spoke softly but sternly to Trace. "Pause the game and talk to your attorney."

Trace leaned to the side and back again as he made one last attempt to kill what looked like a zombie. Then he hit the "Pause" button and set the controller down.

"Thank you, Trace," the foster mother said. She pointed to a chair near a small desk. "Please have a seat, Ms. Brown. Let me know if you need anything," she said as she left the room.

Trace sat down on the twin bed closest to Sabre.

"How are things going here?" Sabre asked.

"Good, but I'd rather be home."

"I know. Are you getting along with your foster parents?"

"Mary is nice, and Rodger likes to tell stories about the Vietnam War. His stories are pretty interesting, but I still want to go home."

"I know you do, and we're working on that. Are you going to school every day?"

"I have to, but I hate it."

"Why's that?"

"It's boring."

More questions about school still didn't reveal anything more definitive, so Sabre broached the subject of the visit with his mother and sisters. All she could get from him was, "It was cool."

* * *

On the drive to see the McFerran girls, Sabre thought about what Conway had said. His concern for his younger siblings was more like that of a father than a teenage brother. He had grown up too quickly and had proven to be more responsible than his mother. He

15

deserved a chance to have a childhood, but Sabre knew it was too late. That ship had sailed. She would see what she could do about getting him his bike.

The two-story, four-bedroom, stucco tract home where the girls were detained was on a cul-de-sac situated among many other homes only yards apart. It was a new development with many unfinished front yards. This home was in one of the first sections built, so most of the homes on this block had grass.

Sabre met with all three girls together in the backyard. They sat on bamboo furniture near the fenced pool.

"Is everything going okay here?"

"Yeah," they all said, nodding.

"Are you all getting along with the foster parents?" Sabre asked.

"They're real nice people," Reba said. "I just wish my brothers were here too."

When neither of the other girls responded, Sabre looked at Dolly. "How about you? Are you doing okay?"

"Yes. It's so clean here. And we have a place to put all our stuff. And we all sit down to the table and eat together. I like it."

"Conway was concerned that you might not be getting to church. Is that an issue for you?"

"My foster mother, Mrs. Smith ... she says we can call her Elizabeth if we want, but it doesn't feel right to me," she said, getting sidetracked. "Anyway, she goes to my church, so she takes me. Everybody else stays home. I think we should all go, but Mrs. Smith says they have a right to choose or that my mother can choose for them. But Mom doesn't care. She never goes to church. I try to get her to, but she won't go."

Taylor commented on the visit with the boys, but she didn't mention her mother. Sabre noticed that none of them mentioned her, other than the comment Dolly made about church.

"Look what Conway brought me," Taylor said, lifting the light green stone in her necklace off her chest with her thumb. The stone was attached with a gold wire that wrapped around it and hung on a black leather cord. "He made it. It's my birthstone."

"That's pretty," Sabre said. "What month is it?"

"August. Conway said it's a peridot."

"He made us each one," Reba added, showing off her necklace. "My birthday is in January. It's a garnet."

Sabre looked at Dolly. Her light, rose-colored stone lay like a precious jewel on her neck. She had her mother's coloring with her blonde hair, blue eyes, and her peaches-and-cream complexion. Unlike her mother, Dolly's hair hung loosely and softly around her face. The soft curls fell nearly to her waist. She had no bangs, but each side was pinned back with a glittering bobby pin. All of the McFerran girls were beautiful, but Dolly was stunning, and she seemed to have no idea how gorgeous she was, which made her even more attractive. She looked the most like her mother, and Sabre imagined Brandy was pretty striking in her youth as well. Brandy was still a pretty woman, but life had taken a toll on her.

"October?" Sabre asked.

Dolly stroked her stone. "Yes."

"That's my birthday month too."

Dolly smiled.

"So did you girls have a nice visit with your mother?"

"I guess," Dolly said.

"Uh-huh," Taylor murmured.

"Sure," Reba said. "Trace told me about a new video game they have at his house. He says maybe I can come over and play with him. Nobody there is that good."

"We'll see what we can work out," Sabre said. "What else did you do with your family?"

"We were swimming most of the time. Conway even swam for a little while."

"Did your mother go swimming?"

"No, she didn't want to get her hair wet. She just had it done," Taylor said.

"She was on the phone most of the time anyway," Reba said with an edge in her tone. "I think she has a new boyfriend."

Chapter 4

Jennifer and Sabre parked in a small parking lot on Boyd Avenue and walked about two hundred feet toward the canyon.

"What does your GPS say?" Sabre asked.

"We have about twenty feet to go."

"Are you sure you have the right coordinates?" Sabre asked, as she ambled through the brush in Tecolote Canyon. She pushed back a bush and peered behind a rock about the size of a football, but found no container.

"Yes, I double-checked them."

"Stop!" Sabre said in a hushed but stern voice. "Did you hear that?"

Both women stood still and listened as the percussive sound emanated from the interlocking segments of keratin knocking together. Sabre's heart pounded.

"It's a rattler," Jennifer whispered, as she pointed just beyond where Sabre was standing.

"Move slowly," Sabre said, as she took a step away from the sound and toward the street. Jennifer followed suit. When Sabre had advanced about ten feet, she picked up her pace. She met up with Jennifer, who had just started to run. Jennifer stood 5'7" tall, about an inch taller than Sabre, but due to the length of her legs, her stride was much longer and the adrenalin had kicked in. Her dark and curly hair, cut just above her shoulders, bounced as she darted through the gully.

"Scared much?" Sabre teased when she reached her car, but she was just as out of breath and as frightened as Jennifer. She hit the button on the key fob, and they hopped in with Sabre behind the wheel.

"I hate snakes," Jennifer bellowed.

"They're not my favorite either." Sabre could still feel her heart racing in her chest. "I think I'll pass on this cache." She looked at her GPS. "There's one near the softball field. It's only a few blocks from here. Want to try that one?"

"Sure." Jennifer inhaled and released a long, deep breath.

Sabre drove up the hill and veered to her right until she reached the softball fields. She pulled into the parking lot against the traffic that was leaving. A girls' softball game had just finished, and parents were heading to their cars with girls about eight or nine years old. One team wore red uniforms. The other wore yellow. You could tell by their jovial behavior that the red team had won. Sabre and Jennifer waited in the car, visiting until most of the cars had left the parking lot.

The GPS led them toward the field. They walked toward the third base dugout on the field closest to the parking lot. The field had emptied except for one man and a teenage boy who were still gathering up equipment in the first base dugout, two young girls in yellow uniforms sitting in the bleachers, and a man in a baseball hat with his back to them standing near a small, black building with red trim where refreshments were sold during the games.

Sabre stepped inside the dugout. It was a metal fence structure covered with red slats. She looked around. The only thing in there was a metal bench, and there was nothing in or around it.

They moved closer to home plate toward the refreshment stand that butted up against the backstop on the field. The man who was there earlier was gone, and the two girls were walking toward the lot with the

20

man and the teenage boy from the first base dugout. No one else was around. Sabre looked up and spotted a plastic container toward the backside of the flat roof.

"I'll bet that's it," she said to Jennifer as she came around the corner of the building.

"You're getting good at this. I think you've found seven out of the last eight caches that we've looked for together."

"Beginner's luck."

"How are we going to get that? It's up too high."

"Just watch."

As soon as the last car left the lot, Sabre stepped over to where the building met the backstop and reached up and slipped her hands into the chain link fence. Raising her right foot up, she said, "Give me a boost."

"Really?" Jennifer said sarcastically.

"Yes, really. Come here."

Jennifer squatted down and cupped her hands so Sabre could step in them.

"Okay, push me up. I'll pull at the same time."

Jennifer raised her hands as she stood up from her squat, stumbling backwards and releasing Sabre's foot as she rose. Sabre held on tightly to the fence with both hands, her left leg flailing around as she tried to find a spot in the fence to rest her left foot. The tip of her tennis shoe barely fit into the opening. She swung her right foot up and stuck her other shoe into the chain link as well. Jennifer caught her balance and braced Sabre's butt with both hands.

"Are you okay?" Jennifer was laughing so hard she could barely get the words out.

Sabre started laughing too. "Yes, just hold on. I need to get a little bit higher, and I'll be able to reach it." She removed her left hand from the fence, stretched her arm up about ten more inches, and grasped the fence again. "I wish I had some gloves."

"Would you like me to run to Target?" Jennifer said between guffaws.

"Just hold on to me." Sabre moved upward with her right hand and then each foot. "I think I can get it from here."

Jennifer shuffled her feet to get better balance. "I hope so. I don't know how much longer I can hold on."

Sabre shifted her left hand toward the building and stretched her right arm out toward the plastic container, but it remained just out of reach.

"Did you get it? My arms are getting tired."

"No. I'm going to lie on the roof. We're going to shift to the right. Ready?"

"No, wait. If you go any higher, I'm not going to be able to brace you. Put your foot on my shoulder."

Sabre removed her right foot from the fence and tried to find Jennifer's shoulder, kicking her in the arm.

"If you keep kicking me, I'm going to let go. Move your foot up a little higher."

They both started laughing again.

"Don't make me laugh," Sabre said and moved her foot up, brushing against Jennifer's arm until she found her shoulder and planted her foot. Then she moved her hands along the fence as close as she could to the building. "Okay, shift to the right."

Jennifer turned. Sabre let go with her right hand and lowered her upper body onto the roof. From there she could easily grab the container. "I got it!"

"Good. Now, how are you going to get down?" Jennifer started toward the car, laughing as she walked away.

"Get back here," Sabre yelled as she stretched out her left leg, reaching her foot toward the fence to find a place to brace herself.

Jennifer walked back, reached up, and guided

Sabre's left foot toward the fence. "Toss me the cache so you have both hands free, and I'll help you down."

Sabre did what she asked.

Jennifer caught the cache and laid it on the ground near her. Then she placed Sabre's right foot on her shoulder, and from there Sabre was able to grab the fence and work her way down.

"Open it. Let's see what we have."

Jennifer opened the small container. It held a single piece of paper rolled up with a rubber band around it. "It must be just a log sheet."

"That's disappointing," Sabre said, as she retrieved something from her pocket. She held it up. "And I have this cool green frog to exchange. I bought it at Target yesterday after you told me the green frog is a geocache symbol."

"Save it for the next one."

Jennifer unrolled the scroll. Her eyebrows furrowed. "It's not a log."

"What is it?"

"It's a note."

Jennifer turned the paper so Sabre could see.

Sabre read it aloud. *Each cache is a clue to the next. You must examine each one more carefully.*

"That's strange," Jennifer said. "It's like a geocache fortune cookie."

"I don't like it," Sabre said, looking around to see if anyone was still at the park, but she saw no one.

Chapter 5

The sun was setting as Sabre jogged along the boardwalk. She stopped to watch for a green flash as the sun dropped into the ocean, but none came. She had seen two in the last month, which was unusual since she had only seen two others in her lifetime. She wondered if the atmosphere had changed and if she could expect to see them more often. The idea excited yet disappointed her. They were fun to see, but they wouldn't be as special if they came too often. She finished her jog and went home.

Once inside her condo, Sabre took a shower, fixed herself a cup of tea, and sat down to review her cases for the next morning's hearings. But the geocache message she had received earlier puzzled her: *Each cache is a clue to the next. You must examine each one more carefully.* It was as if someone were leaving her a message.

She shook it off and thought, *It's just as Jennifer said.* "*It's like a geocache fortune cookie.*" They are written so the reader thinks it's just for him or her.

When she finished perusing her files, she picked up her iPad and looked at the photo of the death certificate she and JP had found. She could see it better on the larger screen. She had just begun to re-examine it when her doorbell rang.

She peeked through her peephole and then opened the door.

"What a nice surprise," Sabre said to JP. "Come in."

"Hi, kid." He kissed her lightly. "I hope you don't mind that I stopped by. I was on my way home from Orange County. I would've called, but my phone went dead."

"You really ought to get a car charger."

"Hey, I'm new at this rodeo. I just got a smartphone. One step at a time."

"It's not rocket science. You plug in one end to the cigarette lighter and the other into your phone."

He shook his head.

"Can I get you something to drink?"

"I'd like a cold beer, but I'll wait until I get home. Are you busy?"

"I should be working on my cases for tomorrow, but I got sidetracked. Come sit for a minute. I was just looking at the cache I found today."

"What! You went geocaching without me?" JP said in an exaggerated tone.

"Like you really wanted to go. I know you hated it yesterday, but I appreciate your giving it a shot."

"Hey, kid, I haven't had that much fun since the hogs ate my little brother." JP's voice got softer. "I would go anywhere with you—even geocaching."

"You don't have to. Jennifer and I do just fine by ourselves. There are plenty of other things you and I can do together."

"I can think of a few."

Sabre smiled and then kissed him.

"Yup, that was one of them." He winked at her. "So show me what you found in the cache today."

Sabre showed him the photo of the note on her iPad.

"I don't get it," JP said.

"I don't either, really, but Jennifer told me there are some caches that are like a treasure hunt, with one giving a clue to the next."

"You think that's what it is?"

"It's not marked that way. The website should indicate that, but someone probably just mixed it up or something. I'll show you what it looks like online. I need to log it, anyway." Sabre brought up www.geocaching.com, signed in, and entered the code for the cache they had been to earlier that day: GC8E999. The page directed to the cache she had brought up earlier. The coordinates were correct, but when she read the description for the cache, it was not the same as the one she had found at the ballpark. The container should have been metal, but the one she found was plastic. It should have contained a baseball card, an eraser shaped like a frog, a small bottle of hand sanitizer, and a bookmark.

"The contents and the container are wrong."

"What does that mean?"

Sabre shrugged. "I'm not sure. I must be doing something wrong because I couldn't find the one we went to yesterday either. It's a totally different cache. Maybe they are just too close to each other, and I'm not finding the right one."

"It sounds too much like work to me."

JP wrapped his arms around Sabre and pulled her toward him, touching his lips on hers. Sabre responded eagerly. After a few minutes, she lay her head on his shoulder and JP held her in his arms for several minutes in silence.

"I suppose I better go. I have a very early start tomorrow."

They stood up and walked to the door. "Lock the door behind me," JP said.

Sabre closed the door and peeked out the peephole. JP remained on her landing until she locked the door. Then he walked to his car.

Sabre sat back down and picked up one of her files for court the next day. She read through the reports and made a couple of notes. She did the same for six others and stacked them in a neat pile, and then she returned to her iPad.

Sabre read the note again: *Each cache is a clue to the next. You must examine each one more carefully.*

It was like someone was speaking to her, telling her she hadn't looked closely enough. She brought the death certificate up on the screen that she had picked up in the cache with JP. She read through it word by word, looking for anything she may have missed. Nothing seemed out of the ordinary, except that she had a death certificate for someone who hadn't died yet.

Suddenly, it hit her. The file number on the death certificate started with the letters GC, the same way all the geocaching codes started. She quickly typed the code GC46987 into www.geocaching.com and hit *Advanced Search*. There it was. She wrote down the coordinates and picked up her cell phone and called Jennifer.

"Can you go geocaching tomorrow at noon?"

"Yes, but what's up?"

Sabre explained what she had found.

"Sweet! I can go about twelve thirty. I don't have another appointment until three."

"Great. Meet me at my house at twelve thirty."

Chapter 6

"How's my little S.O.B. this morning?" Bob asked Sabre as she walked from the parking lot toward the Juvenile Court on Meadowlark. That was Bob's nickname for his best friend, Sabre. It came from her initials—Sabre Orin Brown. He vacillated between calling her "Sobs," "my little S.O.B.," and any number of affectionate terms, like "honey" or "snookums."

"Life is good. We have the McFerran case together this morning. Are you ready?"

"I'm ready for you to send these kids home."

"Yeah, I don't think so. The more I talk with these children, the more I realize how dysfunctional that family is. And there's your client now," Sabre said, nodding her head toward the blonde cowgirl, Brandy McFerran, with her bright pink western hat with a heart of rhinestones on the front and a matching hat band, her too-tight jeans, and her rhinestone-covered cowboy boots. She appeared to be arguing with some man. "Who's that guy?"

"Probably her boyfriend."

"It's not the one she was with last week."

"Maybe she traded him in for a better model. I don't know. She can boink whomever she wants as long as it doesn't affect the kids."

"Maybe this one isn't abusive, although he looks pretty angry." They stopped and watched for a few moments as the couple quarreled. When he raised his hand toward her, Bob stepped forward. Just then a deputy sheriff, Michael McCormick, stepped out of the courthouse, and the man scurried away. Michael remained outside with Brandy while Sabre and Bob went inside.

Once they passed through the metal detector and started down the hallway toward the courtroom, Bob said, "What has this mother really done? She hasn't abused her kids. They have food. She's working on getting the house cleaned up. The kids go to school—okay, they miss a little too much school—but they have the basic needs, and the mother loves those kids."

"Really? That mother loves herself. Everything she does is to advance her career. Those kids go to school looking like ragamuffins, and she looks like she could be a model for *Cosmopolitan Cowgirl* or something."

"Is there a magazine called *Cosmo Cowgirl*?"

"I don't know. I'm just saying she does not put those children first."

"She needs to keep up her appearances for her work. After all, she is an actress."

"My point is Brandy McFerran's first priority is Brandy McFerran. Besides that, she treats Conway like he's the father of the other children. You can hardly get Trace away from the video games. Dolly is gorgeous, but her self-esteem is so low that she thinks she's ugly. Reba is the most adjusted, but she hates men, at least the men who have been involved in your client's life—and there have been plenty of those. And Taylor will hardly eat."

They continued down the hallway to Department Four.

"Maybe Taylor won't eat because she needs her family. As for Conway, it's not unusual to see the oldest child "parentified." I know my client is a little self-absorbed, but not to the level of abuse or neglect. Of course Trace likes video games—he's sixteen. That's not unusual for a kid his age. Hell, my son, Corey, would play all day, every day if I let him. And you're right, Dolly is beautiful, but she's a teenager. Most teenagers have low self-esteem. It comes with the territory."

"There's more to it than that."

"Come on Sobs. You're being unreasonable. This isn't like you. How about a voluntary? If you were okay with it, I think I could convince the social worker."

"Not this one. Set it for trial," Sabre said, as she walked into the courtroom. "It'll give me a little more time to get to know the children, and then we'll see."

"Okay, but I'm going to win this one."

"And maybe you should."

"Did I hear this is a trial set?" the court clerk asked.

"You heard right," Bob said. "Ms. Brown is being very unreasonable this morning."

Just then, Mike McCormick walked into the courtroom.

"Is my client okay?" Bob asked.

"She's fine," Mike said. "The dirtbag left before I could talk to him, and your client refused to tell me his name. You might want to have a talk with her."

"I will."

"Is this case ready?" Mike asked.

"I think so," Sabre said.

"I just saw Attorney Powers outside the courtroom. Who else do we need?" Mike glanced at the court calendar. "Oh," he said dejectedly, "we need Wagner."

"I'm appearing for Wags," Bob said. "I have his available trial dates. Let's do it."

Bob left the courtroom and returned within a couple of minutes with his client. Attorneys Powers, Brown, and Clark sat at the defense table with the mother, Brandy McFerran. The social worker sat next to Sabre, and to her left was Deputy County Counsel, Dave Casey.

When Judge Hekman walked in and took her seat on the bench, Bob whispered something into his client's ear. Brandy removed her hat. Her stiff hair had a ring around it where her hat had been. She fluffed her hair, pulling the creases out with her fingertips. It helped somewhat.

The clerk called the case.

"I understand this is a trial set. Is there anything else we need to discuss besides a date?" Before anyone could answer, Judge Hekman asked, "Ms. Brown, how are the children doing?"

Sabre stood up. "They're adjusting well in their foster homes, Your Honor."

"Are they getting sibling visits?"

"Yes, Your Honor. The social worker did a good job with this placement. The foster parents are friends, and they have made a concerted effort to get the children together. They have a joint camping trip coming up this weekend."

"Good." The judge looked directly at the mother. "There are four fathers for these children. Is that correct?"

"Yes, Your Honor," Bob responded for his client.

"Let me get the players straight here." The judge looked at her file. "Trace's father, Marvin Kline, is represented by Richard Wagner, and you're appearing on his behalf, Mr. Clark?"

"Correct, Your Honor," Bob responded.

"And Mr. Powers, you represent Dolly's father, Earl Wade, correct?"

"That's true, Your Honor," Attorney Powers said.

"And what about the father for Reba and Taylor?" the judge asked, this time addressing the social worker, Penny Armstrong.

Penny said, "According to the mother, their father lives in Winchester, Tennessee. His name is Dwayne Worrell. We've made several attempts to reach him, but he has not responded."

"Does he have any contact with the children, Ms. McFerran?" Judge Hekman said.

"No, ma'am. He hasn't seen them since they were babies. He run off with some young thing that worked at McDonald's. Said he had met the love of his life. I expect he beat her up just the way he done me. She got what she deserved, I'd say."

Bob tapped his client on the arm and whispered, "That's enough."

"And what about Conway's father?"

The social worker spoke again. "The father is listed as 'Unknown' on the birth certificate. According to recent information, the mother is now claiming that she knows who the father is. In fact, I just found out this morning that the mother claims that the biological father comes from a prominent political family in Tennessee. He impregnated Brandy when she was fifteen. When the truth emerged, the father's family covered it up."

"Is that true, Ms. McFerran?"

Brandy nodded.

"You need to speak up for the record," Bob said to her before the judge could.

"Yes, ma'am."

"And who is the father?" the Judge asked.

"His name is Monroe Bullard."

Sabre's head jerked up when she heard the name, but she didn't say anything. She considered telling the court that she had discovered a death certificate in the geocache with the name "Monroe" but decided it was too far-fetched. She needed to do a little more investigating.

"Is he related to Senator Richard Bullard?" Judge Hekman asked.

"Yes, Monroe is the senator's older brother."

"Did you have a paternity test run on Conway and

Mr. Bullard?"

"We did, but the Bullards must have greased some palms because it came back negative. I know it was Monroe because I'd never been with anyone else."

Chapter 7

" **S** obs, wait up," Bob called to Sabre, as she left the courtroom and started down the hall.

Sabre stopped.

"Are you okay?" Bob asked. "Your face turned white when my client said the name of Conway's father."

"It's just not very often we get big political names in here. Look, I have to go. I have another case in Department One. They're waiting for me."

Sabre would normally have told Bob about the strange events from her geocaching over the weekend, but she hadn't seen or talked to him since she had found the death certificate. He was her best friend, and they shared most everything that went on in their lives. This time she was glad she hadn't had the chance to tell him because if it turned out to be the same guy, she could potentially have a conflict on the McFerran case.

As Sabre walked down the hallway, she thought about the name "Monroe." It was an unusual name if it was a first name. She was certain there were a lot of people with the surname Monroe, however. It was most likely a coincidence and not worth stirring everyone up over. She would do some research when she got back to her computer.

When Sabre finished her morning calendar, Bob was waiting outside the courthouse for her.

"Want to go to Pho's for lunch? We haven't eaten there all week," Bob asked.

"Bob, it's Monday."

"I know, but I'm craving a Number 124."

"I would like to, but I promised Jennifer I would

meet her at twelve thirty. I can go tomorrow, though."

"It's just as well. I have some work I can do at my office."

***

Back at her condo, Sabre Googled "Monroe Bullard." She found a lot of information on the very politically active family. Monroe's father, Attorney William Bullard, had an abundance of political connections. He ran for political office on two occasions but was unsuccessful in both attempts. He represented several big names in politics and in entertainment, especially in the country western music industry.

Monroe graduated from Harvard with a degree in political science. He returned home and was being primed for greatness in the political arena in spite of his tendency to be a little wild. At twenty-eight, it was known that he would be a contender for the House of Representatives, but he suddenly stopped campaigning and disappeared from the limelight.

Four years later, his brother ran for the same spot and won. Richard Bullard served three terms in the House and then ran for the Senate, which he won. Richard was now serving his second term.

That's about all she could glean from the Internet, but she would ask JP to investigate further. She needed to know for Conway's sake, but she also wanted to make sure it wasn't the same Monroe as the death certificate named. She emailed JP and asked him to find out anything he could about Monroe Bullard, brother to Tennessee Senator Richard Bullard.

Sabre changed into a pair of jeans, a pink T-shirt, and a pair of walking shoes. Then she returned to her computer and printed out the coordinates for Cache GC46987, the file number on the death certificate. She reached for her phone to call JP to see if he wanted to go with them. Just then the doorbell rang. It was Jennifer.

"Are you ready?"

"Absolutely," Sabre said. "Are you driving?"

"Sure. Let's go."

On the way to the geocache site, Sabre told Jennifer what she had deduced from the numbers on the death certificate.

"That's so cool. This is the best kind of cache search. I did one of these before where one led to another. I just stumbled across it, but it was loads of fun."

Sabre didn't tell Jennifer about the "coincidental name" on her case.

Jennifer pulled into a diagonal parking space on East Main Street in El Cajon. "I love these parking spots. They are so much easier than regular parking. It's like something out of an old fifties movie."

"Talk about old fifties movies, there's Rock-A-Betties hair salon," Sabre said, nodding toward the salon. "I hear they're really good."

"They do some great hairstyles. I went there once when I was going to a costume party. With this curly hair, I was limited. If I wanted to dye it red I could have come out looking like Lucille Ball, but I wasn't willing to go that far."

"So what did you choose?"

"They gave me a Katherine Hepburn style."

"Really? She's one of my favorite actresses of all time," Sabre said.

They walked along the concrete squares, following the coordinates toward some wrought iron tables and chairs, each with its own red and yellow umbrella. A black, three-foot, wrought iron fence surrounded the tables, with three or four openings where people could enter. All along the inside of the fence were pots of varying sizes filled with plants, some of them as tall as the umbrellas. About every twenty feet, there was a concrete square filled with dirt where a tree had been planted.

"We're really close," Jennifer said. "It must be in one of those planters."

About half of the tables were filled with people eating lunch. Sabre looked around. "This feels strange with all these people around."

"Who cares?"

People stared at them as they started looking through the planters. One woman gave Jennifer a dirty look as she reached inside the fence and into a plant that was sitting right next to her.

"Sorry, my friend was here earlier and she left something. I told her I would come look for it."

"What is it you're looking for?"

"It's a little, container-like thing, about this big—" She held her hands about four inches apart and then moved them further apart and back again. "It's not here. Sorry."

Sabre was about to walk away. She whispered to her friend. "We'll come back later when there are not so many people here."

But Jennifer just moved to another planter. "Oh, here it is," she said, holding it up. "Sorry, everyone."

She scurried toward the car, with Sabre trying to keep up.

"You can't take it with you," Sabre said.

"What else are we going to do? We told them we were looking for something we lost."

"We? We didn't tell them anything. You did."

"We'll bring it back later when there are not so many people around. No one will know the difference."

As they got inside the car, Sabre said, "You

could've just told them what we were doing."

"That would take too much explaining. Besides, this was more fun. It's like old times. Remember when we followed my ex and found out he was cheating on me?"

Sabre laughed. "I remember. We watched him leave, and then we snuck into his apartment and listened to his messages on his answering machine."

"Yeah, and he came back to get something, and we had to hide in the closet until he left. That was close."

"Did he ever figure out what you did?"

"I never told him. The jerk. I just dumped his ass."

Sabre turned her head to the side and looked at Jennifer with a raised eyebrow.

"Okay, so I went back to him after that. But I finally figured it out. It just took me a little longer than it should have. Now I have Alex, and he's wonderful."

"Open up the cache. Let's see what's in it."

Jennifer opened the little plastic container and removed a piece of paper.

"It's a riddle. I don't get it."

"Let me see." Sabre read it aloud.

Riddle me this:
Go get the cache,
Cause you need it to know,
What to do next,
And who kills Monroe.
6 or 8 or maybe even 9 more places to go.

Sabre's face lost a little color as she read the note.

"What is that? Who kills Monroe," Jennifer asked. "Isn't Monroe the name on your death certificate?"

"Yes, it is. But I guess it makes sense because they are connected. After all, we were led to this one from the number on the death certificate."

"It's like a clue game. I think the butler did it in the

parlor with poison."

"What if it's not a game?"

Chapter 8

"Damn it, Sabre. No more geocaching without me," JP said after Sabre told him what had happened earlier today.

Sabre's face tightened.

"Please," he said, his tone more subdued. "Not until we know what's going on."

"Fair enough, but I still think it's a hoax."

JP stood up from the sofa and walked into the kitchen. "I need a drink."

"There's a Shiner Bock in the refrigerator. Help yourself."

JP whipped around. "You're kidding, right?"

Sabre chuckled. "Of course I'm kidding, although Bob has threatened to stock my refrigerator with them just to get your goat."

Sabre checked the geocache online in order to sign the log, but this time it led to a page with a confused looking green frog and the words, "*404—File Not Found. We're sorry the page you are looking for could not be found.*" It went on to list several reasons for the error message, including that the page may no longer exist, that it may have moved to another location, or perhaps she mistyped something. She explained what she found to JP when he returned.

"This is all starting to get a little frightening," JP said. "I don't like the idea of you chasing clues that may lead to a dead guy."

"The first thing we need to do is find out if there is any connection to this and the 'Monroe' on the McFerran case. If not, then it's likely just a silly game. If it is connected, that's a whole different ball game."

"I did a little checking on Monroe Bullard this

afternoon, but I didn't get very far. I'll have more time tomorrow. I did find out that the family has high hopes for Senator Bullard. It looks like they are priming him for the presidency. But that might all be wishful thinking on behalf of his mother. The rumor is that she's like a chicken on a June bug when it comes to boosting her son's career."

"If what Brandy McFerran says is true, Mother Bullard must have been furious at Monroe when Brandy became pregnant."

"And if it's not true, she must have been furious at Brandy."

"Either way, it apparently ended his career. There must be some record of the scandal somewhere."

"I have a friend who has a finger on the political scene. I have a call in to her."

Sabre stared at the McFerran file sitting on her coffee table.

"What's the matter?" JP asked.

"I'm wondering what Brandy has told Conway about his father." Sabre picked up her cell phone and called Bob.

"Hi, Sobs," Bob said.

Sabre pushed the speaker button on. "I'm here with JP, and we're working on the McFerran case."

"Yeah, I bet you're working."

Sabre ignored his remark. "Any chance I could talk to your client about Conway's father? I need to talk with Conway. When I do, I'd like to know what she has told him so I know how to proceed. It would also be good to know who Conway's father really is. I would expect you to be there, of course."

"I'm meeting with Brandy tomorrow about noon thirty in my office. Why don't you come by about one. That will give me time to do what I need to do, and then we can talk together."

"Thanks, honey." Sabre hung up.

"Are you going to question Conway about his father?" JP asked.

"It depends on what his mother has told him. If he doesn't know about Monroe, I won't bring it up. We don't even know if it's true. I'm going to see him tomorrow anyway, so I want to be prepared. That reminds me. Are you busy tomorrow around five?"

"Never too busy for you," he grinned. "What do you need?"

"I talked to the social worker and the foster parents, and I've worked it out so Conway can have his bike to ride to school and to work. I just need to get it to him. I was hoping we could use your pickup to move it."

"Only if you let me take you to dinner afterwards."

"It's a date."

JP took a swig of his beer and shifted back on the sofa. Sabre snuggled up to him, and he wrapped his arm around her.

"Are you really concerned about this 'Monroe' thing?" Sabre asked.

"I'm always concerned when you go off investigating without me. That's what you pay me for. Let me do my job."

"In my defense, I haven't really been investigating. I was merely geocaching. I just keep finding strange caches."

"Let me see that note again that you found today," JP said as he sat up straight, gently moving Sabre forward.

Sabre brought it up on her iPad screen and read it.
Riddle me this:
Go get the cache,
Cause you need it to know,
What to do next,
And who kills Monroe.

6 or 8 or maybe even 9 more places to go.

"Do you think it means something other than the obvious?" Sabre asked.

"You mean more than 'you need to find the next cache to get the next clue, and it will take six to nine more before you know'?"

"Yeah, is that it? Or is there some subliminal meaning that I don't see?"

"I think there's more. He comes right out and tells you it's a riddle. And the first cache led you to this one. The part that concerns me is that he planted another in between to make sure you were figuring it out. I definitely think there is something else here."

"Me too."

"I'm not very good at these kinds of puzzles, but I'm sure you'll figure it out." JP raised an eyebrow. "You said there were some caches that led from one to another. Is this how they work?"

"I don't know. I asked Jennifer, but she didn't know either. She hasn't really done this type before, except once by accident. But I'll do some research and find out more about it." Sabre picked up her file. "Meanwhile, I need you to investigate each of the fathers on this case. I know you're already looking into Monroe, but see what you can find out about the others as well. Marvin Kline and Earl Wade are represented by counsel so you can't talk to them, but if you find Dwayne Worrell, he's fair game. By the way, he also goes by 'Squeak.'"

"Squeak?"

"Yes. I have no idea where the name came from. I do know that he has spent his share of time in prison."

"Will do."

"Oh, and see what you can find out about Brandy McFerran's new boyfriend. According to the social study, his name is Doug Griffin."

43

JP finished his beer. "I'd better be going."

He stood up, walked to the kitchen, and dropped the can in the recycle bin. Sabre met him when he came back and walked with him to the door.

"Oh, I almost forgot to tell you. I followed up on Dr. Perry Lane Martin, the doctor named on the death certificate."

"Is he a real doctor?"

"Yeah, but he's on vacation in Australia. Apparently he's in the Outback and can't be reached. I left a message in case he called in to his service. They didn't expect that he would until he's ready to come home."

"Do they know when that is?"

"About three weeks."

"After the murder takes place."

"That's right. I was wondering if you want to send me to Australia to investigate. Aye?" He smirked.

"No, I don't think so, unless we go together." She smiled.

"That works for me." JP kissed her goodnight. "I'll see you tomorrow."

Sabre closed and locked the door behind him.

Chapter 9

Sabre waited with the receptionist in the lobby at Bob's office. The two other attorneys who shared the suite with him were both out to lunch. John Merrifield was a tax attorney, and Timothy Lindgren did trusts and estates. Bob had only been in this office for about a year. For years he partnered with his good friend RJ, whom he met in law school. One day, Bob came back from court and found his partner face down on his desk. He had died from a heart attack.

Bob stayed until the lease ran out, and then he moved to this office. Sabre missed RJ. He was her friend as well. They had all started on the juvenile panel about the same time. When the three of them were on the same side on a case, they were a force to be reckoned with. But most of the time, one or the other would be on the opposite side. That always proved to be a challenge, but it never affected their friendship. They would have a full-on fight at trial against one another and then leave it all in the courtroom and go to lunch. Or leave almost all of it. Sometimes there was a little gloating when one side beat the other.

The phone dinged on the receptionist's desk. "You can go in now, Ms. Brown."

"Thank you," Sabre said, as she stood and went into Bob's office.

Brandy McFerran sat across from Bob's huge, antique oak desk.

"You know Ms. Brown," Bob said, nodding at Sabre.

"Yes," Brandy said.

"Hello, Brandy. Thanks for meeting with me. I just

have a few questions about Conway's father."

"We just discussed that, and Brandy told me that Monroe Bullard is Conway's father," Bob said. "I'll give you a brief synopsis of what happened, and if you have any other questions, you can ask." Bob looked at his client. "Please stop me if I misspeak."

Bob returned his gaze to Sabre. "Brandy was only fifteen years old when she met Monroe. He was in his mid to late twenties. He lavished her with gifts and swept her off her feet. He seduced her and promised to use his influence to get her singing career in motion. She fell for him, and when she told him she was pregnant with his baby, he dumped her." He looked again at Brandy. "Is that correct?"

"Yes, when I threatened to tell the world what he had done, his mother promised to help me with my career." She spoke in a dramatic voice as if she were on stage. "I believed her, and so when I was questioned by the press, I denied everything. She convinced me that I needed to wait until after I had the baby and got my shape back before I should start auditioning. She said I would only get one good chance and that I needed to not lose it because I didn't look good or lacked morals. It was almost a year before I was back in shape. She set up one audition for me that got me a couple of singing engagements at local clubs. Then I got pregnant again, and she wouldn't do anything more until after that baby was born."

"Did she help you then?" Bob asked.

"No, she said it didn't matter anymore because Monroe wasn't running for any more offices. His brother, Richard, was taking his place."

"You said in court that you had a paternity test done on Monroe?" Sabre asked. "Is that correct?"

"Yes. When I threatened to go to court, his mother set up a test, and I went. Monroe went too, but not at the same time. I knew it would show that he was the father because I hadn't been with anyone else."

"But it came back different from what you expected?"

"Yeah." Brandy dragged the word out like a teenage girl talking to her friends. "They had it rigged. I know he's the father."

"And his mother was still willing to help you get the auditions, even though the test was negative?"

"I told her I would tell the reporters. I knew it would be enough for the press to know Monroe had been with a fifteen-year-old. She acted like she was just doing it to 'help' me, but I know she was still afraid."

"Did Monroe ever admit to being the father?"

"He got real angry when I told him I was pregnant. He slapped me and called me names and said it couldn't be his." Brandy emphasized "slapped," almost making it sound like a slapping sound. "Then his mother came to see me, and Monroe denied ever being with me, but that was for his mother's sake and his political stuff. I was pretty devastated because I loved him—or at least I thought I did. A few weeks later, he got drunk, which he did a lot. He was actually nicer when he was drunk than when he was sober. Anyway, this time he came to me and said he knew he was the father, but because he was going to be running for office, he couldn't do anything about it. He encouraged me to let his mother help me get what I wanted. That way we were both better off."

"Did he ever pay any support?" Sabre asked.

"No. He bought me lots of pretty things in the beginning, jewelry and stuff, but nothing after he found out about the baby."

"Does Conway know who his father is?"

"Of course not. His father never had any interest in him, so there was no need for him to know."

"What did you tell Conway about who his father was?" Sabre asked.

"I didn't. He thought it was Marvin for a while."

"Marvin?"

"Marvin Kline—Trace's dad. He lived with us when Conway was first talking. He called him 'Dad' for a long time. Then when Earl moved in—that's Dolly's father—he called him 'Dad.' I don't know whether or not he thought he was his father, but he never called Reba and Taylor's father anything but 'Squeak.' I tried to get him to show more respect. You know, call him, 'Dad,' or 'Pa,' or something, but he never would. Conway said he had had enough 'dads.' Even at five years old, he was already set in his ways."

"So, Conway doesn't know that Monroe is his real father?"

"No. He couldn't. I never told him. I started to once, but he said he knew who his father was."

"But you didn't believe him?"

"No. There's no way he could really know."

"And you didn't ask him who he thought it was?"

"No. I think he just didn't want to talk about it. Or maybe he had this image in his head about some hero father, and I didn't want to ruin that for him," Brandy orated.

Every time Brandy spoke, Sabre felt like she was in the middle of a 1950s B-movie melodrama.

"Are you going to tell Conway about Monroe?" Brandy asked Sabre.

"No, not right away. If he asks me who his father is, I will have to answer honestly that I don't know for certain. But eventually he'll have to know. It might be better coming from you. You may want to think about telling Conway when you have a private moment with him."

Sabre looked at Bob, and he nodded.

"Brandy," Sabre said, "please don't tell him that Monroe is the father unless you are one hundred percent certain. He doesn't need any more confusion in his life."

"I can see why people would question me. I'm just poor white trash with a fancy name, and he's some big shot with lots of money. But I'm the only one who knows for sure, and unless this was some kind of Immaculate Deception or somethin', Monroe is my baby daddy."

Chapter 10

After waiting around the courthouse for most of the afternoon, Sabre's trial was continued. She called Conway to see if she could go see him. Then she drove to De Jong's Dairy in Lakeside. She wanted to see where he worked and to make sure it was an appropriate place for him.

The smell of cow manure was overwhelming. Although it was strong and unpleasant, there was something about the farm that made her feel warm and happy inside. She remembered her grandfather's farm in Minnesota. They only went there once, and Sabre was very young when they visited her grandparents. She remembered watching her grandpa milk the cows and playing in the hay with her brother, Ron. The vision of the rooster chasing her and Ron's laughter were vivid in her mind, as well as the sound of Ron's shrieks when the rooster turned course and went after him.

Sabre parked in front of the huge barn and stepped out onto the gravel, her heels giving way to the pebbles as she walked. She wished she had gone home to change clothes before coming here. She made a mental note to put a pair of sneakers back in her trunk.

When she walked inside the barn, a fair-skinned man with blue eyes who looked to be about sixty-five greeted her. He was dressed in jeans, a T-shirt, and a fisherman's hat.

"Hi," Sabre said, extending her hand. "I'm Sabre Brown. I'm here to see Conway McFerran."

"Nice to meet you, Ms. Brown. I'm Jan De Jong," the man said in a slight Dutch accent. "Conway said you were coming. He's in the milk room. Right over there." He pointed to a door to his left. "Tell him I said to take a break."

Sabre walked into the cold room where Conway was working on one of the many chrome machines that filled the room.

"Got a minute?" Sabre asked. "Mr. De Jong said you could take a break."

Conway finished checking the dials on one of the machines, and walked out with Sabre. "We can sit out back. There's a bench there where we eat lunch sometimes."

He led Sabre through the barn, past an enormous bull that snorted when they got close, and out the back door.

"That bull looks mean."

"He is. We don't get too close to him unless we have to, and then we are very careful."

Sabre stepped prudently over a fresh cow pie as she walked outside and toward the bench. The pungent smell made her cough.

"Sorry. I didn't get that cleaned up when the cows came in."

"It's okay." They sat down, and Sabre gazed around at the fenced fields that seemed to go on for miles.

"I can see why you like it here," Sabre said.

"I do like it. There's something very comfortable about this place. I don't even mind the smells."

"And the job is going well?"

"Yes. Mr. De Jong is very good to work for."

"Did you ride your bike here?"

"Yes. Thank you for getting it to me."

"You're welcome."

"It's not that far. My foster father got me a light for it in case I get done late. And he told me to call if it gets too late and he'll come pick me up."

"That was very nice of him," Sabre said. "Conway, I want to ask you a couple of questions about some of the men you've dealt with in your life."

Conway nodded.

"Do you remember Dwayne Worrell?"

"We called him Squeak. Everyone did. He's Reba's and Taylor's father. What do you want to know?"

"Did you get along with him?"

"When he was sober he was alright."

"And when he wasn't?"

"I would stay away from him."

"Did he ever hurt you?"

"He only whooped me once with a belt, but he would whoop Trace all the time. I would try to get Trace to steer clear of him, but he wouldn't, especially when Squeak was hitting our mother." Conway looked away from Sabre and he lowered his chin toward his chest. "I'm the oldest. I should have done more. I tried at first to stop him when he hit her, but that's when he whooped me." He brought his head up and looked at Sabre. "I told Mom over and over again to leave him, but she wouldn't."

"But they eventually split up. What happened?"

"I think he found a new girlfriend. That's usually what happened to the men in my mom's life—that or they went to jail. She's been pretty unlucky."

Sabre thought it was interesting that he thought his mother was unlucky in love. He didn't blame her for her choices.

"What about Dolly's father, Earl Wade?"

"I remember him a little. I don't think I liked him much either."

"And Marvin Kline?"

"Trace's father. He lived with us for a while, but I don't really remember much about that. After Earl moved in, he came around sometimes to see Trace. He came to see me too, I guess. He was good to us, never hit us or anything, but I think he hit Mom some. Then he went to prison for a few years, and we didn't see him. He came around a couple of times after that, but we haven't seen or heard from him since we moved to California. He might be back in prison for all I know."

Sabre knew that he was in prison, but she didn't think it would serve any purpose to tell Conway.

"What about your father? Do you know him?"

"No. I never met him." He paused and looked out at the field. He didn't say anything for a few seconds, and then he added, "But I know who he is. Mom doesn't know that I know, but I do."

"And who is he?"

"His name is Monroe Bullard. He's some hotshot politician back in Tennessee. Or at least he used to be. His brother is a senator."

"How do you know that?" Sabre asked.

"Mom's been talking about it for years. She says stuff all the time to her friends and to Grandma. I even heard my mom talk to him a couple of times on the phone. I've known since I was pretty little. I looked him up on the Internet a couple of years back. I thought I might try to go see him, but then I decided that if he didn't want anything to do with me, why should I bother?"

Chapter 11

S̲abre read through the riddle again for about the tenth time. She still wasn't getting a hidden message from it. It seemed pretty clear what he was trying to say, but that didn't lead her anywhere. She was about to give up when the doorbell rang. Since she wasn't expecting company, she peeked through the peephole and then opened the door to her brother.

"You're back. Is Mom with you?"

"No," Ron said, as he walked in. "I dropped her off at the house. She was tired and wanted to clean up. She has some social event this evening, bridge or something. You know Mom."

"And you didn't want to play bridge with a bunch of old ladies?"

"Not exactly my thing, although her friends find me charming, especially the older ones. She has one woman she plays bridge with who is ninety-one. She's still sharp as a tack. And she loves me."

Sabre shrugged. "What's not to love?"

Ron walked into the kitchen. Sabre followed.

"Are you hungry?" Sabre asked.

Ron opened the refrigerator. "Better pickings at Mom's, but that's no surprise." He removed a can of Dr Pepper and popped it open.

"How was San Francisco?" Sabre asked.

"Great. It's changed a bit since I was there last, especially at the wharf, which is more commercial than it used to be. It was a good trip, and I think Mom really enjoyed it. We took Route 101 on the drive up, so we saw some nice scenery. We stopped a few places and took some nice little hikes and walks by the ocean. On the way back we came straight down I-5 all the way without stopping except for gas. It's good to be out of the car."

"So what are your plans now?"

"I need to find a job. I've been doing a few odd jobs for Mom's friends, but I need to find something steady. Mom has been wonderful, but I need my own place." Ron moved his elbows in a backward motion as far as he could, stretching his shoulders and back muscles. "What have you been up to?"

"Mostly work." She picked up her cell phone, brought up the photo of the riddle, and handed it to Ron. "And I've been trying to figure out this riddle. You're good at this sort of stuff. Maybe you can solve it."

Ron read it. "Where did you get this?"

"From a geocache."

Ron raised a quizzical eyebrow. "You geocache?"

"I've only gone a few times. My friend Jennifer got me started. Do you know about geocaching?"

"You bet. It's one of my favorite pastimes. Outdoors. Treasures. Solving puzzles. What could be better?"

"Of course; I might have known. Well, maybe you can help me. I'll even pay you for your time, assuming you're any good at it."

Sabre told Ron everything she had found in her geocaching adventure. Then she printed two copies of the riddle on her desktop printer, and handed him one. "I'm stuck. I can't figure out what he or she is trying to tell me. I think it should lead to the next cache, but I can't see anything that leads me there."

"A death certificate, huh?"

"Yes."

"In the future?"

"Yes."

"That's wicked clever. Do you think this 'Monroe'

guy is really going to be bumped off?"

"No, and neither do the cops, but you never know. There are a lot of crazy people out there."

"I'll be glad to help you, but you don't have to pay me. It'll be fun."

"I kinda do need to pay you." Sabre paused.

"What aren't you telling me?"

"There's one other thing I haven't mentioned. I'm working on a case right now in juvenile court that may be connected to this geocaching thing. If so, I can't tell you about it unless you're working for me. If I hire you, you can help me find out if there is a connection and help me work my way through the geocaching since I'm a novice at it."

"Whatever you need to do." Ron extended his hand palm up. "Give me a dollar. That'll be my retainer. That's the way they do it in the movies, right?"

Sabre laughed, reached in her pocket, and handed him a quarter.

"Dang, you're cheap."

"I learned that from you."

"Tell me, how is the case connected?"

"Like I said, I'm not certain if it is, but the father of one of my minor clients is named Monroe."

"That's quite a coincidence if it's not connected. Monroe isn't that common a name, is it?"

"I Googled it and discovered it was used quite a bit thirty or forty years ago for male children. Now it's more common for a girl. Go figure."

"Do you know if the Monroe on the death certificate is a man or a woman?"

"He's a male, according to the certificate." Sabre handed him a copy of the death certificate that she had printed earlier.

"Hmm..." Ron said and laid it down. He retrieved the riddle from the coffee table and read it aloud.

Riddle me this:
Go get the cache,
Cause you need it to know,
What to do next,
And who kills Monroe.
6 or 8 or maybe even 9 more places to go.

Ron stared at the paper, mumbling to himself. He stood up and paced with the paper in his hand, reading it over and over. His face burst out with a smile. "I think I've got it."

"What is it?" Sabre asked.

Ron walked back to the sofa. "Do you have your geocaching site open?"

"Yes, why?"

"What do all the codes start with?"

"GC, which I assume stands for Geo Cache."

"Yup. And look at the first two lines of the riddle: Go get the cache, Cause you need it to know. The first letter in the first line is "G," and in the second line it's "C." Try this: GCWA689. It's the first letter of each line and then the numbers. Pretty simple code actually."

Sabre typed it into the search line and pushed enter.

"It brings up a cache in San Diego."

"Let's go see what's in it."

"Right now?" Sabre asked.

"Sure, why not?"

"I better call JP. He asked me not to go geocaching without him."

"JP? Really?" He brushed his hand through his blond hair. "I didn't figure him for a geocaching kind of guy."

Sabre chuckled. "He's not. In fact, I think he hates it, but I sort of promised him I wouldn't follow up on this 'death certificate thing' without him. He's worried that there might be more to it, especially if it's connected to this case."

"I think it's getting too late anyway today. We won't have daylight much longer. Why don't you tell JP what we discovered so he's in the loop. If he wants to go with us, he can. If not, your big brother will take care of you."

"Fair enough."

"Can you go tomorrow?"

"I'll be done early at court tomorrow. I only have a couple of cases on calendar and no trial in the afternoon. I'll call you when I'm done, and we can go then."

Chapter 12

By 5:30 a.m., JP was already on his second cup of coffee. With his beagle, Louie, at his feet, he parked himself at his computer. He was frustrated because so many of the players in this case were in Nashville or its surrounding area. He much preferred talking to people in person as opposed to the phone. When he lost the element of surprise, he couldn't read their body language. But he had no choice since it wasn't likely Sabre was going to send him to Tennessee.

He checked the databases he had access to regarding criminal offenses by each one of the fathers on the McFerran case, as well as the new boyfriend. Most of the information wasn't anything different than what was in the social study provided by the Department of Social Services. Each of the men had at least one arrest for domestic violence, except Monroe Bullard. He had no record of any kind.

The new boyfriend, Doug Griffin, was a local guy. He was considerably younger than Brandy—nearly eight years—which meant he was slightly closer in age to Conway than Brandy. He had one domestic violence arrest but no conviction, a DUI, and a misdemeanor drug charge for which he was presently on probation. He was also an actor who hadn't quite caught his big break yet.

Louie went to the sliding glass door and stood looking out. When JP ignored him, he gave a short, sharp bark.

"Okay, Louie. I hear you."

JP let Louie out, leaving the door open so he could come back inside on his own, and returned to the computer. He had done what research he could on the Internet regarding the Bullard family. Most of the information appeared to be filtered, most likely by Mother Bullard. She still appeared to have a lot of influence on the family, although Senator Bullard seemed to try to keep her out of the picture. JP still hadn't heard back from his political reporter friend, Pauline Vasquez. She was an excellent resource for this sort of thing, but he hadn't been comfortable calling her since they hadn't parted on the best of terms the last time that he saw her. He did it for Sabre.

He and Pauline had met a few years back and became good friends—friends with benefits. That's all she wanted because she was so wrapped up in her career. JP was okay with that for a while, but then he met Sabre and he stopped calling her. It wasn't that noticeable at first because Pauline traveled so much, but a couple of times when she was in town, he was simply not available. They never really argued about it. They just sort of stopped communicating.

The phone rang. It was Sabre.

"Good morning, kid," JP answered.

"Are you working already this morning?"

"Absolutely." He told her what little he knew so far, and she told him how Ron had solved the riddle.

"Don't go geocaching alone. And don't go with Jennifer." JP's voice sounded a little stern. Then he tempered it. "Please. This is all a little too odd."

"I told you I wouldn't. I'm not going alone. Ron is going with me. It turns out he is quite adept at this sport. We're going as soon as I finish at court this morning. You're welcome to come along if you'd like."

"You're in good hands with your brother. Besides, I want to drop in on Doug Griffin and see what I can find out, maybe talk to a few neighbors. Will you please call me when you find the next cache?"

"Will do."

JP spent the next couple of hours rifling through obituaries looking for anyone named Monroe in San Diego County. In the past year, eight people with that last name and one with Monroe as the first name had died. The one whose given name was Monroe was eighty-four years old and died of a heart attack. The eight with the same surname included a family of three who were killed together in a car crash; two had died from cancer; one died in a skiing accident; one died from kidney failure; and one was a stillborn baby girl. None died from poison or even anything that could have been mistaken for poison, except perhaps the heart attack victim. Upon further investigation, JP determined the eighty-four-year-old had a long history of heart disease.

JP had only covered one year's worth of obituaries. He considered going back another year but decided his time would be better spent elsewhere.

He worked for another hour researching, Googling, and reading trash magazines about the Bullard family. Most of the gossip was not substantiated, but the general tenor of the attitude of Mother Bullard came through loud and clear. She was the driving force behind her husband and her two boys. She was ruthless and cold, but she was also very effective.

JP even discovered a few tidbits about actress/singer Brandy McFerran. JP surmised it was paid-for publicity because it was so intermittent and inconsequential.

***

JP drove to the address he had for Doug Griffin. He approached the small apartment complex in El Cajon that looked like it hadn't been painted in thirty years. In a small patch of weeds that grew next to the steps of Doug's apartment were a Budweiser can, a discarded bag from McDonald's, a rolled-up dirty diaper, and numerous cigarette butts.

JP knocked. A woman in her mid-fifties opened the door wearing a flimsy, coral-colored robe and holding a cigarette in one hand and a cup of coffee in the other.

She looked him over from the top of his black Stetson down to the tip of his Tony Lama boots. "What can I do for you, cowboy?"

"I'm looking for Doug Griffin. Is he home?"

"You're not a cop, are you?"

"No, ma'am. I'm certainly not."

"Come on in. He's in bed with his woman." She pointed to the sofa about ten feet from them. Two lumps protruded from the open sofa bed. JP could see the top of a head at one end and two feet sticking out at the other end—one with hot pink nail polish, the other larger and rougher. "Feel free to wake him up."

"Are you sure?"

"Yeah, he needs to find a job."

JP remained standing near the door. "Perhaps you could do it for me, ma'am," he said in his sweetest voice. "I wouldn't want to take him by surprise."

She gave a half smile. "Sure. I kinda enjoy ousting his butt." She walked to the sofa, smacked him on the rear end and yelled, "Get up, you lazy bum."

"Ma, I'm trying to sleep," Doug moaned.

"I got that, but it's time you got outta bed. You got company."

Doug wriggled under the covers but didn't uncover his head.

"I think it may be that agent you been waitin' for. He looks important, and he says he isn't a cop."

Doug sat up, flashing his bare butt before he could get the covers in place around him. He also pulled the blanket off Brandy McFerran when he scooted to the edge of the sofa bed, exposing more than JP cared to see.

"You an agent?" Doug asked JP.

"No, I'm not an agent, but I do need to talk to you."

"About what?"

Brandy remained in a prone position but stuck her head around the side of Doug.

"Hello, Brandy," JP said.

"Good morning," she said sweetly, fluffing her hair.

Doug's head spun around to Brandy. "Who the hell is this guy?"

Doug made a move as if he were about to stand up. JP did not relish seeing his bare body and spoke up. "I'm a private investigator. I work for Sabre Brown, the attorney for Brandy's children."

"What the hell do they need an attorney for?"

"How about you get some pants on and come outside and talk to me a bit? I'll be glad to explain it to you. I'm sure you want to help Brandy any way you can to get her kids back, right?"

Brandy put her hand on Doug's bare back. "Go on, honey. Just go talk to him."

***

Once outside, JP explained, in as few words as possible, how the system worked and why the children had representation. Doug stood there with his bare chest, his jeans hanging just below his navel, and his bare feet. His body was in good shape, but JP surmised it had more to do with his youth than any real effort he had put into it.

"I understand you're an actor," JP said.

"Yeah, I also do some modeling, and I've been on a few commercials. I'll be discovered one of these days." He put the tips of two fingers under his own chin and pushed his head up slightly, turning his head sideways showing JP his profile. "A pretty face like this can't go undiscovered too long."

JP couldn't decide if he wanted to punch the "pretty face" or puke. "Is that how you met Brandy? Through your acting?"

"Yeah, we were at an audition for a Steven Spielberg movie. They were looking for extras. I don't know why, but they didn't pick either of us. I guess they wanted ordinary, ugly people. Sometimes I'm just too good-looking for jobs."

"How long ago was that?"

"A couple weeks."

"You know Brandy is trying to get her kids back, right?"

"Yeah, I know."

"You okay with that?"

"Sure. I love kids."

"Do you have any of your own?"

"I have two, but my old lady won't let me see them."

"Your old lady?" JP wasn't certain if he was referring to his own mother who he lived with, or the mother of his children. Either way, he never liked the term.

"My ex. She went to court and got a restraining order."

"That can be tough." JP feigned concern. "Why the restraining order?"

"She said I hit her, but it was all a misunderstanding. She lied about a lot of things. I just finally quit fighting it. It wasn't good for my career. It won't be long before I'm *directing* movies, you know. I don't plan to stop acting, but I already dabble in directing a little. I'm just waiting for the right script to come along."

JP encouraged his delusion. "I'll bet you'd be good at that."

"I've written a script myself that I might use. I'm thinking about producing it. I've got a couple of investors who are pretty interested. I had a meeting last week in Orange County with a big money guy." Doug lowered his voice and said, "I can't mention any names right now, but he's real interested."

JP nodded. "That's what it's all about, having the right connections."

"It's important to have good connections. That's why Brandy is so good for me. Don't get me wrong. She's hot for an older gal, but she knows some real influential people."

"Really? I didn't know that. Sounds like you two make a good pair." JP continued to play the game with him, hoping he might say something that would help Sabre.

"And publicity. Any publicity—good or bad. Just getting the attention of the press helps. I just haven't had the time to pull it all together."

"What do you do in your spare time, when you're not modeling, acting, or writing?"

"I'm mostly out there looking for jobs to further my career."

"Do you ever do any geocaching?" JP asked.

"Geo what?"

"Geocaching. Have you ever heard of it?"

"No, but if it has anything to do with cash, I'm in."

"No, wrong kind of cache."

"What does that have to do with anything?"

"It doesn't. I was just curious." JP turned to go. "Thanks, Doug, for being so cooperative. I appreciate it."

When JP arrived at his car, he called Sabre and

reached her voice mail. He left a message: "I just got Doug Griffin out of bed with Brandy. I didn't get much, except I don't think he knows anything about geocaching. Mostly, it was a colossal waste of time. Call me when you can."

Chapter 13

"You sure you have the coordinates right?" Sabre asked.

"Yes," Ron responded. "It has to be pretty close to where we are."

They had been searching an area in front of a condo development for nearly fifteen minutes. The sloping ground was landscaped with aquamarine colored rock in an area about sixty feet long. It was about twenty feet wide at the top and ten feet wide at the bottom. Every two or three feet there was a plant that was ecologically friendly. One large tree stood at the west end. The entire area was surrounded by sidewalk.

Ron picked up an empty liquor bottle and placed it in a plastic bag he had brought with him.

"What are you going to do with that?"

"CITO."

"See to what?" Sabre asked.

"C-I-T-O. It's the first rule of geocaching. Cache In Trash Out. All good geocachers bring a trash bag with them to help clean up."

"I like that."

"They even have a CITO event once a year where lots of geocachers participate in cleanup. They've been doing it since 2002. I've joined in with them the last four years."

Sabre looked at her brother with admiration.

"Are you surprised that I would do that?"

"No, it's just that there is so much I don't know about you. So much we missed when you were gone."

Ron hugged her. "I'm back now, Sis, and I'm not going anywhere soon." Then he yanked on her braid and jumped back. "I think we've checked every bush, nook, and cranny here."

"And all we found is an empty booze bottle. Maybe someone beat us to it."

"Or maybe we just missed it. Or maybe we're not in the right spot."

"It has to be on this common ground. There are condos on three sides and the road on the other. They're not going to put it on someone's porch." She paused. "Do you think?"

"No. We can rule out the porches." Ron laid the bag with the bottle down. Then he crossed the street and stepped onto the sidewalk that abutted an eight-foot fence. "According to the GPS I'm just getting further away," he called out and walked back. "Now I'm getting closer. Let's check every bush again. You start at the top, and I'll work from the bottom up. Remember, it could be as small as a pill box."

Sabre methodically worked her way from plant to plant, pushing aside the stems and leaves, looking in and around each one, moving rocks that might be big enough to conceal a cache, but to no avail. Ron did the same working his way up the hill. Approximately twenty minutes later they met near the middle in front of a large rock where Sabre sat down.

"This place is as clean as a whistle," Sabre said. "There's not even a scrap of paper."

"Nothing besides the bottle," Ron said.

"The maintenance here is pretty exceptional. How do you suppose that got there when everything else is so clean?"

"Someone recently driving or walking by probably tossed it. Most likely an underage drinker."

Sabre straightened her posture. "Maybe the bottle is the cache. Did you look inside to make sure there's nothing there?"

Ron and Sabre walked to where Ron had left the trash bag and retrieved the bottle. Ron removed it and turned it upside down over his left palm. Nothing came out. He held it up and peeked inside through the small opening, but couldn't see anything.

"What kind of alcohol is it?" Sabre asked, trying to see the outside label as Ron peeked inside.

Ron brought it down and turned it so they both could read the label. "It looks like it's brandy."

"Brandy?" Sabre said, wrinkling her brow.

"Yeah, brandy. Isn't that the name of the mother on your case?"

"Yes, but that has to be a coincidence. That's just too weird."

"This whole geocaching adventure is weird. First Monroe and now Brandy."

She shook her head. "I think we're reading too much into this," Sabre said. She took the bottle and read the name on it. "Germain-Robin Coast Road Reserve California Brandy. I've never heard of it."

"Me neither, but then I'm not exactly a brandy connoisseur."

***

Sabre sat down at her laptop in her living room and typed in the name they had found on the liquor bottle. "How large is the bottle?" Sabre asked.

Ron sat next to her on the sofa holding the bottle. "It's seven hundred and fifty milliliters."

Sabre typed it in. "It's made in California by a man named Hubert Germain-Robin. His family, the Jules Robin family, has been distilling cognac since 1782. The Coast Road Reserve bottles are aged longer than most of his brandy. It says here that it's aged from eight to twenty-two years."

"Hmm, is it expensive?"

"It's not cheap. It's eighty dollars a bottle at BevMo!" She checked several more sites where the brandy was sold. "It ranges from about sixty-five to ninety dollars a bottle, depending on the store and the quantity you purchase."

"I guess I won't be drinking any Coast Road Reserve anytime soon."

"Me neither. And I do think we are just chasing our tails. I'm not convinced we found the cache."

"Bring up the cache again. I didn't check to see if there were any clues."

"I didn't know there could be clues," Sabre said, as she opened the site.

"A lot of the caches have clues. They're in code, but they provide the codes so you can easily figure them out. Sometimes they tell you what kind of container it is, or what size, or things like 'look up' if it's in a tree or on top of something."

"Now you tell me," Sabre said.

She typed in GCWA689. Once again the page read, "*404—File Not Found.*"

"It's gone, just like the last one," Sabre said.

"Do you mind if I take the bottle home with me?" Ron asked. "You're probably right. This is likely just a bottle someone threw away, but I want to study it a little further."

"No problem. Just let me get some photos of it in case JP wants to see it."

Chapter 14

JP sat at one of the small tables outside Jitter's Coffee Shop in La Mesa with his second cup of decaf. He attempted to read his emails on his cell phone, but he couldn't remember how to find them. Technology was not his thing, but Sabre had been teaching him slowly. He knew he needed to learn, but it didn't make the process any less painful.

"Well hello, handsome," Pauline Vasquez said, as she walked up to the table. She leaned down and kissed him lightly on his cheek.

"Hi, Pauline. Thanks for coming. What can I get you?"

"I'm good," she said, as she set a blue Contigo mug filled with water on the table. "I know this is not a social call, which is very disappointing because I would so much like it to be, but I'm here as your friend. We are still friends, aren't we?"

"I hope so." JP smiled. "I apologize for not keeping in touch."

"No excuse?"

"Excuses are like backsides. Everyone's got one, and they all stink."

"That's the cowboy I know and love." She slowly slid her hand down the side of his face and onto his neck, reaching his chest before she removed it. "So why am I here?"

"I'm trying to get some information on Monroe Bullard."

"Senator Bullard's brother?"

"Yes, do you know much about the family?"

"I know their mother is the moving force behind that family. She came from old southern money, one of the few families in the south that had prestige and still maintained its fortune. She married Attorney James Bullard and provided him with a lot of well-known clients, mostly in politics—governors, senators, and representatives like Bill Frist and John and Jimmy Duncan."

"Sorry, those names don't mean anything to me."

"All very important politicians. James Bullard also worked with Chet Atkins, who was a close personal friend of his father-in-law."

"Now that name I know. I guess I'm more in step with country music than politics."

"Most people don't know much about the senators and representatives of other states. A lot don't even follow the leaders of their own state." She flung her head to one side, tossing her hair back. "But enough of my soapbox. What specifically do you need to know?"

"I'd like to know why Monroe ended his political career. There's reason to believe he fathered a child about seventeen years ago with a minor. Is there any truth to that? It may be helpful to know what he's doing now and what he has done for the last seventeen years. Oh, and a current address if possible. Can you do that for me?"

"I haven't paid much attention to the Bullards lately, but I'll see what I can find out for you. I have a couple of friends in Tennessee who may be able to help."

"I'd appreciate that."

Pauline checked the time on her phone. "I've got to run." She stood up and placed her hand on his. "Now that we've established we're still friends, let me know if you want to reconsider that 'benefits' thing."

JP nodded and smiled but gave no verbal response.

"Ta-ta," she said and left. Instead of watching her

walk away as he normally would have, he called Sabre.

"Hi, kid, are you available for dinner tonight?"

"I have a trial tomorrow that I need to work on, so I can't be late."

"No problem. I'll pick you up at six thirty and have you home by eight. Just dinner."

***

Ron set the empty brandy bottle on the coffee table and sat down on the sofa.

"What's that?" his mother asked.

"Do you remember I told you that I was going geocaching today with Sabre?"

"Yes."

"We didn't find the cache. Or at least we don't think we did, unless this is it because it's all we found."

"I thought they were like treasure boxes or containers."

"They are. That's why this is probably not it. But this geocache is unusual. One cache leads to the next, and I'm wondering if this bottle is somehow a clue to something."

His mother caressed his shoulder. "You and your puzzles. Always trying to figure something out. I guess some things never change." She walked toward the kitchen. "Have fun. I'll let you know when dinner is ready."

"Thanks, Mom."

Ron picked up the bottle and examined it from top to bottom, reading every word on the label. The information included how the brandy was brewed at an antique cognac distillery since 1982. The distillery had plenty of pinot noir brandy and was located on the Pomo Indian Nature Trail. It was a 750 mL bottle with forty percent alcohol. The only other thing on the bottle was a map of the trail. Nothing seemed very relevant to his task at hand.

He turned on the flashlight on his phone and shined it down inside the bottle to make sure he hadn't missed a note that had stuck to the side or perhaps some other clue. When he found nothing, he set it back down.

He got up and went to the den and retrieved a pen and a pad of paper. Then he picked up the bottle again and started to write on his pad. He wrote the full name on the label: Germain-Robin Coast Road Reserve California Brandy. Then he wrote out the first letter of each word: G-R-C-R-R-C-B. He tried making words out of the letters: Grucrsb, graserusb, Grace Rosab.

He texted Sabre: *Does the name Grace Rosab or just Grace mean anything to you?*

Sabre: *No, should it?*

Ron: *Probably not. I'm just playing with the brandy bottle. Later.*

Then it hit him. Germain-Robin was one word, which would make the first two letters GC. That was the first two letters of every geocache code. Now he just had to figure out the rest.

Ron opened his laptop, typed in www.geocaching.com, and entered his password. When the site opened, he wrote in the search window the code GCRRCB. It led him to a cache in Northern Cape, South Africa.

"That can't be it," he mumbled.

"Did you say something, Ronnie?" his mother called from the kitchen.

"Just talking to myself."

Ron looked at the bottle for more clues. He jotted down anything on the bottle that might be a hint: *Pomo Indian Trail, 1982, antique, cognac, distillery, pinot noir, 750 mL, 40 percent.*

On the site he tried GCRRCB82, but no file existed. He dropped the C for California—still nothing. He dropped the B and found a cache in British Columbia, Canada. Too far away. He tried several combinations with the word Pomo but found no caches.

Next he tried the number 40 in several combinations. GC40RRC was in Southern England. Other combinations with the number 40 gave the error message "*404—File Not Found.*" He finally tried GCRR40 and found a cache near Manhattan Beach, California. That was only a few hours away, but Ron thought it could be possible. Then he realized the cache had already been archived. He sighed. It was a relief, since he didn't relish driving into L.A. traffic to hunt for something he wasn't even sure was there.

He tried similar combinations of letters and 750, the only other number on the bottle. This led him to caches in Washington, Georgia, and Stuttgart, Germany, and finally, San Diego.

"That's it," Ron said, louder than he intended.

His mother returned to the room. "Did you figure it out?"

"I think so."

"Good, now come eat. Dinner is ready."

Ron felt good. It was nice to be home and eating his mother's cooking again. But mostly he felt good helping his sister. She had done so much for him recently; he just wanted to give back a little.

"I'll be right in, Mom."

He called Sabre and gave her the code. "If you want to go out tomorrow, I'll be glad to go with you, or if you just want me to do it, I can."

"Let me see how long I'm stuck in court. I'll text you tomorrow when I'm done."

Chapter 15

JP stopped to see his friend Ernie Madrigal at the El Cajon Sheriff's Department.

"You look to me like you have your 'this-is-business' face on," Ernie said. "What's up?"

"Remember the geocache we brought in with the death certificate?"

"Yes, do you have anything new on it?"

"It just so happens that the name 'Monroe' came up on one of Sabre's cases. Monroe Bullard. He's from an old-money, political family in Tennessee. His brother is a U.S. senator. Besides that, Sabre figured out that the number on the death certificate was not a filing or an account number, but the code for another cache. That cache was a riddle that led her to another." JP stopped.

"And that led to another cache?" Ernie prompted.

"Sort of. They didn't find a typical container with anything in it, but they did find an empty alcohol bottle—a brandy bottle."

"Your point?"

"The mother's name on Sabre's case is Brandy. I know this is a stretch, and it might not be anything, but there are only two days left until this death certificate comes to fruition—assuming it's real. I wouldn't want to think I let someone die because I didn't take it seriously."

"I still don't see that a crime has been committed. What is it you want me to do?"

"My sources are trying to get me information on Monroe Bullard. I'd like you to do the same. I have a political reporter friend who can get me the inside scoop, but I don't know if she'll be able to track his whereabouts. I was hoping you could."

"I'll see what I can do, but first tell me about your political reporter friend. Is that Pauline Vasquez, the one you used to date?"

JP said, "Yes," without any change of expression.

"That woman is hot!"

"She's just a friend."

Ernie cocked his head to one side and raised one eyebrow. "Does Sabre know about your 'friendship'?" He made air quotes when he said "friendship."

"She knows I have friends, and she knows I have a past. So does she. I don't want to know about the men she's been with; I doubt if she wants to know about my past relationships either."

Ernie shook his head. "I don't know. You're in a committed relationship. You might want to select your sources a little more carefully."

"Yeah, like you for instance." They both laughed.

"I'll let you know when I find something on Monroe Bullard."

"Thanks, I'd like to let him know that he may be going home to meet Elvis in a few days."

***

Sabre's court hearings lasted well into the late morning. She still had one case to go, but Attorney Richard Wagner was on it and he was tied up in Department One. Sabre paced back and forth in front of Department Four.

"Do you have somewhere you need to be?" Bob asked.

"I'm supposed to meet my brother and run an errand with him, but I have to get this case done first. I have a trial this afternoon, so I was hoping we could get it done before then."

"I would appear for you, but since we are on opposing sides, I guess I can't do that."

"Or, you could convince your client that unsupervised visits are out of the question until she gets rid of the man who molested her daughter."

"Sorry. She's in love," Bob dragged out the word "love." "You can't argue with a woman in love." He extended the word "love" again. "Besides, she doesn't believe he did anything wrong."

"What do you mean she doesn't believe it? She caught him in bed with her."

"Yeah, but he was drunk and he thought it was my client."

Sabre chuckled. "And that's the argument you're going to make to Judge Hekman? That the perpetrator couldn't tell the difference between his extremely voluptuous wife and an eight-year-old girl?"

"I have to go with what I have, but I'll do it in a very persuasive voice."

***

It was 12:16 when Sabre and Bob finished their last hearing.

"That went well," Bob said, as they walked out of the courtroom.

"You mean that your client didn't get held in contempt for calling the judge an idiot?"

"She didn't exactly call the judge an idiot. She mumbled it after the judge ruled."

"That was a smart move on your part to suggest your client was probably talking about you," Sabre said. "Given the argument you made, Hekman probably agreed with her."

"My client's the idiot. She actually thought that argument would work." They walked out of the courthouse. "Enough of that. Let's go to Pho's. You don't have time to run your errands with your brother now."

"You're right." Sabre called Ron and explained they would have to go after her trial, if she was done in time. Otherwise, it would have to wait until tomorrow.

"If I don't hear from you by two thirty, I'll go on my own. For all we know, this isn't even the cache we're looking for."

"If you don't mind, that would be great."

"Anything for my favorite sister," Ron said and hung up.

Bob looked at Sabre. His face was solemn. "Is everything okay, Sobs?"

"Yeah, it's fine."

"Do you want me to cover your trial this afternoon?"

"No. I need to be there. If I'm not done early enough, Ron can go on his own."

"What is he doing?"

"Nothing important." She took his arm in hers. "It's no big thing." She didn't like keeping things from Bob. He was always a great sounding board for her. But until she knew whether the caches were connected to the McFerran case, she couldn't discuss it with Bob. "Let's go eat. Do you know what you're having?"

"Of course, Number 124. It's the best thing on the menu."

"How would you know? You've never tried anything else."

Chapter 16

JP sat at the bar at Jake's in Del Mar waiting for Pauline. The stools on either side of him were empty, as well as seven or eight others along the bar. It was nearly 8:30 p.m. and he was tired, but Pauline had insisted on meeting rather than having a phone conversation. He had already been there for over half an hour. He hoped it was worth the wait.

He positioned himself at the curve of the bar so he could see the door when she entered. He took the last swig of his beer and set the empty bottle down. Two attractive women in their early-to-mid-twenties approached.

"Are these seats taken?" the blonde with a purple streak in her hair asked.

"I'm afraid one of them is," JP said.

"Your date?"

JP started to say "no," but decided a "yes" gave way to far less explanation and showed less interest on his part.

"Afraid so," he said.

The blonde leaned down close to his ear and spoke softly. "A word of advice, cowboy. If you aren't looking, you might want to ditch the hat. It's a real turn-on to some of us."

JP tipped his black Stetson. "I'll keep that in mind, ma'am."

Just as the women started to walk away, Pauline approached, wearing a slinky, black cocktail dress and some of the tallest heels he had ever seen.

"Sorry I'm so late. I was at a work-related party in Rancho Santa Fe." She leaned over and pecked JP on the cheek. She had the move down pat—quick, soft, and never bumping his hat.

"Hobnobbing with the big wigs, huh?"

"That's my life."

She turned as the bartender walked up and set a cocktail napkin in front of her. Before he could ask what she wanted, she said, "Do you have Finlandia Vodka?"

"Yes, we do."

"How about Cointreau?"

"Absolutely. Would you like a cosmo?"

"Yes, with lime not lemon, but not too heavy on the lime."

"You got it."

Pauline turned back to JP before the bartender walked away. "It's nice to see you again. Two days in a row. We haven't done that in a while."

"It's nice to see you too, Pauline. What did you find out about Monroe?"

She caressed his arm. "Please give me a few minutes to relax. I've been working all day and half the night."

He looked at her dress. "You don't look like you've been working that hard."

"Are you kidding me? The parties are the worst. A bunch of old, inebriated politicians hanging on me. Most of them hate their wives, but they're stuck with them. They wouldn't give a second thought to cheating on them. There are two things they have no respect for: their wives and the tax laws. And a lot of them are gropers. I hate the gropers."

"They can't all be like that."

"No, of course not, but there are more than I care to deal with."

The bartender brought the cosmo. "Can I get you another Coors Light?"

JP hadn't planned on having another, but it didn't look like he was going to get out of there any too soon.

"Yes, please."

Pauline picked up her cosmopolitan and held it for a few seconds before she brought it to her lips. She took such a small sip that JP wondered if it even wet her tongue. He immediately dismissed the thought of her wet tongue.

"I'm hungry. Let's get something to eat."

"Really?" JP said. "Are you going to put me through this?"

"Is my company so bad?" She cocked her head to one side and pouted her lips.

"No, you know I enjoy your company, Pauline. It's just getting late."

"We'll just have an appetizer. Please."

The bartender returned with his beer, and JP paid for the drinks and left a generous tip.

Pauline stood up with her drink in her hand and spoke to the bartender. "We're moving to the patio for an appetizer." Then she moved toward the door that led outside.

JP thanked him, picked up his beer, and followed her.

An hour later Pauline had consumed an order of macadamia-nut-crusted calamari, a few spoonfuls of seafood chowder, her second cosmo, and a scotch. JP stopped after his second beer.

After the second time that Pauline ran her foot up JP's leg, he said, "It's been fun catching up, but I really need to go. What can you tell me about Bullard?"

She wrinkled her nose and pouted for a couple of seconds, and then she said, "Monroe was the golden boy until he became a teenager. I couldn't get his juvenile record, but there are plenty of rumors about how many times his parents had to step in and save him. I guess they thought he would outgrow his delinquency because they continued to further him on the path to greatness. He settled down some when he went to college, but he still had a reputation for being a playboy who got a little rough with his women."

"I couldn't find any convictions or even arrests on him," JP said. "Are you aware of any?"

"No, he has no record. Mother Bullard saw to that."

"Anything else?"

She took a drink of her scotch before she continued. "There was an incident with a young singer. There are a couple of photos of the two of them together but nothing really incriminating. I'm trying to get those for you, but that's for another time." She ran her finger along the back of JP's hand and then moved it back to her glass in one smooth move.

JP didn't respond.

"A couple of rag papers ran one or two articles, but then the publicity stopped," she continued. "I'm sure they were paid off. I have a good friend in Nashville who knows there was a paternity test run, but the results were never revealed. The test was done by a private facility."

"If he wasn't the father, do you think the test would have been used to squelch further investigation by the media?"

"Not necessarily. It was really a two-edged sword. They couldn't admit that he had sex with her, and if he didn't, why would he need a test? The issue wasn't whether or not he was the father; it was whether or not he was with an underage girl."

"We have a client involved in a juvenile court case who claims Monroe is the father of her eldest child. She says there was a test taken and that Monroe told her the test came out negative, but she claims that it had to be him because he was the only one she had been with."

"Is she credible?"

"No, not really."

"I think she's probably telling the truth. Anyway, it looks like the scandal started to come out, the family hushed it up, and it all went away. My source is still trying to get the test results. I haven't given up yet." She winked at him. "By the way, the girl never made it as a singer, at least not in Nashville."

"Did you get her name?"

"She went by the name Brandy, just Brandy, no last name. I don't know if that was her stage name or if it was real. I'll find that out for you."

"No need."

"It ended Monroe's political career, or at least that was the final straw. His brother, Richard, became the main focus of the family and, as you can see, that was a wise choice."

"What has Monroe been doing since then?"

"Not much of anything. They try to keep him out of the public eye, but every once in a while he surfaces and proves to be an embarrassment."

"In what way?"

"There was a hooker scandal about ten years ago. She claimed he got too rough, but that went away and she apologized to the family for 'lying' to them." Pauline made quotation signs in the air as she said the word "lying."

"Do you have any more information on the woman involved?"

"My guess is that 'Haley Hooker' is either living quite well now, or she had one heck of a high for a while. I haven't been able to follow up on that yet. Do you need it?"

"If you can get it without too much trouble. At least a name might help."

She ran her finger along his, from the tip to the back of his hand. "Anything for you, darling."

"Where is Monroe now? I have an address for him in Clarksville, Tennessee, but when I followed up on it, he was no longer living there."

"I don't know where he is exactly. I do know where he *isn't*, however. He *isn't* in Tennessee. He left a few months back, but I don't know where he went yet. That shouldn't be too hard to find." She smiled. "I'll have it for you next time we get together."

JP decided the next time would be earlier in the day.

The waitress came by and asked if she could get them anything else. When Pauline started to order another scotch, JP asked, "How are you getting home?"

She pointed a finger at him. "You're taking me, darling. I certainly can't drive. I've had way too much to drink."

"If you're going with me, we're leaving now." JP looked at the waitress. "Please just bring the check."

"I love it when you get all manly on me." She leaned close to JP and smiled.

When the waitress returned with the bill, Pauline insisted on paying for it. Having a woman pay for dinner, or anything, didn't set well with JP. He knew that was considered chauvinistic, but to him it was just good manners. His grandpappy had taught him well. Besides, she was doing him a favor by providing the information.

"Please, let me get it," he said, as he reached for the check.

She placed her hand on top of his. "Honey, it was my food and my drinks. Besides, I make tons more money than you do. Let me." She stood up.

He knew she did make a lot more money than he did, but that didn't make it feel any better. JP didn't want to make a scene in the restaurant, even though there were only a few people left. That would be even more embarrassing to him than having a woman pay for the check, so he let it go.

As they left the table, JP looked at Pauline and wondered how she was going to be able to walk on those spikes she came in with, but she did so with complete grace, in spite of the alcohol she had consumed. He chalked it up to years of practice.

***

The drive to Pauline's house in La Jolla was uncomfortable for JP. He knew it would be, but he couldn't let her drive herself. Every time she spoke, she would touch his shoulder, his arm, or his leg—only for a second, but just long enough for JP to know her intentions.

He drove up the hill and pulled in the driveway in front of her house. The home was not as large as many that surrounded it, but the view was spectacular. The ocean loomed below, just past the city lights. Although JP appreciated the view, he still preferred a ranch or a place in the mountains.

"You coming in?" Pauline asked, giving him her sweetest smile.

"No," he said without hesitation, "but I'll walk you to your door." He stepped out, and she waited until he opened her car door. He accompanied her to her door, made sure she was inside, and before she could say "ta-ta" or make any kind of move, he walked away. She was a beautiful woman with no strings attached, but all he could think of was Sabre.

Chapter 17

"**I** can't get away," Sabre said to Ron on the phone. "I'm stuck in court again. Can you go check on the cache? We've only got one day left before the date on the death certificate, and I don't know when I'm going to get out of here."

"No problem. I'll talk to you this afternoon."

"Thanks, Bro."

Sabre hung up just as Bob walked up. "Hi, honey. I have some news for you on McFerran."

"Ah, my client, the lovely Brandy McFerran," Bob said, "mother of five children with four different fathers. You gotta love a woman who isn't afraid to experiment a little."

"A little?" Sabre said. "Anyway, it's not that she has so many different men in her life; it's her choice of men. Nearly every one of them has knocked her around."

"So what's your news?"

"First of all, Conway knows about Monroe. He believes that Monroe is his father because he has heard Brandy talking about it—many times."

"Yeah, she's not the most discreet woman around. What else?"

"There may be some truth to Brandy's story about the Bullard family and how it all went down. Most of it doesn't matter to the case right now, but it would be important to establish who Conway's father is, if possible."

"Imagine that, my client might be telling the truth. To listen to her tales of her singing career, you'd think she was Dolly Parton herself. I figured she was just blowing smoke about the senator connection. She's quite the name-dropper—mentions every star she ever had the slightest contact with, like her tales of Chet Atkins." Bob looked at Sabre with scrutiny. "You know who Chet Atkins is, right? Of course you do. You're a country music gal. Not exactly my kind of music, but it's nice that you and JP have that in common—although JP's old enough to have toured with him."

"JP's not that old. And really, this is coming from a guy who worships Leonard Cohen? Now, are you done ragging on me?"

"For the moment."

"Brandy may be telling the truth when she tells stories about Chet Atkins, or at least stories she has heard about him. Apparently, Monroe's grandfather was a good friend of Atkins."

An announcement came over the intercom: "Regina Collicott, Jerry Leahy, Robert Clark, and Sabre Brown, please come to Department One."

"That's us," Sabre said, as they moved through the crowded courthouse.

Just before she reached Department One, Sabre received a text.

Ron: *Have you tried to log in to yesterday's cache?*

Sabre: *You mean the one we didn't find? The brandy bottle?*

Ron: *Yes.*

Sabre: *No.*

Ron: *I did, and it's gone, like the last one.*

Sabre: *So you think we may have found the right one?*

Ron: *That's what I'm thinking. Going out to see if the code I found works.*

***

The sun was shining as Ron pulled into the parking lot. He checked his GPS coordinates and felt comfortable that he was as close as he was going to get in a vehicle. He exited the car and looked around. It reminded him of a place he had visited in Idaho just a few months ago. But on that day, he'd had company. He thought of Gina Basham. Ron had geocached many times by himself and found it to be relatively enjoyable. And then he met Gina, who really made it exciting for him. She seemed to be as interested in the sport as he was, and for the first time he had a partner. He sighed. *That's all in the past,* he thought.

The coordinates led him to a wooden sign about ten feet wide and four feet tall. It was secured in concrete and surrounded by trees and bushes. It read:

> *Mission Trails*
> *Regional Park*
> *Cowles Mountain*

This signpost marked the main junction to the mile-and-a-half trail to the summit. The cache was clearly close to it, so Ron started moving his way through the brush. It didn't take long to find the blue plastic container wedged between two rocks and hidden by a laurel sumac bush just beginning to bloom. The container was approximately ten inches long, six inches wide, and four inches deep.

He picked it up, leaned against the sign, and opened the cover. Inside was a rubber green frog, a baseball trading card, a bookmark for an author he didn't recognize, a Monopoly thimble, a complimentary-sized bar of soap, and a travel-sized package of Kleenex tissues.

This was very different from the other caches that appeared to be connected to Sabre's case. All the rest had only a single item. This one also contained a log sheet, which the other caches didn't have. Ron was convinced he had found the wrong cache, but just to be certain, he carefully photographed each and every item in the box. He removed the bookmark and replaced it with a pocket-sized, plastic pencil sharpener he had brought with him just in case he needed it for the cache. He'd also brought a deck of cards and a small notepad. He always wanted to make sure he made an appropriate exchange.

Ron was disappointed about the find. He was so sure he had figured out the right code in the last cache, and there was no doubt in his mind that the bottle was the clue. Now he would have to try some different combinations on the brandy bottle. His thoughts turned to the contents of the cache he just found. Perhaps this was the right cache and the clues were in there. As the thoughts bounced around in his head, he decided to try something that might rid his brain of all the inconsequential clutter; he would hike the mountain before he went back to his code-breaking. It had been nearly ten years since he climbed Cowles Mountain. Prior to that, he and his girlfriend, Carla, made the hike many times.

He started up the mountain, hoping to clear his head.

Chapter 18

"Where's JP tonight?" Ron asked. "I thought you two would be out dancing the night away."

"He's working on a case."

"You made him work instead of going out with you tonight? Shame on you."

"He's not working for me. It's for another attorney, and he's on a stakeout. He hates to do those. Most of the time, they're just boring."

"Yeah, I guess it's not like he can play on a tablet or anything because he'd probably miss what he's watching for."

"He'll call later if he's somewhere he can talk," Sabre said. She shifted forward on the sofa. "So you struck out today?"

"Yes, but I had a great hike up Cowles Mountain. It felt good to reach the top. It made me think of Carla. Remember our first hike up the mountain with her?"

"Yes, you were mean, telling her there was a Starbucks coffee cart at the top."

"It motivated her to climb it, didn't it? She really didn't want to go up."

"I don't know how you did it with a straight face. And how you got her to believe it is beyond me."

"I think the clincher was when I sent her back to her car to get her money."

"That was just mean."

"Once she climbed it, she loved it. We went climbing many times after that." Ron sighed. "Do you think I should go see her?"

Carla had been through a lot the last ten years. She lost her father, then her mother, and she was dating Ron off and on before he went into the Witness

Protection Program. Neither Carla, Sabre, nor his mother knew that Ron was even alive. Carla finally snapped and spent months in a mental hospital. Sabre had helped her as much as she could, but it never seemed like enough to Sabre. Carla eventually improved with a lot of therapy, was released several years ago, and was living a normal life.

"I'll call her and set something up," Sabre said. "You don't want to just run into her on the street."

"Thanks." Ron stood up and took a step toward the kitchen. "Do you have anything to eat?"

"I ordered us a large, vegetarian pizza. It'll be here shortly. Come sit."

Ron turned back and sat next to Sabre on the sofa in front of the computer on the coffee table. Next to the computer were Ron's notepad, the Germain-Robin brandy bottle, a copy of the death certificate, the note from the second cache, and the bookmark Ron had retrieved in the last cache.

"Yes, I struck out today. When I got home, I attempted to form all kinds of codes with the junk I found in the cache, but nothing seemed plausible."

"And you logged into the code online?"

"Yes, it's still there. It didn't go away like the others."

"So the bottle is probably nothing either."

"Or I just came up with the wrong code. There are still some possible combinations." Ron's stomach growled. "And I'm sure I could figure it out if I just had some food."

Sabre picked up the bookmark, read it over, and then laid it back down.

Ron retrieved the liquor bottle. "I know it's here. Let's try some more combinations."

"I think we're wasting our time." She looked again at the items. "You know, we really have nothing other than the death certificate, and that's probably just a hoax."

Ron shrugged.

Sabre knew how much fun Ron was having, and it helped fill his time between job applications. "We'll give it one more shot. That's if we can find another code that works from the bottle. If not, we bag it, okay?"

"Fair enough." Ron picked up his notepad and opened it to where he had played with the codes the day before. He scribbled a couple of letters on the pad just as the doorbell rang. He stood up. "That's probably the pizza."

Sabre reached in her pocket for some money, but Ron already had his wallet out and was paying for it. He took the pizza and closed the door. Sabre handed Ron a twenty, but he pushed it away.

"I got this. I still have a little money saved from my last job."

"But you won't if you don't find a job soon."

"I will, don't worry. Just let me treat my little sis. If I run out, you'll be the first I borrow from." He smiled his charming smile.

"Fair enough." They walked into the kitchen and sat down at the table.

Sabre ate one slice of pizza. Ron ate three. When they stood to go back to work, Ron picked up the pizza box and a couple of napkins. Sabre looked at him.

"In case I want some more," he said, and followed her into the living room.

They spent nearly an hour coming up with possible geocache codes from the bottle before they felt like they had exhausted all combinations. They had three more that fit the pattern. One was in Texas. That was out. One was in Bakersfield, California, about 400 miles away. Even if that was the one they were looking for, they weren't driving there. The last one was in

Pacific Beach, a beach community in San Diego.

"Can you go out tomorrow, or do you want me to go without you?" Ron asked.

"I can go first thing in the morning. How about seven thirty?"

"That's not first thing. That's halfway through the morning."

"Just be here at seven thirty. Now go home. I have real work to do."

Ron stood up and walked toward the door. Sabre picked up the pizza box and handed it to him. Ron took it and pecked her on the cheek.

"It's sure nice to have you home, Bro," she said and closed the door.

***

"Are you sure you have the coordinates right?" Sabre asked.

"Yes," Ron said. "I checked them several times." He walked along the boardwalk near the bay in Crown Point with Sabre following closely behind, each of them looking at every clump of plant life, bench, or crevice they could find. Ron picked up an empty Miller can, looked inside, and then carried it to the trashcan and dropped it in. "We're moving away from the coordinates. It should be closer to the steps."

They turned and walked back to the concrete steps. While climbing the thirty steps that led up to the street, Ron and Sabre crouched down and rummaged through the ice plant that lined each of the stairs.

About a third of the way up, Sabre picked up a plastic prescription bottle tucked right up against the step where a chunk of the concrete had chipped away. Part of the label was missing from the bottle, but the name of the drug was legible. It read "Fluoxetine."

"I think I found it," Sabre said.

Ron walked down the two steps to be on her level. "A prescription bottle? Is there something inside?"

"I don't know. I haven't looked yet, but this is the same drug that is listed as a consequence of the cause of death on Monroe's death certificate."

"But this says 'Fluoxetine.' The death certificate says 'Prozac.'"

"Prozac is the brand name."

"Really? Let me see that," Ron reached for the bottle.

"Be careful," Sabre said. "Don't put any more fingerprints on it. I'm afraid it already has mine."

Ron pulled out a pair of latex gloves from his pocket and put them on.

"Why do you have gloves in your pocket?" Sabre asked with a hint of incredulity in her voice.

"I always carry them when I geocache."

"Of course you do." Sabre smiled.

"You scoff, but there are times when I have to look through things I'm not sure I want to touch."

Ron removed the lid from the bottle and shook out a note. He opened it up and read it. "Good job."

"That's it? That's all it says?" Sabre said, positioning herself where she could see the note. Ron turned it toward her.

"That's it." He looked the bottle over carefully, turning it all around. "Look, you can see part of the patient's name on the label. It starts with B-r—as in Brandy," Ron said, raising his voice when he said her name.

"You don't think we're just stretching this thing to fit?" Sabre said.

"It's quite a coincidence that we would find a bottle with the same drug that is on the death certificate, don't you think?"

"Yes, but this may not even be the cache."

"Oh, it's the cache all right." He turned the bottle so Sabre could see the label. "Look at the prescription number. It starts with GC, just like the codes. Prescriptions don't start with GC."

Chapter 19

Sabre and Ron sat down on a cement bench along the boardwalk about thirty feet from where they found the cache. Sabre pulled her iPad out of her backpack and opened it up to the geocaching site.

"What is that code on the prescription bottle?"

Ron read it to her, and she typed it in the search window. A cache page appeared.

"It's close to here."

"Let me see," Ron said. "You're right. It's real close." Ron put the coordinates in his GPS. "Let's go."

They walked on the boardwalk for about five hundred feet and stopped in front of seven catamarans lined up in a row along the beach. "It should be around here," Ron said, as he donned his latex gloves again. "You start at that end. I'll start here."

A homeless person lay on the beach about twenty feet away. They couldn't tell if it was a man or a woman because his or her head was covered. The person was completely immersed in a tattered sleeping bag, the rest of the belongings tucked alongside.

"If I were homeless and sleeping on the beach at night," Ron said, "I would climb under one of these catamarans. It would give you lots of shelter."

"I've often thought that too, yet I've never seen anyone under them."

"Perhaps they've tried it and someone chases them away."

Sabre looked all around the first boat, on top of it, under it, and in the crevices of the sails that were wrapped up tightly, but found nothing. She moved on to the next one.

"Do you find it odd that there are two caches along

the path where I walk nearly every day with Jennifer?"

"Maybe Jennifer has hidden this stuff. She's a geocacher herself, right?"

"Yes, but she wouldn't do that."

"She's quite a character. She loves to play tricks on people. You told me about the time you two laid a costume jewelry ring on the boardwalk near the beach and watched as people came by to see what they would do. Wasn't that her idea?"

"Yes, she loved to do that. Sometimes she would put money on the ground; sometimes it was jewelry. Some people would pick it up and set it on the wall. Most of the time when they took it with them, they would look around all sneaky-like and then stick it in their pocket."

"This certainly sounds like something she would do."

"It's exactly the kind of thing she would do. It's also the kind of thing you would do, but neither of you knew about Monroe. I didn't even know about Monroe."

"That's true." Ron examined the next boat. "By the way, it's not me doing this. I haven't stopped playing tricks on you, and I have years of missed jokes to catch up on. But with all the things you've been through with your cases, I wouldn't do anything that frightened you."

"I know," Sabre said. "Actually, this would be kind of fun if it weren't so bizarre." She stopped searching when she spotted a rectangular plastic container on the inside of a catamaran. "Hey, I may have something here."

Ron walked around the boats to where she was standing.

"Why don't you see what's in it? It may be better if we don't get any fingerprints on it."

"Sure."

The plastic box sat on a bar that dropped down

several inches on the inside of the catamaran. The box was about six inches long and four inches wide. Ron picked it up and popped open the latches on each side of it that held it shut. A typed note read: *2 of 3*. Ron picked up the note and underneath he found a photograph.

"Is that who I think it is?" Sabre asked.

"I don't know. Who do you think it is?"

"It looks like Chet Atkins."

"The country singer?"

"Yes." Sabre retrieved her phone from her bag and Googled images of Chet Atkins. "Yeah. That's him. Look."

"That's weird."

"Not all that weird. This case has a connection to Chet Atkins."

"The country singer?"

"You keep saying that. Yes, the country singer."

"How?"

"It's not important at the moment. There's no log or anything else in the box?"

"Nope. That's it."

"The note says 'two of three.' Do you suppose that means there are two more?"

"It sure sounds like it."

Ron returned to where he had stopped searching, and within minutes he found a second plastic container about the same size as the first. This one was tucked inside a fold of the sail, held there by a rope that wrapped around the sails. Sabre reached his side just as he opened it up and saw another typewritten note: *1 of 3*. Underneath the note was another photograph but nothing else. Ron held it up.

"That's George Clooney," Sabre said. "Dang, he's good looking." She made a funny face. "George Clooney? I'm not complaining, mind you. He's quite a treasure, but why George Clooney?"

"Is this case connected to him too?" Ron asked.

"Not that I know of, but I wouldn't mind if it were." She smirked. "There has to be one more cache. Let's find it."

Ron found the third container underneath one of the boats. It was difficult to find because it was tucked into some tall weeds. He carried it to Sabre before he opened it.

This one read: *3 of 3*. Underneath was the front part of a greeting card that had been torn apart. It had a picture of a big-breasted cowgirl in skimpy cut-off blue jeans, lizard-skin cowboy boots, and a red raffia cowboy hat. Across the top were two words: *Happy Birthday*.

Chapter 20

When JP arrived at Sabre's house, she and Ron had the newfound caches spread out on the coffee table in order by number. JP handed Sabre a large, white envelope.

"Here's the report on the McFerran case, for what it's worth. There's not much there yet."

JP observed the layout on the table. Underneath the *1 of 3* note was the picture of George Clooney. Next to it, was the *2 of 3* note with the photo of Chet Atkins. On its right was the *3 of 3* note with the greeting card that read *Happy Birthday.* Sabre and her brother had been studying them for some time.

JP stood over them and looked at the spread before him. "I don't like this, Sabre. Especially the Chet Atkins thing."

"What is the Chet Atkins thing?" Ron asked.

"Atkins was apparently a good friend of Monroe Bullard's parents or grandparents," Sabre said.

"So this can't be a coincidence."

"I don't think it is," JP said. "The real question is whether these were meant for Sabre to find. And if so, why?"

"And how they knew we would find them in the first place." Sabre said.

"Have you told anyone involved in this case that you geocache?" JP asked.

"No. I'm sure I haven't, and there would be no reason for it to come up in conversation."

"Could you have mentioned it in court, where it could have been overheard?"

"I don't think so." Sabre thought about any conversations she may have had while waiting for this case to be heard. "Bob and I talk about all sorts of stuff when we're waiting for a case to be heard, but we're usually not around the clients."

"Think," JP said, his voice a little harsher than usual. "Who else knows you geocache?"

"Jennifer, but it can't be her, and who is she going to tell?"

"I don't know. You need to ask her."

"You're really concerned about this, aren't you?" Ron interjected.

JP rubbed his chin and looked directly at Sabre. "Someone may die tomorrow and you, Sabre, have been warned about it. The victim has been directly connected to a case you're involved in. And you have been targeted to follow clues to solve his murder." He turned back to Ron. "Yes, I'm concerned."

"You were at the first geocache when the death certificate was found," Ron said. "And you're on the case too. Maybe it was you who was targeted?"

"I thought about that, but that was my first time geocaching. How would anyone know I was going? And I wasn't on the case until after this was discovered. No, it was meant for Sabre."

"I haven't been able to sleep well since we found the first cache, but it's not me I'm concerned about," Sabre said. "It's Monroe. We need to find him so we can warn him. We're all going to feel horrible if he dies and we could have saved him."

"I'm doing everything I can to locate him. I asked Ernie to try to find him, too. He told me yesterday that he had contacted the police department in Nashville, but I'm not sure that will do any good since he's apparently not there." JP took a deep breath. "Sabre, who else knows that you geocache?"

"I don't think I've told anyone else. However—" She paused.

"However, what?"

"Everyone on geocaching dot com knows because I have an account and a profile on there. It doesn't have my personal information, but anyone with a little savvy could figure it out. And I may have mentioned it on Facebook."

"So pretty much the whole world," JP mumbled.

Sabre tossed her hair back and took a deep breath. "Have you had any luck finding Monroe?" Sabre asked JP.

"I don't have an address yet, but I'm working on it."

"What happens now?" Ron asked.

JP swept his hand over the coffee table. "Now that we have more information, I'm going to take all this to my friend at the Sheriff's Department and see if he can do anything. In the meantime, we need to figure out what this cache means."

"I don't think it means anything except the code for the next cache, and maybe the Chet Atkins thing has a double meaning," Sabre said.

"How's that?" JP asked.

"George Clooney, Geo Cache, the codes all start with 'GC.'"

"And the next two letters are probably 'CA,'" Ron added. "And using Atkins also made sure you knew it was connected."

"That's what I'm thinking," Sabre said. "The big question is the rest of the code. We checked online for the code GCCAHB, the 'HB' standing for 'Happy Birthday,' but it wasn't a cache. I'm guessing it's someone's birthday, but that could be anyone."

"Is there any way to run the different combinations and check them without doing it manually?" JP asked.

"Not that I know of," Sabre said.

"Me, neither," Ron added. "But we can try some combinations, starting with you and Sabre."

"And even that will take some work. We don't know if it is the month and day; the month, day, and year; or just the year or some combination thereof."

"Can you put this stuff in a bag for me, and I'll take it to Ernie."

Ron put his latex gloves back on and took front and back photos of each piece so he and Sabre could continue to work with them. Then he bagged the caches and handed them to JP.

JP walked toward the door. "See what you can come up with. I'm going to take this stuff to Ernie, and I'm going to push my source for more info on Monroe's whereabouts—before he ends up dead."

Chapter 21

JP dropped the caches off with Ernie, who had agreed to run them for fingerprints and investigate further. JP knew Ernie couldn't spend a lot of time on the case since they still had no crime, but he had agreed to do what he could.

From there he drove to Jitter's Coffee Shop in La Mesa to meet with Pauline. He was reluctant to meet with her again because she had been so flirtatious the last time. He hoped it was the alcohol and the moonlight at their last meeting in Del Mar that spurred her on. He liked Pauline. She was intelligent, uncomplicated, and she was hot, but he didn't want anything to interfere with his chances with Sabre. They had come too far to let anything mess up their relationship now.

JP made a few phone calls on some other things he was working on. He laid his phone on the table when he finished and sat back and sipped his coffee. He had been waiting nearly half an hour when Pauline showed up wearing a white blouse, a dark blue skirt that lay a few inches above her knee, and pumps the same color as her skirt. The heels on her shoes were considerably lower than what she'd worn to Jake's. She looked very professional except for the open top button on her blouse that exposed a little too much cleavage. A large, leather purse hung from her left shoulder, and she carried her ever-present blue Contigo mug in her right hand.

JP had tried to obtain the information from Pauline over the phone, but she insisted on meeting with him.

"Thanks for coming," JP said.

She leaned in and pecked him on the cheek. "Of

course." She sat down in the seat closest to him on the cafe's patio, placing her mug on the wrought iron table and her bag on the chair next to her. She retrieved a large, white envelope from her bag and playfully dangled it out in front of her.

"Would you like anything to drink?" JP asked. "I'll go get you something. Coffee? Tea?"

"No, thanks." She nodded toward her mug. "I have my water."

"You said you have something new on Monroe?"

She sighed. "Yes." She opened the envelope, removed a photograph, and handed it to JP.

The face of the woman in the photograph was bruised on both cheeks and around her eyes. Her eyes appeared to be swollen shut. It was a full body shot of a well-dressed woman who was probably quite attractive if not for the bruises and swelling.

"That's the hooker Monroe allegedly beat up about ten years back. This is the result of his handiwork. Her name is Susan James. She's from a small town in Kentucky. The name she used at the time of this incident was Della Street. We know she was paid about a hundred grand to make a public apology. Of course, nothing about the payoff ever made the press. Then she disappeared. She returned a couple of years ago, probably to get more money, but my sources don't think she got any. Her full name, last known address, birthdate, and a few other details are in the envelope."

"Thanks, I'll follow up and see if I can find her now."

Pauline took another photo from the envelope. "Here's a shot of Monroe kissing Brandy. As you can see, she's pretty young. They both are. The date is on the back. There are more in the envelope."

JP turned it over. "This is before her oldest son was born."

Pauline tilted her head to the side. "Do you think they have any soda water in this little coffee shop? I think that would be just what I need right now."

"I'll go check." JP stood up and walked to the end of the sidewalk and into the coffee shop.

Pauline checked her phone for new messages while she waited. She was reading an email from a coworker when JP's phone rang. She reached over and picked it up. The name on the screen read, *"Sabre."* Pauline tapped the phone and said, "Hello."

"Oh, I'm sorry. I must have called the wrong number."

"Are you calling JP?"

"Yes. May I speak to him?"

"He just went to get me something to drink. I'll tell him you called. Ta-ta." Pauline hung up. She started to lay the phone down and then smirked. She pushed the top of her blouse open a little further and took a selfie. Then she opened the Contacts folder and dropped the photo in so it would show up whenever she called. Before she laid the phone back on the table, she changed the ringtone on her contact to "Timba" so it would be distinctive.

Moments later JP returned carrying a bottle of soda water and a cup of ice. He handed them both to Pauline. "Here you go."

"Thank you." She poured the water into the cup, took a sip, and set the bottle and cup down. "I also found out that Monroe received a substantial trust fund from his grandparents. I don't know the terms of the trust, but I can probably get that for you too."

JP shook his head, "I'm afraid to ask how you get this stuff."

"Don't." She laid her hand on his for a brief moment and then retreated. "He started to receive the funds when he turned thirty. Monroe hasn't worked since, and he has dropped out of mainstream political society. He has been reported to be seen occasionally at parties with some big name entertainers, but mostly he keeps to himself and out of the limelight."

JP continued to look at the photo of Della Street, avoiding any extra eye contact with Pauline. "Any more domestic violence incidents?"

"Not that are recorded anywhere."

"Did you find out where he's living now?"

"I have an address for him, but I don't know if it is current. It was accurate a month ago. He's not that far from here, actually."

"Really?" JP raised his head and looked directly at Pauline. "Where is he?"

"Monroe has a house in Laguna Beach."

"That's a little over an hour away. Any idea what brought him here?"

"Of course I do, darling," she laid her hand on his. "I'm really good at what I do."

"So are you going to tell me?"

"He's been diagnosed with a rare type of cancer. It seems he came here so he could go to the City of Hope."

"Why wouldn't he live in L.A. then? He would be a lot closer."

"There's a doctor he is friends with who lives somewhere in Orange County—in Laguna Beach, I think. I don't have his name yet, but I'm sure with a little work I can get it. Anyway, he seems to be the reason Monroe landed where he did. The doctor is apparently helping him through this."

"You've been very helpful, Pauline. I can't thank you enough."

"I'm sure you'll think of a way." She stood up and handed him the envelope. "There's also the paternity test in here that shows Monroe is not the father of

Conway Twitty McFerran, but I think if you investigate further you'll find it has been altered. You should have enough information in there to follow the trail."

"Thank you." JP stood up.

Pauline gave him a hug. She whispered in his ear. "Call me when you need me, or even if you don't. Ta-ta."

Chapter 22

JP drove back to his house before he opened the envelope Pauline had given him. He perused each photo, note, and document. *She was nothing if not thorough*, JP thought. The paternity test had a document that listed the name of the facility and the name of the person who performed the test and wrote the report, along with his phone number and address. He tried the phone number but reached a voice mail. JP left his first name and phone number but didn't explain who he was.

Next, JP read through the one-page document Pauline had left on Monroe Bullard. He was listed as having Mantle Cell Lymphoma, a rare, aggressive cancer. Monroe had undergone a bone marrow biopsy to determine if it was in his bone marrow and a lumbar puncture to determine if the cancer had metastasized to the brain. It was in his bone marrow but not yet in his brain.

JP shook his head. *How does she get this information?*

Not only did she have the information, but most of the time she also had documentation to back it up. Attached to her note was a page that appeared to be right out of Monroe's medical records. JP was glad she had added her note because the handwriting was not that legible in the medical record. Apparently, this doctor was not using computers to type the information.

The first photo of Brandy and Monroe proved there was a connection between them, but not much else. The other photos provided a more complete picture. Another six photos depicting intimate moments between the couple were inside the envelope. The dates were specific and spanned just over six months, all prior to Brandy's sixteenth birthday. In each, she was wearing different clothes and shoes and the length of her hair had changed slightly from the first picture to the last. JP was convinced they weren't staged. Although they didn't prove paternity, they did make Brandy look a little more credible.

JP was deep in thought when his phone rang.

"There are no fingerprints on any of the containers or the contents," Ernie said. "They've been wiped completely clean. There still isn't a crime here as far as I can tell, and even if this Monroe guy were in danger, didn't you say he was in Tennessee?"

"He was, but now I have an address in Laguna Beach."

"That's still out of my jurisdiction."

"I know the whole thing seems a little hokey, but I don't like the way they have involved Sabre. She would feel terrible if someone died and we could have prevented it," JP said. "But I understand there isn't anything you can do."

"Hey, do you remember Bradford Williams?" Ernie asked.

"Yeah, he was in the department with us when we were in Vista."

"Didn't he join the Laguna Beach Police Department when he left here?"

"That's right. He was living in Orange County and commuting, and when an opening came up, he left. I'll call and see if he's still there. Thanks, Ernie."

As soon as he hung up, JP looked up the number on his computer and called the Laguna Beach Police Department. Brad was still working there as a homicide detective, but he wasn't on duty. JP was assured they would give him the message.

Susan James, aka Della Street, the professional Monroe had beaten up, was the subject of the next document. It contained not only her phone number and last known address but also a brief history of where she had been until a few years ago. According to this report, Susan was last living with her sister, Belle James, in Tustin, California.

JP tried the phone number for Susan.

"Yo," a young man answered.

"May I speak to Susan?"

"Ain't no Susan here. You got the wrong number, dude."

"Sorry about that. I'm just trying to find my friend. I haven't spoken to her in quite a while. Have you had this number for a long time?"

"'Bout two years. You should keep in better touch with your friends, dude."

Before JP could say anything else, the young man hung up.

JP opened his computer and searched for the address that Pauline had given him. After checking through several classified databases he had access to, he was satisfied that the home was still owned by Belle James. He was unable to establish where Susan was living.

Since JP couldn't reach anyone, and he had exhausted his resources for the moment, he decided to drive to Tustin and see if he could find Susan James. JP had a gut feeling that it would help lead him to Monroe. Hopefully, he would hear back from Bradford Williams before he returned, but if not, he would stop at the address he had for Monroe and talk to him. He had no idea what he might say to the guy, but somehow he felt he had to do it.

***

JP knocked on the door of the residence owned by Belle James. A tall woman, who appeared to be in her late forties, answered the door. Her hair was short and straight. She wore no makeup and was dressed in gray sweats and a plain white T-shirt.

"Hi, my name is JP Torn and I'm looking for Susan James."

A look of anguish flashed across the woman's face. "What do you want from her?"

JP often used a cover story when he was in this kind of situation, but he decided something close to the truth would work best. "I'm sorry to bother you, but I'm a private investigator, and I'm working on a child abuse case. Susan appears to have been a victim in another case that may be related. I'd like to ask her some questions if it's not too much trouble."

"She's not here."

"Are you her sister, Belle James?"

"Yes, but Susan's not here." The woman stepped back as if she were about to close the door.

"Maybe you can help. Do you know a man named Monroe Bullard?"

The woman reopened the door and stood there for a second in silence. She looked JP up and down and then settled on his face. "Did he kill someone else?"

"Someone else? You think he killed someone?"

"Come on in."

JP followed her inside. The house was small with minimal furniture and simply decorated. Only a few pictures hung on the walls, and with the exception of what appeared to be three family photographs sitting on the fireplace mantle, little else adorned the room.

The woman pointed to the sofa and said, "Please have a seat." She sat down in a recliner next to the couch. "I'm Belle James, Susan's sister. She came to live with me about three years ago."

"Was that after Monroe beat her up?"

"Yes." She paused. "How much do you know about Susan?"

"Very little. I know that she was a victim of abuse by Monroe, that she received some money for not exposing him, and that she may have tried to get more money from him later."

"That's all true, and you were kind enough to leave the part out about her career as a prostitute. I'm sure that's why little was done." Belle took a deep breath. "I should've been there for her, but I didn't know what to do. There was a big age gap between Susan and me. I left home when she was just a little girl. Our mother spent most of her time in a drunken stupor, and I couldn't take any more abuse from the jerks she brought home from the bars. I should've taken Susan with me when I left, but I thought she'd be all right because she was so young. By the time I figured out what she was up to, it was too late. She was hooking and stuck in the lifestyle."

JP just listened as Belle poured out her story.

"Then she had the incident with Monroe. I didn't know anything about that until much later. Susan told me about it when she came to me for help. She said that Monroe's mother approached her and offered her two hundred thousand dollars to drop the charges against Monroe, make a public apology, and leave town."

"Did she come to you after the apology?"

"No. She went to New York City and tried to get into acting. She blew through her money in less than a year. She went back to Monroe's mother and tried to get more money. Mrs. Bullard refused to pay her. She said it wouldn't matter since she had already made a public statement, and that no one would believe her now. When Susan tried to call her bluff, the old lady threatened to have her killed."

"Did that scare Susan off?"

"Not at first. She wasn't afraid of much, but she noticed that she was being followed, or at least she thought she was. The next day, she was walking down the street, and a car almost hit her. A soldier saw her and yanked her out of the way. She decided the old woman meant business. That's when she came here."

Belle took a deep breath and let it out. "She stayed here for almost a year. She tried to find work, but she wasn't really qualified for anything. After a few months, she told me she had a job at a warehouse. She was supposedly working the night shift. I believed her at first, but then one morning she came home and she had been beaten up. She tried to tell me she had been mugged, but I knew then she had gone back to prostitution."

"Is she still working?"

"No." Belle's eyes were watery.

JP thought she was trying to keep from crying. He waited.

"She finally fessed up, but not until she was picked up by the cops."

"Was she arrested?"

"She was, and she told them about a pimp who was using really young girls. Susan had tried to help the girls, but she couldn't do much. The cops made a deal with her, put her back on the street, and used her as a snitch. I think they had her involved in a sting operation."

"How did that pan out?"

"They busted the operation with the young girls. Susan swore to me she was going to stop prostituting."

"Did she?"

Susan swallowed. "She never got the chance. She was found dead in an alley about a week later."

"Was she murdered?"

"The coroner wrote it up as an 'accidental overdose,' but I never believed it. She didn't use drugs. She hated them. She had tried a few things when she was younger, but she didn't like to not have control. She always said it was difficult enough to stay safe without adding drugs to the mix."

"Did you tell the cops that?"

"Yes, but no one would listen to me. I don't think there was much of an investigation. They just figured that since she was a hooker, she must be into drugs. I did find one homicide detective, Gene Mick, who said he would look into it, but he couldn't find any evidence that led back to the pimp." She shook her head. "Susan was a good person at heart, but no one really got to know her. I didn't either until she came to live with me. Even then, she was very private. I know she felt terrible about those young girls, and she really wanted to help them."

"So you think the guys she snitched on killed her?"

"It's possible, but I really think it was either Monroe or his mother who had her killed."

"Why's that?"

"Because Susan was suddenly afraid of them again. She wouldn't tell me why, but I think someone from Nashville had contacted her. She thought she was being followed again too, but there was more that she didn't tell. I know there was more because she was really afraid. Besides, Detective Mick told me that if the pimp were going to kill her, he would likely have done it before she could testify."

"That makes sense." JP waited to see if she was going to say more. When she didn't, he asked, "Do you know what precinct this detective was from, or do you have a phone number? Maybe I can get a little more information for you."

She stood up. "I have his card. Let me get it for you." She walked to a little writing desk on a nearby wall. She opened the top drawer and removed a card and brought it to JP. "Here you go. Please let me know if you learn anything new. She had a pretty rotten life, you know, from the day she was born. I should have taken her with me when I left."

"You were just a kid yourself. You did the best you could." JP stood and handed Belle his card. "If you think of anything else that you might have forgotten, please call me."

"I will."

"I'm really sorry about your sister."

"She was a good person."

"I'm sure she was."

Chapter 23

Sabre and Ron tried every combination of Sabre's and JP's birthdays that they could come up with, in every order possible, with no luck.

"Maybe the day should be first and the month second, like the Europeans do," Ron said.

"It's worth a try," Sabre said. She punched in the codes with and without the year, but found "*404—File Not Found*" for three of the combinations and a cache in Quebec, Canada for one of them.

"We need to try someone else," Ron said.

"How about Monroe? After all, this is all about him."

"Now you're thinking, Sis." He waited in silence for a few seconds, looking directly at Sabre.

"What?"

"What's his birthday?"

"Sorry." Sabre reached for the file.

"Are you okay? You seem a little befuddled."

"I was just thinking about an earlier phone call. It was nothing." She looked through the file, found Monroe's birthdate, and gave it to Ron.

He created all the different combinations he could derive, including the European version.

"None of these seem to be working. The nearest cache I found was in Sacramento," Ron said. "We need to try another birthdate."

"How about Brandy's?" Sabre glanced through the file without waiting for a response. "This is interesting. Tomorrow is her birthday, which ..."

"... is the same day Monroe is supposed to die," Ron finished her sentence. That can't be a coincidence."

It didn't take them long to figure out a combination that provided a local geocache site. They continued to look for other combinations to make sure they had the right one. Satisfied there were no others, they stopped searching.

Ron stood up, picked up his keys, and walked toward the door. "Let's go geocaching."

***

Once JP was past Red Hill Road in Tustin, the traffic lessened. He wondered what it was about that street that always created traffic jams. He was hoping Bradford Williams would call back when the phone rang. It was Sabre.

"We think we found the code for the next cache. We used Brandy's birthday."

"Really?"

"Yes, and get this, it's tomorrow."

"What's tomorrow?"

"Her birthday. It's tomorrow—the same day that Monroe is supposed to die."

"This is crazy. Everything we turn up appears to lead to something else in the McFerran case, yet nothing really makes sense. We're investigating a crime that hasn't even happened yet, and we don't even know if it will. Someone is pulling the strings, but we aren't even sure if the cache was meant for us. I just discovered another murder victim that may not be a murder, and she may or may not be connected. I've never worked on such a crazy case. I feel like a gnat in a hailstorm."

"Now, that's a visual."

"Are you going to try to find the cache?"

"We're on our way right now."

"Just be careful."

"I tried to call you earlier," Sabre said.

"I didn't get a message or a missed call. Sorry about that."

"Who ans—?" Sabre stopped. "It doesn't matter. I'll let you know what we find. When will you be back?"

"I have one more stop. I should be back in a couple of hours. Are we still on for tonight?"

"Absolutely."

JP headed south on I-5. When he saw the sign for Laguna Beach, he pulled off the highway and stopped at a gas station. Then he entered Monroe's last known address on his GPS. *What the heck*, he thought. *I may as well see if he's still vertical.*

Ten minutes later he was in front of a large custom home that overlooked the city. In the distance, he could see a spectacular view of the ocean. The yard was perfectly manicured. The grass was dark green and thicker than he had ever seen. Several king palms lined the side of the house.

As JP walked up the white steps and approached the door, he could hear soft music coming from within. He rang the doorbell. After a few seconds with no response, he rang it again. He could hear the chimes from the bell ring out like the sound of an old church calling its parishioners. But no one came. The front door was made of mahogany with a peacock etched onto three large, cut-glass panes. There were only a few spots where JP could see through, and he couldn't see any movement. He rang the bell a third time. Still nothing.

JP walked down the steps and around the left side of the house. He could only go a short distance before he reached a six-foot fence. All he could see over the fence was the tip of a swimming pool. He walked around to the other side and saw the same thing, the end of a swimming pool. The house was approximately fifty feet wide. JP couldn't tell if there was more than one pool in the backyard or if the pool extended the entire length of the house. Behind the pool, JP could see a tennis court. The tenants of this house certainly had no reason to not stay in shape. He just wasn't sure if Monroe was the tenant.

JP drove down the street to the nearest neighbor's house, which was about a hundred feet away. There was a construction crew working on the house. JP stopped and chatted with one of the workers, who told him the house he was working on was being totally remodeled to the tune of about three million dollars.

"I could build ten houses for that and still have money for beer," JP said.

"Me too," the man said.

"Do you know who lives in the house next door?" JP nodded toward the house he had just left.

"All I've ever seen is one man coming and going. He has never stopped, so I don't know anything about him."

"What does he look like?"

"About forty or forty-five, I'd say. Blondish hair. I couldn't tell you his height or anything. I've only seen him in his car. He looked kind of tall from the way he sat in his seat, but I couldn't be certain."

"You've never seen anyone else there? No women?"

"I leave here before dark, so he could have them coming and going all night for all I know, but not during the day. Except for once, last week. There was a couple, a man and a woman, who came to his house in an old, beat-up Nissan. I remember because the car just didn't belong in this neighborhood."

"What color was it?"

"A light blue, I think. The back fender on the passenger side was a different color, like a darker blue or maybe even black. I'm not sure."

"Is there anything else about the car that stood out?"

"Not really."

"Did you see who was in it?"

"Yes, they drove right past me when they left, and with all this construction, they couldn't go very fast. The woman was driving. She was an attractive blonde, probably in her late thirties."

"Anything else you remember about her?"

"She wore a lot of makeup and had big hair. Her cleavage was exposed, so it was hard to look at much else."

"And the guy?"

"I couldn't see him that well, but he looked younger. I'm just not sure." He paused. "Why all the questions? Are you a cop or something?"

"No, I'm a private investigator."

"Cheating spouse?"

"Not exactly." JP gave him his business card. "Would you mind calling me if you see any activity at that house? Like any visitors or anything unusual."

"Sure, man." He put the card in his back pocket.

Chapter 24

Ron and Sabre followed the GPS north on Interstate 5 to the Carmel Valley Road off-ramp. They drove west for about a mile, passing some condos and a few businesses, and then turned left onto Torrey Pines Road in Del Mar, a small beach community near San Diego. They passed through the town and just as they came down the hill from Del Mar, the street curved and the ocean appeared.

After parking the car near the ocean in a small parking lot, they walked across the street to a grassy area that surrounded the swamps in the Torrey Pines State Reserve. They tromped around the reserve near the edge of the parking lot. The area had a gorgeous beach and incredible views. Sabre wondered why the master of this treasure hunt had chosen this spot.

They looked along the edge of the grass line and worked their way further into the swampy grass. A couple of creeks ran through the reserve, and the recent rains had made them overflow, making the area muddier than usual.

"Are you finding anything?" Sabre called out to her brother.

"Not a thing. I take it you haven't either."

"Nope. I hope we have the right coordinates."

Sabre searched through some low bushes, found nothing but some loose rocks, and then stepped toward the creek. Her right foot sunk into the ground, but before she could get it out, the mud had covered up about an inch of her walking shoe. She moved to her left and tried to plant her left foot on the ground, but the grass was slick and she slipped. Grabbing a nearby bush, she managed to break her fall, but her right hand hit the ground before she could steady herself. She stood up and pushed her hair back from her face, leaving a streak of mud across her forehead. She turned around to the sound of Ron's laughter, which only got louder when he saw her muddy face.

"Are you okay?" Ron asked.

"I'm fine, just a little dirtier than when I came." She moved toward the railroad tracks in the direction of the parking lot. "I don't think the cache is down here, and if it is, it's covered in water. There are some bushes in that strip over there." Sabre pointed. "Maybe it's in there."

Ron followed her, watching carefully as he walked. When he reached the tracks, he said, "Look." He pointed toward a shiny object about twenty feet north lying against the track. "Maybe that's the cache."

As they approached the silver container with a big "L" imprinted in the metal, Ron put his latex gloves on.

"That's a Lush container," Sabre said, as Ron picked it up.

"What's a Lush container?"

"It's a company that makes natural cleansers, soaps, shampoos, stuff like that. I use a few of their products."

Ron opened it up. A note on bright pink paper read, "You're too late to save Monroe!"

"Oh no!" Sabre took a deep breath.

"Do you think he's dead?"

"I don't know. This whole thing is so crazy. I talked to JP just before we left, and he said he had stopped by Monroe's house in Orange County, or what was his last known address. No one answered the door."

"Maybe he was already dead. That would explain why no one answered." Ron held the note up and read it again, then started to place it back in the receptacle.

"Wait," Sabre said. "There's something on the

back."

Ron turned it over and read, "GC89742."

"Another cache."

Ron bagged the container and walked to the car, where Sabre retrieved her iPad. She opened the geocache site and put in the code. It referred them to a cache in Laguna Beach.

"That's where Monroe lives."

"That exact spot? That address?"

"I don't know. I just know that JP said he lived in Laguna Beach."

Sabre called JP, got the address, and then ran it against the coordinates she had for the cache on the note. The cache appeared to be on Monroe's property. She informed JP of what she had discovered.

"We're going to check the cache," Sabre said.

"Not without me. I just passed the Del Mar Heights exit. I'll take the next off-ramp and pick up the two of you. We'll go back there together."

Chapter 25

JP headed north on Interstate 5 for the second time that day. They had only been on the freeway about twenty minutes when JP's phone rang.

"Well I'll be, if it isn't our resident cowboy," Bradford Williams said when JP answered the phone. "How the hell are ya?"

"I'm still on the north side of the grass," JP said. "I see you're still in homicide. How do you like working in Laguna Beach?"

"It's a good department. A little less action than we had in San Diego, but enough just the same. In my spare time, I volunteer with the Civil Air Patrol. That keeps me out of trouble. I only have thirty-three days left until I can take early retirement from the department. I've been offered a part-time job with the U.S. Food and Drug Administration, which I have accepted. So I'll be moving to Falling Waters, West Virginia, and finally putting my chemistry major to some use." He paused for a second. "But I'm guessing you didn't call to catch up. I heard you were in the private sector, and I'm thinking you might need something in my jurisdiction."

"Yes, I could use your help. Especially right now."

"You always had my back on the force, cowboy, so I'm here for you. What is it you need?"

"Ever heard of geocaching?"

"Yes, I've been a few times with my oldest daughter. She's kind of a fanatic. Why?"

"It's a rather strange request, but we think someone in a big, fancy house in Laguna Beach may have been murdered—or is about to be murdered. His name is Monroe Bullard. He's the brother to the

126

Tennessee senator, Richard Bullard."

"Why do you think he's in danger? And what, pray tell, does that have to do with geocaching?"

"That's the strange part. It all started with a geocache that my attorney friend and I found a couple of weeks ago. It had an authentic-looking death certificate with the name Monroe on it and today's date as the date of his murder."

"And that's it?"

"No, there's a lot more to the story, but the simple version is that Monroe appears to be connected to a juvenile dependency case that my friend is working on. There have been more geocaches and more clues, and each one brings the case closer to Monroe Bullard. The last cache, the one they found today, says, and I quote, 'It's too late for Monroe.' On the back was another code for a geocache with the same coordinates as the last known address for Monroe Bullard."

"What's the address?"

JP gave it to him. "I'm on my way there now. I'm about twenty or twenty-five minutes away."

"My partner and I will meet you there. Don't start without us."

"Got it," JP said. "Thanks, Brad."

***

Detective Bradford Williams was parked in front of the house when JP arrived. When he stepped out of the car, JP thought he hadn't changed much since he last saw him. Same buzz haircut, long enough to prove he had a full head of hair, but short enough to know he was a cop. The hair was a little grayer than before. He stood about six feet tall and had a slight paunch. He always threatened to work out, but never seemed to get around to it. JP guessed that still hadn't changed.

Another man exited Brad's car, and the two of them approached JP, who had also left his truck.

"This is my partner, Eric Ridenour," Brad said. "This is JP. We worked together on the force in San Diego. He's a PI now, but he can still be trusted." Brad smiled a half-smile.

"Nice to meet you," the younger detective said.

Eric appeared to be less than thirty years old, had dark hair, and carried himself with confidence.

"Who's with you?" Eric asked.

"My friend, the attorney whose case this is related to, and her brother. I asked them to wait in the truck." JP turned to Brad. "Do you mind if I go in with you?"

"Just stay back a little ways until we find out what's going on."

"Will do."

Eric and Brad approached the house with JP just behind them. Eric rang the bell. No one answered. He tried again. Still nothing.

"Police!" Eric shouted. "Open up!"

No response.

"We're coming in," Eric yelled, as he turned the door handle. "It's unlocked."

Eric went in first with his gun drawn, followed by Brad, and then JP. The house looked spotless and in perfect order. "Live Like You Were Dying" by Tim McGraw played softly on an iPod in the front room. It ended and started again as the three of them made their way through the first floor of the house. No one was around. They went up the stairway and when they reached the top, they began checking each room.

"He's in here," Brad yelled from the master bedroom.

JP ran into the room and saw a blond-haired man convulsing on the floor near an open liquor cabinet. He was clutching the neck of an unopened, bell-shaped bottle that read "Conde de Osborne Brandy de Jerez" across the front.

"Call the paramedics," Brad yelled.

JP dialed 9-1-1 and reported the seizure as Brad kneeled down by the side of the man. The man lay on his back and continued to twitch and jerk. When he flopped toward a large stuffed chair, JP grabbed the chair and pulled it out of the way, just missing the spew as it flew out of the man's mouth. Brad grabbed hold of the man and turned him onto his side to keep him from choking. JP dropped down next to Brad and helped him hold the man on his side. A smell of bitter almonds lingered in the air.

"Don't force him down. Just help me keep him on his side in case he vomits again," Brad said.

Eric returned. "There's no one else here."

"Check on the ambulance," Brad said, as he moved with the man's seizures. "He's still alive."

Things calmed for about two seconds, and the man tried to lift the bottle in his hand, but it only came a few inches off the floor. He mumbled, "Pois—" Brad and JP exchanged glances. The man's body went limp and fell back onto the floor, the bottle rolled out of his hand, and he lay still.

Brad leaned down closer to his red face. "He's still breathing, but it's light."

Sirens could be heard approaching. Brad pushed the man back onto his side. "Eric, get down here and make sure he doesn't fall onto his back again. If he vomits again, he could choke." Then he looked up at JP. "You better step out before it gets too crowded in here. We don't want anyone to think we contaminated the crime scene."

Before JP left, he looked around the huge room. The covers on the bed were disheveled, there were pillows on the floor, and the sheets were wrinkled. In addition to the usual things you find in a bedroom, this one had a sitting area with a love seat and coffee table in front of a panoramic window that looked out at the distant ocean. On the coffee table were two short-stemmed, globular glasses and a decanter about three-quarters full of golden liquid. One glass had lipstick on the rim and some liquid residue in the bottom. The other contained about a half-inch of the same color liquid as the decanter. The only other item on the table was a tacky, gold-colored box, about six inches wide, nine inches long, and approximately four inches tall, with a cowboy painted on the side of it. Glittering stones were embedded in the hat, the boots, the belt, and the clothes of the cowboy. In a sea of expensive furnishings, this box looked like something from Big Lots! He snapped a quick photo.

JP's feet sunk into the plush carpet as he left the room. He heard the ambulance pull into the yard. As he reached the bottom of the marble steps, he saw something sparkly lying on the floor near the door. He walked over to it and took a photo of the bobby pin with a cut-glass flower on the end of it.

Just as JP stepped outside, the paramedics dashed past him and into the mansion. JP continued to where Sabre was waiting and told her what had transpired upstairs. Ron was looking around rocks and bushes near the street.

"What's he doing?" JP asked.

"He's looking for the cache in case there is one. But I told him not to disturb anything, so he's only looking along the edges."

"I think it may be upstairs on the coffee table. There was a hideous box sitting on the table that really looked out of place in all the splendor in the room," JP said. "I'll ask Brad about it later."

"Do you think it was Monroe in the bedroom?" Sabre asked.

"I would say so from the photos of him that I've seen. Even though the pics weren't that recent, it sure looked like the same man to me."

The front door opened, and several paramedics carried a gurney with the man's body down the steps, out the front door, and then into the back of the ambulance. Sabre couldn't see exactly what they were doing, but it looked like they hooked him up to some machine before they closed the door and drove away.

Several other black and white police cars pulled up to the house with their sirens blaring. Men in uniform unloaded from the cars and went inside.

Brad and Eric came outside and approached JP. "It doesn't look like he's going to make it. He may already be gone."

"Dang! I should've gotten hold of you sooner."

"We're going to need more details," Brad said. "I'd like to talk to all of you. Can you follow me to the office?"

"Sure," JP said. "Do you think somebody tried to murder him?"

"We probably would think it was an attempted suicide if it weren't for what you told me, and I do believe he was trying to say 'poison.' Is that what you heard?"

"That's what I heard," JP said.

"Either way, we would've investigated, especially since he's from a prominent political family. Our chief wouldn't have it any other way. After all, it's an election year. Just so you know, so far we haven't found a suicide note."

JP told Brad about the sparkly pin he saw near the door.

"We've already bagged it. There's not much else

out of place. This guy was a real neat freak."

***

At the police station, Brad spoke with Sabre, JP, and Ron individually. JP went first, then Sabre, and then Ron. Afterward, he called them all in together.

"The ID on the victim says that he is Monroe Bullard from Tennessee. There are lots of pictures of him online, so even though we don't have a positive ID, we're convinced that's who he is."

The phone on Brad's desk rang. He picked it up.

"Detective Williams," he said. He listened for a few seconds. "Thanks for the call." He hung up. "Monroe Bullard didn't make it. They think he died from potassium cyanide poisoning, but we'll know more when they do the autopsy." He looked directly at Sabre, then JP. "Isn't that what was named the cause of death on his death certificate? 'Murder by Poison.'"

"Yes," Sabre and JP said in unison.

Chapter 26

"Are you okay?" JP asked Sabre, as he drove home from the Laguna Beach Police Department with Sabre in the passenger seat and Ron in the back.

"Yes." She sighed. "I'm just wondering what and how I'm going to tell Conway about Monroe."

"Do you have to tell him anything?"

"I'm sure it will be national news since Monroe's brother is a senator. It'll be on television and the Internet by morning if it isn't already." She shook her head. "I need to tell Conway something, and hopefully he hears it from me first. I just don't know what to say. Do I tell him that his father—who denied being his father and may or may not be his father since the paternity test says he's not the father, but we have reason to believe he is his father—is dead? Possibly murdered. And to top that, there's a good chance his mother may be involved."

"Do you think Brandy killed him?"

"I hope not. Brandy is a mess, but I hope for those kids' sake that she wasn't a part of this."

"It's a shame Monroe couldn't tell us more before he died."

"Was his house beautiful inside?" Sabre asked.

"It was pretty impressive. Not a place I'd want to live, but it had a nice view, and someone has been keeping it really clean." He told her about the glasses on the table and the bobby pin he saw. "I took a couple of photos before I left." He handed her his phone. "Look."

Sabre took the phone and brought up the photos, starting with the last one taken. "Oh no."

"What is it?"

"Dolly was wearing a couple of those bobby pins in her hair when I saw her last."

"I'm sure she didn't have anything to do with this. She doesn't even know Monroe." He paused. "Does she?"

"Not that I'm aware of."

Sabre looked at the next photo of the sitting area in Monroe's bedroom. "Two glasses? So he had company."

"I don't know if you can tell from the photo, but there is lipstick on one of them. And the bed looked to me like someone had recently had sex in it. Either that or Monroe is quite a wild sleeper."

Sabre hit the *Back* button to the next photo. It was a picture of a beautiful, dark-haired woman with her cleavage prominently displayed. She felt her stomach do a little flip. She was sure it was nothing, probably another case JP was working on. At first she wasn't going to say anything, but she couldn't stop herself.

"Who's the beauty with the big boobs?"

"What?"

"The picture on your phone." Sabre held it up so JP could see.

"Eww ... let me see," Ron said from the back seat.

Sabre handed Ron the phone, scowling at him as she did.

"I didn't take that," JP said.

"It looks like a selfie," Ron said. "You have random women taking photos of themselves with your phone? I'm impressed."

"No, that's not it," JP said.

Sabre could see his face tighten. "You know this woman?"

"Yes. She's my source to the political underworld."

"I should've been a politician," Ron spouted. "Maybe I still can be. Can you hook me up, JP?"

JP didn't respond.

Sabre didn't know what to say. She was sorry she had asked about the photo, but it took her by surprise. Jealousy was never a part of her makeup. As far as she was concerned, jealousy was a wasted emotion. Either you trusted the person you were with or you didn't, and if you didn't, you shouldn't be with him. She did trust JP, but after the phone call earlier when a woman answered his phone, she had to admit she felt a little uneasy. She decided she wasn't going to stew over it. Instead she would tell JP about the phone call and let him explain—but not with Ron in the car. It would have to wait until later.

The rest of the ride back to San Diego was done in silence, except for the occasional comment from the back seat.

They reached Ron's car in Del Mar about a quarter past nine.

"Is anyone hungry?" Ron asked.

"No," the response came in unison from both JP and Sabre.

"Okay," Ron said. "I guess I'll get something on my own. You two—" He stopped, got out of the car, and said, "Thanks for the adventure. Love you, Sis. See you soon."

Few words were exchanged on the twenty-minute ride from Del Mar to Sabre's condo. She was frustrated with herself for letting the phone call and the picture bother her. She and JP had a good thing going, and she didn't want to mess it up. She knew if they didn't deal with it, though, she would start to pull back and distance herself until it didn't matter anymore because she didn't care enough. But she couldn't get herself to say anything more. Instead, she talked about work.

"The McFerran kids have a visit with their mother tomorrow. I think I'll stop by and see the children after their visit."

"Have you ever seen them with their mother? Just to see how they react to her?"

"I did early on in the case. I don't really want to go when they are with her because they only get limited time together, and I don't want to intrude. It's hard on both the children and the parents. She has supervised visits right now, so she already has a social worker or someone watching them."

"That makes sense."

JP pulled up in front of Sabre's condo. "Are you hungry?" he asked.

"Not really." Sabre wanted to invite him in, but she couldn't get herself to say the words. "It's a little late for our date, I guess."

"Yeah, I guess so."

JP walked Sabre to her door, kissed her goodnight, waited for her to lock her door, and drove away. All the way home he stewed about what Pauline had done and how he left things with Sabre. He wanted to say, "No, it's not too late for our date." But he didn't. He had such a hard time opening up. *Why didn't I just explain about Pauline?*

Chapter 27

Sabre was waiting on the park bench near her car until the end of the hour that would mark the conclusion of Brandy's visit with her children. An older model car with two different colored fenders was parked in front of hers. At first she thought the car was empty, but then a man sat up in the passenger seat, opened the door, and stepped out. He lit up a cigarette and then walked over to the bench and sat down next to Sabre. She raised her eyes toward the "No Smoking in the Park" sign and then back at the man. He looked up, took another drag, and then leaned down and crushed the end of the cigarette into the ground, putting it out.

"Sorry, I didn't see the sign," he said. He pinched the hot end of the cigarette off and then dropped the butt in his T-shirt pocket. He looked Sabre over from top to bottom. "How you doing?" he said in a poor imitation of Joey on the sitcom *Friends*.

Sabre didn't react to his obvious flirtation. She just said, "I'm fine." She checked her watch. It was 12:03. Then she looked out at her clients, who were sitting near their mother at a picnic table. Taylor sat on one side of Brandy and Dolly was on the other. Brandy appeared to be conversing with Dolly. Trace and Reba were engaged with one another and sat on the backside of the table. Conway stood at the end of the table as if to oversee it all. The attendant from the Department of Social Services leaned against a tree about fifteen feet away.

"You with them?" the man asked, nodding his head toward the McFerrans.

"Yes." Sabre stood up.

"Me too," he said.

"Really? Are you a relative?"

"I'm the dad."

Sabre looked closer at his face. He looked too young to be any of the fathers. She wasn't even sure he was of drinking age. That's when she realized he must be Brandy's new boy toy.

"I'm just messing with you," he said. "Brandy's my main squeeze. I'm an actor. You may have heard of me, Doug Griffin."

"I can't say as I have."

He looked her over again. "I wouldn't mind trading my old lady in for a younger model, though. You interested?"

"Not really," Sabre said and walked away.

The kids were saying their goodbyes to their mother just as Sabre walked up to them. Sabre was fascinated as she observed the children and their interactions with their mother. Conway gave his mother a hug and then stood back to gather up his siblings. Trace pecked his mother on the cheek and dashed off toward Conway. While Dolly was hugging her mother, Reba waved as she flit by, not intruding on her sibling's embrace. She made no attempt to get close enough to her mother for a hug or a kiss. Conway placed his hand on Reba's shoulder, leaned down, and said something to Reba that Sabre couldn't hear. Reba turned around and walked back to her mom.

By then, Taylor was hugging her mother, clinging to her as if she didn't want to let go. Reba sneaked in, pecked Brandy on the cheek, and swooped toward Trace, where she remained. Conway stepped forward and gently pulled Taylor away. Brandy straightened her blouse and touched her hair as if to make sure it was all in place. Then she reached into her purse and brought out a compact, looked in the mirror, and reapplied her lipstick.

Sabre acknowledged her and then greeted the children. She explained that she wanted to talk with each of them. She was going to start with Taylor, but Taylor was still clinging to Conway, so Sabre asked Trace to join her first.

Sabre was facing the street where her car was parked, so she was able to observe Brandy as she approached her boyfriend. He greeted her like she had been gone for a week, laying a lip-lock on her. Sabre glanced around at the children. Most were not even looking at their mother, except for Taylor and Reba. Reba opened her mouth wide and pointed her finger down at the open space, making an "induce-vomiting" gesture.

"How have you been, Trace?"

"Good."

"Anything new going on at home or at school?"

"Naw."

"No problems?"

"Naw."

After a few minutes of similar conversation, she switched up and spoke with Taylor, who was now playing with Reba.

When Sabre asked Taylor how things were going, her response was, "I really miss my mom. When can we go home?"

"I don't know the answer to that. Your mom is attending some programs to learn how to make a better life for all of you."

"Then why can't I live with Conway until she's done? He takes real good care of us. He makes our breakfast in the morning and gets us off to school. He always tells me bedtime stories and tucks me in at night. He's big. We could go live with him."

Taylor seemed to be the child who missed her

mother the most, but she missed Conway equally as much. Sabre had tried to get more visits for the siblings, but with school and Conway's job it had been difficult.

Reba was next. She was an interesting child and probably the most independent of them all. She was bright, confident, and spoke her mind.

"I take it you didn't like the display of affection between your mother and Doug," Sabre said.

"He's a loser."

Sabre knew that Brandy's court-ordered visits did not include any guests. "Have you met him?"

"No. Mom talks about him like he's some famous actor, but all he has done is some stupid commercial that no one has ever seen. Oh, and there's his part in a big movie with Johnny Depp where he doesn't even talk. But soon he will be a star." She rolled her eyes. "Just like her. She's just dreaming as usual."

Upon further questioning from Sabre, Reba explained that everything was fine at her foster home. She didn't request more time with her mother, but she did express the desire to see more of Trace.

"Trace's foster father said he would take us geocaching next Saturday."

Sabre was surprised to hear the word, but then she remembered that millions of people go geocaching.

"I've been saving things to exchange in the cache," Reba said. "I can't wait to go again."

"So you've been before?"

"Yeah, a lot of times. Mom used to take us all the time. It was the most fun when we all went, but then Mom stopped taking us because the others didn't want to go. Only me and Trace really liked going. Sometimes just Trace and me would go places that were close to home—places we could walk to."

"Do you know if your mom has done any geocaching since you've been gone?"

"Yeah, she and Doug go all the time." Reba made a face when she said his name. "She's always bragging about it."

Reba turned and walked back towards her siblings. Conway gently pushed Dolly in Sabre's direction.

"Are we going to get to go home soon?" Dolly asked. "I don't think Mom is doing that well. She's having a hard time keeping up with the cleaning and cooking."

"But she only has herself to care for now," Sabre said.

"I know, but she's been real busy with acting and singing auditions. She's pretty sure she's getting a big part soon. They're starting the filming of a movie here in San Diego next month with Sandra Bullock, and Mom auditioned for it. She hasn't heard back yet, but she's pretty sure she'll get it. She said there wasn't anyone else as good as her trying out for the part."

"I'm sure she did a good job." Sabre thought how different Dolly was from Reba. Dolly seemed very gullible and wanted to believe the best in her Mom. Reba, on the other hand, was far more skeptical and didn't trust much of what her mother told her.

"She says she may have to go back to Nashville and try out for that TV series. You know, *Nashville*."

"Yeah, it's a good show."

"I like it. We always watched it together at home. Mom never misses an episode. She has all the shows recorded and watches them over and over. She loves Deacon. She's sure she could get a job on that show because she is all country, and she can sing and act."

"What do you think?"

"She's a good singer. When we were kids, she

would always sing us to sleep."

Sabre opened the photo app on her cell phone and found the picture of the bobby pin that JP had found at Monroe's house. Sabre had sent herself a copy of it from JP's phone last night so she would have it. She showed the photo to Dolly.

"You were wearing a bobby pin similar to this when I saw you last time. Was it the same as this one?"

Dolly looked at the photo. "Yes. That's the same as mine."

"Do you remember where you got it?"

"Yeah. It's my mom's. She has a bunch of them. She wears them all the time. She gave me four of them a couple of weeks ago because my hair was hanging down in my face. She doesn't like that. She pinned it back for me so it hung down in the back. I don't really like my hair like that, but I pin it back on the sides sometimes."

"You said your mother had a bunch of them. Does she have more than the four she gave you?" Sabre asked, and then added, "Just like this one?"

"Yes, she got a package with about twenty of them at a garage sale last year. She was so excited. Mom loves the bling."

Conway was the last to meet with Sabre. He thanked her again for getting him the bike, said work and school were both going well, and asked again about going home.

"We don't know anything yet about returning home," Sabre said. "But there is something else I need to tell you."

"It's about Monroe, right?"

"Yes."

"I already know he's dead."

Chapter 28

Sabre's phone rang. When she saw it was her friend Bob, she answered, "Hello, honey."

"Are you watching the news?"

"No, I was cleaning out a closet."

"Turn it on. Quick! Channel 10."

Sabre picked up her remote and found the channel. The first thing she spotted was Brandy McFerran's big hair. Next to her stood Doug Griffin. The screen split, and a still shot of Monroe Bullard flashed on the screen, followed by videos of Senator Richard Bullard.

"Oh my God," Sabre muttered.

A news reporter stood next to Brandy. She asked, "How well did you know Monroe Bullard?"

"We've been friends since I was a teenager. We met in Nashville, where I used to live. You see, I'm a singer—"

The reporter pulled the microphone back and asked, "Did you know the senator's brother well?"

"He's the baby daddy of my firstborn, Conway Twitty McFerran. He's seventeen now. Not much older than I was when I got pregnant with him."

"How old were you?" the reporter asked.

"Fifteen. Just turned. I used to live in Nashville, but I came to California to pursue my acting career."

"Did Monroe know he was the father of your child?"

"He knew, but he denied it. His mother paid me to shut me up, but I can't keep quiet any longer. My kid has a right to know. The world has a right to know."

It looked like Brandy was going to say something else, but they cut away to show more shots of Monroe and his family.

"Is this live?" Sabre asked Bob.

"It appears so."

"What the heck is she doing?"

"Looks to me like she's getting her fifteen minutes of fame."

"Your client is an idiot," Sabre said.

"Ya think?" Bob chuckled.

"I hope Conway doesn't see this. He already knew about Monroe being dead when I talked with him yesterday. He said he saw it on the news. Apparently, his foster father watches the news regularly, and Conway happened to see it. I expect he has seen this too."

***

JP met Detective Bradford Williams at the Starbucks on the corner of Balboa and Genesee. Brad had requested that JP join him, and JP had already agreed to work with Brad and provide whatever assistance he could to help solve his case.

"The coroner is officially calling Monroe's death a murder. There was a pill bottle found in his pocket for a prescription of fluoxetine."

"Prozac?"

"That's right, in enteric-coated capsules, but that's not what was in the bottle. When they tested the pills, they found that the Prozac inside the capsules had been replaced with cyanide."

"Isn't that what the Tylenol Terrorist did back in 1982?"

"Exactly. He used enteric-coated capsules so the victims wouldn't die right away. The coating dissolves when the capsule enters the small intestine. It varies with each person, but the coroner said it could take up to two hours after ingestion to go into effect. In this case, it appears that someone switched his Prozac with cyanide. The coroner also said that when a person has ingested cyanide, his vomit often smells like almonds or Amaretto."

"That explains the smell," JP said.

"Yes. They not only found it in the bottle, but his blood tested positive for it as well."

"So it's official?"

"Murder by cyanide poisoning. That, coupled with no suicide note, the glasses on the table, and the information you provided, ties it into a nice little package. Now all we have to do is find out who killed him."

"Here is everything I have from the geocaches. Once we became suspicious, we stopped handling them. Prior to that, you'll find a lot of my fingerprints and Sabre's on them."

JP handed Brad a box with the contents of the caches they had found. It contained the death certificate; the note that said to read the caches more carefully; the riddle; the brandy bottle; the prescription bottle; and the boxes with the photos of George Clooney and Chet Atkins, as well as the Happy Birthday note. Sabre had already given Brad the note in the last cache that led them to the house in Laguna Beach.

"We ran the last note for prints but found nothing," Brad said.

"Have you interrogated anyone on this case yet? Besides us?"

"We talked to some neighbors, but no one saw anything. We're going to question Brandy McFerran and her boyfriend, Doug Griffin, as soon as we leave here. We plan to speak to the children as well."

"Does Sabre know that? I'm sure she'll want to be present, and since they are minors with counsel, she's required to be there."

"I spoke with Ms. Brown on the way here. She said she'd arrange the interviews. She has one set for later today and the others for tomorrow. She's been very cooperative."

"Oh, she'll cooperate alright, but she's tougher than a one-eared alley cat when it comes to protecting her kids. Just giving you fair warning."

"Yeah, I kinda got that from our conversation."

"Do you mind if I tag along when you interview Brandy McFerran and her latest boyfriend?"

"Not at all, as long as you can keep your mouth shut."

"I know the drill," JP said. "By the way, they are likely at Doug's mother's house. That's where they seem to have set up housekeeping."

***

Brandy answered the door wearing short shorts, a low-cut tank top, and bare feet. Her hair was stiff with spray without a hair out of place, and her makeup painstakingly but thickly applied. She looked right past Brad and focused on his younger, more handsome partner, Eric.

"Are you Brandy McFerran?" Brad asked.

"Yes."

Brad flashed his badge. "Detective Bradford Williams, Laguna Beach PD. This is my partner, Eric Ridenour. I think you already know JP Torn."

Brandy nodded.

"We'd like to speak to you, if you don't mind," Brad said.

"Sure. Is this about Monroe?" Her voice suddenly became guttural and dramatic as she asked the question.

"Yes, it is. Is Douglas Griffin here?"

"Yeah, he's in the bedroom." Brandy dropped the dramatic voice.

"Could you get him, please? We have a few questions for him as well."

"Sure, come on in."

"Is anyone else here, Ms. McFerran?"

"No. Doug's mother lives here, but she's at work right now."

Brandy walked toward the bedroom while Brad, Eric, and JP remained in the living room. It reeked with the smell of cigarette smoke. Several ashtrays were strewn about the room, and all were filled with butts and ashes.

"Doug, there are some detectives here who want to talk to us," Brandy called out in that guttural voice again. "It's about Monroe."

Doug appeared in the hallway without a shirt, barefoot, and wearing jeans. His hair was disheveled, and he obviously hadn't shaved recently.

Before Brad could ask any questions, Brandy started talking in her drama queen voice. "I feel terrible about him dying, but he wasn't a very nice man, if you know what I mean."

"What do you mean, ma'am?"

"He took advantage of me when I was a minor. Got me pregnant and then dumped me." Her acting voice continued for several statements and then faded to normal.

"That must have made you pretty upset. Did you try to get him to take responsibility for the child?"

"I tried, but his bitch of a mother got involved. She said it wasn't his kid, but I know it was because he was my first—that I went all the way with, that is. The old lady threatened me and then offered me money if I'd keep my mouth shut."

"I told her I'd be quiet until the baby was born, and then we could take a paternity test." Brandy looked around the room, pushing things aside on the coffee table and the end tables.

"She agreed to that?"

"Yes, and we took the test, but it came out that he wasn't the baby daddy. But I know that wasn't right, so I figure they paid someone off there too." She continued her search, picking up one empty pack of cigarettes after another, searching for one that had something in it. Instead of throwing the empties in the trash, they landed right back where she had found them.

"But you never told anyone?"

"No. What was I going to do? Old Mother Bullard gave me money to not tell anyone. She said if the press got ahold of it, it would ruin her son's chances of becoming a big politician. You can see how that turned out. He never got elected to nothing."

Brandy walked over to the chest of drawers where the television sat and ran her hand along the top of the chest behind the television.

Brad reached in his jacket pocket and pulled out a pack of cigarettes. "Would you like a smoke?"

"Oh, yes," she said in her most dramatic voice. She reached out her hand for him to shake one out, but instead he handed her the pack.

"Take two. You'll have one for later."

She shook two cigarettes out and handed the pack back to Brad. He handled the pack with just his index finger and thumb on the top and bottom of the pack and dropped it back in his pocket.

"But you took the money?"

"I did," she elongated the word "did," speaking slowly and deliberately. "But only because I didn't think I could do anything else. I was afraid, you know."

"Afraid of who?"

"Monroe smacked me around a few times. I was afraid he'd hurt my baby. But no one was as scary as Old Mother Bullard. Besides her threats and the money, she also offered to get me started in my singing career. That was real important to me back then. It still is, except I'm leaning more toward acting now than singing. Or maybe I could do both."

"I'm an actor too," Doug added, as if Brad were a talent scout instead of a detective.

"When did you last see Monroe Bullard?" The question was aimed at Brandy, but Doug shifted his feet, looked at Brandy, and then looked away.

"It's been years," Brandy said, once again speaking as if she were in front of a camera for a low-budget film.

More twitching from Doug. Brad looked at Eric and nodded his head.

"Doug, would you mind stepping outside and talking to me for a minute? We could get through this a lot faster." Eric touched him lightly on the arm and guided him to the door. "I know you must have a real busy schedule with your career."

JP remained inside with Brad and watched the performance.

"How many years since you saw Monroe?"

"I saw him a few months before I left Nashville. Been more than three years, I'd say."

"Did you know he was in California?"

"No, I had no idea." She stretched out the words "no" and "idea."

JP turned so Brandy wouldn't see the smile that popped up on his face from her dramatic answer. He figured Brad had had enough as well because he changed the subject.

"Ms. McFerran, have you ever been geocaching?"

149

"Why, yes. Do you geocache?" She was speaking again in her normal tone without the drama.

"I think the cameras stopped," JP mumbled.

Brad turned and furrowed his brow at JP. Brandy didn't appear to hear him or see Brad's look because she continued to talk.

"I love to geocache. The kids and I do it all the time."

"When was the last time you went?"

"It was when the kids were still living with me. We went a lot back then." She paused. "No, that's not true. I went once after that with Doug. He'd never been, and he wanted to know how it worked, so I took him."

"When was that?"

"A week or so ago. I'm not sure exactly."

"Whose idea was it to go geocaching? Yours or Doug's?" A soft beeping sound came from Brad's pocket. He pulled his phone out, glanced at the text message, and then placed it back in his pocket.

"I think it was his. I guess he heard me talking about it, and he asked if I'd take him." She looked at JP and then at Brad. "What does this have to do with Monroe?" She paused, lowered her head, and looked up at Brad, blinking her eyelashes. "Or are you just curious about what an actress does in her spare time?"

Brad gave her a half smile as if he were really interested in her personal life. "When was it you said you last saw Monroe?"

"More than three years ago."

"Have you talked to him or had any contact with him of any sort since then?"

"No, none."

"I'm curious. Have you ever hidden a cache?"

She shook her head. "No. That seems way too complicated. We just like looking for them." Brandy looked at the clock on the wall. "I really have to get going. I have an important appointment this morning."

"Are you planning to leave town any time soon?"

"No, not for a few days anyway. I may be getting an audition in L.A. in a week or so, though. I've got some pretty interesting things going on right now."

"Good, because I'm sure we'll have more questions. Please stick around, okay? We may need your help."

"Sure. No problem. I'm glad to help."

"One more thing, so you don't end up as a suspect: where were you yesterday morning?"

"I was right here with Doug. We didn't get up until about ten. It was nearly two before we went anywhere." She tilted her head and smiled at Brad. "It takes me a while to make myself this beautiful."

"You've been very helpful, Ms. McFerran."

JP and Brad walked outside. Doug and Detective Ridenour were standing near the car about twenty-five feet away.

JP said, "Could she be any more dramatic?"

"If she talks like that at her auditions, it's pretty easy to see why she's unemployed. Besides that, she was lying through her pearly whites."

"About the geocaching?"

"Probably that too, but she lied about having contact with Monroe for sure. That text I got a while ago was from the precinct. They said Monroe's cell phone showed calls to and from Brandy's cell phone number last week and again yesterday."

They walked toward the car. "You don't smoke, do you?"

"Nope, haven't touched them in twenty years, but they sure come in handy when I need a set of fingerprints."

Chapter 29

Sabre met with Conway for the second time that day. This time it was at his foster home. They sat on a bench in the shade of several large eucalyptus trees. "I wanted to talk with you before Detective Williams arrives to see if you have any questions. Do you?"

"Not really. I don't know anything about Monroe except that he may be my father." Conway pursed his lips and wiggled his shoulders in apparent discomfort.

"Is there something else I should know?" Sabre asked.

"Sort of."

"What's that? You can tell me anything, you know. I am your attorney and what you tell me will be kept in confidence. You understand that, right?"

"Yeah. It's not like that. It's just that I ... I know there are tests to see if someone is the father of a kid. I was wondering if that could be done for me and him. I would really like to know who my father is."

Sabre didn't have the heart to tell him that a test had already been done and it was negative, especially since the source of the information thought it was invalid. "Let me see what I can do." At the very least, she decided she would ask the court for an order.

Detective Brad Williams pulled up to the yard and parked about thirty feet from where Sabre and Conway were sitting. Sabre waved when he stepped out of the car, and he walked toward them.

"I used to think I wanted to be a cop," Conway said.

"That's a good profession. Are you no longer interested?"

"No. I think I want to go to law school and then maybe be a lawyer like you or a politician. I've held a couple of offices at school, and I really liked it."

"Those are both good professions." Sabre smiled. "Hello, Detective. Nice to see you again." She turned to her client. "This is Conway McFerran. He's the eldest of the children and a very responsible young man."

Brad extended his hand. "Hello, Conway. I'm Detective Williams. It's nice to meet you."

Conway shook his hand. "Likewise."

After a few questions about school and Conway's work, the detective asked, "Did you ever meet Monroe Bullard?"

"No, sir."

"Did he ever try to make contact with you, maybe a phone call or a visit of any kind that you're aware of?"

"No, sir."

"Have you talked to any strangers in the past few months? Perhaps he approached you and you didn't know it was him."

"I'm sure he hasn't been around. I would have recognized him if I saw him."

"How's that? Do you know what he looks like?"

"I've seen lots of pictures of him online. I've been following him on Google for years."

If Detective Williams was surprised by his answer, he didn't show it. "Why is that?"

"My mom has always claimed he was my father. Not to me she didn't. To me, she made up some soldier who died in Afghanistan. But then later she told me he was killed in a car accident. When I asked her about it, she said that he died in a car accident right after he got back from Afghanistan. His name changed too. Besides, I heard her talking to her friends about Monroe when she didn't know I was listening. I think I always knew he was my father, or at least thought he was, because I was pretty young when she would talk about it. There are no secrets in our house. Mom doesn't realize how much she talks about stuff that kids probably shouldn't hear."

Brad looked directly at Conway. "I'll do my best to figure out why he had to die."

"Was he murdered?" Conway asked.

"We believe so," Brad said. "Conway, did you ever go geocaching with your mom?" Then he added, "Or with anyone?"

Sabre's experience and instincts kicked in. She glared at the detective and prepared herself to stop the questioning if it appeared accusatory. She was used to protecting her clients when the questions turned on them.

"I went a few times with Mom and my brother and sisters. I wasn't really into it that much, though. Trace and Reba enjoyed it the most. They kept going even after Mom stopped doing it with us."

"Do you know Doug Griffin?" the detective asked.

"You mean Mom's boyfriend? That Doug?"

"Yes. Have you ever met him?"

"No. I see him waiting for my mom after visits. She asked me once if I wanted to meet him, but I said no. I told her it was against the court order."

"Good man. It's real important that you follow court orders." Brad gave Conway a comfortable smile. "So you must be pretty proficient on the computer?"

"I guess so. I use it a lot for school. Mom's always pretty much let us do whatever we wanted on the computer."

"So the other kids are good on it too."

"Yes, especially Trace. He plays a lot of games, but he knows his way around the computer when it comes to other things as well. Whenever one of us gets stuck, he's our go-to guy."

"How about your mother? Does she use the computer too?"

"She's pretty good, but she spends most of her time on Facebook or reading about movie stars and singers. She applies for a lot of auditions online too."

"Does your mom get a lot of acting parts?"

"No, not really, but she tries."

"One more thing," Brad said. He showed Conway a picture of the bobby pin. "Does this look familiar to you?"

"My mom has some like that. I don't know if they are exactly like that, though. I never paid that much attention."

"Thank you, Conway. You've been very helpful. If you ever need anything that I might be able to help with, your attorney has my number."

***

Sabre introduced Brad to the girls and they spoke briefly with all of them present. When Brad showed them the photo, they all agreed that their mother had some reasonable facsimile of the bobby pin. Dolly said they were exactly like her mother's, and she had some that her mother had given her.

"Reba and Taylor, if you don't mind, we would like to speak to Dolly alone for a few minutes. Then we'll speak to each of you."

The younger girls dashed off, seemingly eager to go.

Brad spoke directly to Dolly. "When did your mother give them to you?" Brad asked.

"About a week ago. No, it would be two weeks now. It was at our Sunday visit, the one before last."

"Do you know Monroe Bullard?"

"I never met him, but Mom used to brag about

155

dating this rich, important guy from a very influential family when she was young. She said his mother was a b-i-t-c-h." Dolly lowered her voice when she said it as if she were uncomfortable even spelling the word.

Brad finished his interview and then questioned Reba and then Taylor. The interviews with the rest of the children didn't reveal much more than what Conway had already provided the detective. None of them had ever met Doug, but their mother had asked each one of them if they wanted to. Trace and Reba had told her "no." Dolly and Taylor were indifferent about it. Sabre wondered if Brandy was going to use "the kids want to see him" as a way to get permission from the court to allow Doug at the visits, or if she would have just violated the order. Either way, it didn't sit well with Sabre. It always irritated her when the parents put their needs above those of their children.

All the children had good computer skills, but none as good as Trace. All except Taylor had heard conversations about Monroe being Conway's father, although they didn't show the interest that Conway did.

Brad and Sabre were just getting ready to leave when Reba ran up and said, "Mom's gonna be on television again." Then she ran off toward the house. Brad, Sabre, and Taylor followed her.

They arrived just as the commercial was ending, and the news was showing more photos of Monroe Bullard.

The news reporter stood with Brandy, without Doug, in front of what appeared to be a backdrop.

"They must be in the television studio," Brad said.

"We've been recently informed that the coroner in Orange County, California, has declared the cause of Monroe Bullard's death to be murder. Do you have any information to add to that, Ms. McFerran?"

"Some detectives were at my house an hour or so

ago asking lots of questions. I helped them the best I could. I just want the family to know how sorry I am. Even when someone is a bad seed, the family usually loves them."

"How is your son taking the loss?" the reporter asked.

"He's very upset. His father has rejected him all his life, and death is the ultimate rejection," Brandy said in the most dramatic tone she could summon, and then looked up and smiled at the camera.

"Oh my God," Reba shouted. "Did you see her smile at the camera? And that voice? Does she ever stop acting?"

Dolly put her arm around Reba. Reba seemed to succumb for a moment to the empathy, but then she pulled away and ran to her room.

Chapter 30

"Hello, this is Chuck Shafer," the man said to JP on the phone. "We met a couple of days ago in Laguna Beach. I was on the construction site next to Monroe Bullard's house."

"Oh, yes, Chuck. What can I do for you?"

"You said to call if I saw or remembered anything else. There's a woman on the news tonight—a busty, blonde woman who sounds very strange when she talks. Her name, according to the news reporter, is Brandy McFerran."

"Yes, I saw that."

"She's the same woman who was here that day in that beat-up Nissan."

"Are you sure?"

"She's hard to forget. She did sound a little stranger on TV than she did when I talked to her, but it was definitely her."

"Thanks, Chuck, that's a big help."

"One more thing. I was there on Saturday morning for just a few minutes. I stopped to pick up a tool that I had inadvertently left behind. Just as I was walking to my truck, I saw a car hurry past the house. It looked like the same car."

"The Nissan?"

"Yes. It was a Nissan for sure, and it had the two different-colored fenders, but I couldn't tell you who was driving it. I didn't really notice it until it was already past me. I didn't call you right away because I wasn't positive it was the same car."

JP thanked him. "Detective Brad Williams at the Laguna Beach Police Department is handling the homicide investigation. I'm sure he'll be very interested in what you told me. I will pass it on, but I expect he'll be calling you for more details. Is this the best number to reach you?"

"Yes, this is my cell. I'll be glad to help."

JP passed the information on to Brad and then resumed his research.

***

Early Monday morning Sabre sat in her office drafting a request for a special hearing to attempt to get a court order for a paternity test on Monroe. Conway had a right to know who his father was for many reasons. That was the easy part of the request. However, she knew she had lots of other legal and practical hurdles to jump through. At least the case was in Judge Hekman's courtroom. If anyone would order the test, it would be her. But she knew even Hekman was unlikely to make the order since a test had already been done, and without proof that the earlier test was invalid, it was a long shot.

Sabre finished up the forms, made ample copies, and drove to the courthouse. Her phone rang.

"Hi, Bro," she said.

"Good morning, Sis. Are you on your way to court?"

"Yes, what's up?"

"I think there's still another cache. And I think it's at Monroe's house."

"Or, whoever has been doing this was just leading us to the house to find the body," Sabre said. "I guess they didn't think we would be so quick since he was still alive when we got there."

"I'm thinking we should go do a more extensive search of that place."

"Ron, don't even think about it. It's still a crime

scene, and at best you could only look around the perimeter, the road, or the hills near there, but not the grounds and certainly not the house."

"You're right."

"Ron, I mean it. You could mess things up for me on this case, not to mention getting yourself in a whole lot of trouble."

"I hear ya, Sis," he said.

"Promise me."

There was silence for a few seconds. "Alright. I promise I won't go there. But if the cache shows up, you have to let me know what's in it."

"You bet," Sabre said and hung up.

She arrived at juvenile court a few minutes later, met up with Bob, and they proceeded to Department Four to seek her hearing. She gave Bob a copy of her request, which she already knew he fully supported.

"Well, if it's not the King and Queen of juvenile court," Jeanette, the court clerk, said when they walked into the courtroom. "What are you two up to?"

"I need to set a special hearing, and time is of the essence."

"What's it for?"

"She needs a paternity test on a dead guy," Bob chimed in.

Sabre handed the paperwork to the clerk. "He died two days ago. He was murdered, so the body likely won't be disposed of too soon, but from what I have read, the tests are better if the specimens are gathered within five days of the death. Also, when the police release the body, it will probably be shipped out of state."

"You two sure keep this job interesting." She looked at the paperwork. "Let me go check with the judge."

While she was gone, David Casey, the Deputy

County Counsel, came into the courtroom and took his seat at the table. Sabre handed him a copy of the paperwork, explaining her request.

"What do you think?" Sabre asked.

"I can't see why the department would object, but I'm not sure how you're going to enforce it, even if Hekman orders it."

"One step at a time," Sabre said.

Jeanette returned with papers in hand. "The hearing is on for one-thirty this afternoon. The judge would like to have the mother present, if possible. She's your client, right, Bob?"

"Yes, I'll see if I can get her here."

Jeanette turned to Mr. Casey. "Will you be handling this case this afternoon, Dave?"

"Yes. The social worker is going to be here anyway on another case, so that'll work out just fine."

Sabre and Bob finished their morning calendars, had lunch at Pho's, and returned for the special hearing. They were waiting outside of Department Four when Brandy and Doug walked up to them.

"Thanks for coming. The judge may want to ask you some questions about Conway's father."

"I'll be glad to tell her anything. Monroe is the father. That's for sure." She exaggerated every word as she spoke.

Bob leaned in and said softly, "You need to try to speak a little less dramatically when you answer the judge's questions. Being that you're an actress, we need to make sure the judge doesn't think you're playing a role. I can tell how good you are, but if you sound too good, then she may not trust what you say."

Sabre rolled her eyes. Bob really knew how to work his clients.

When the bailiff came out to get them for the hearing, they walked into the courtroom. Doug followed

Brandy inside. Sabre saw it and nudged Bob, gesturing her head toward Doug.

Bob stepped toward him. "I'm afraid you'll have to wait outside."

"Why?" Brandy asked. "I don't have any secrets from him."

"These are confidential hearings, so only people with standing can be in here."

"Can't I waive that? I don't mind if he's here."

"No, I'm afraid you can't waive it. You're not the only party to this action. Just let him go. He can wait for you outside. I'll explain it all later."

Sabre knew Bob was anxious to get him out before the judge saw him. Hekman didn't like mothers bringing their boyfriends to court hearings.

Doug left the room and Bob, Sabre, and Brandy took their seats at the table just before the judge entered.

"Ms. Brown, you're requesting a paternity test on the late Monroe Bullard on behalf of your client, Conway Twitty McFerran, is that correct?"

"That's correct, Your Honor."

"Didn't we already deal with this at an earlier hearing?"

"No, Your Honor. There was some discussion about Mr. Bullard being the father, but there was no ruling on the paternity issue. There was actually no request made at that hearing."

"If I recall, there was already a paternity test done on this man." She turned to Brandy. "Is that correct, Ms. McFerran?"

"Yes, ma'am."

"And he was not the father, correct?"

"He is the father, ma'am." Brandy started to slip into her "acting" voice. Bob gave her a stern look. "I know he's the father because I never had sex with anyone else during that time. I was a virgin when I started dating Monroe." A little too much emphasis on "virgin" got her another look from her attorney. "That's how I know the test wasn't right."

The judge looked at Sabre. "Do you have anything to add?"

"My client is extremely anxious to know who his father is, Your Honor. He is seventeen years old and has lived his entire life wondering about this. It would go a long way toward easing his mind if he knew. It would be helpful for him to know if there are any genetic health issues he needs to be aware of as well. And, he would like to know more about his extended family."

"Ms. Brown, I know all the reasons why a child should know who his parents are, and I agree with all of them. I would be delighted to make the order, except that this has already been decided by an earlier test. Unless you can come up with some proof that the first test was invalid, I'm afraid my hands are tied."

Chapter 31

JP's cell phone suddenly made a strange sound like someone playing bongos. He picked it up and saw Pauline's name and the photo she had apparently taken with his phone. JP was new to technology and he'd had his smartphone for only about a year. He hadn't really mastered it yet.

"Hello, Pauline," he said when he answered.

"Oh good. The photo helped you recognize who was calling. Soon you'll be used to the ringtone too."

He thought about asking her why she did that, but he didn't really want to know. "Yeah, thanks."

"Listen, sweet cheeks, I saw that Monroe Bullard cashed in. I started digging, and I found more information that I think will be helpful to you."

"I'm listening," JP said.

"The trust fund that Monroe was living on is huge. When his grandfather died, he made sure Monroe would be taken care of for life. He also knew how irresponsible Monroe had become, or maybe always was. Anyway, he pretty much bypassed his daughter, Mother Bullard, and split the estate between Richard and Monroe. Monroe had his inheritance 'for life,' and then it went to the oldest of Monroe's living children."

"Did Monroe have any other children besides Conway?"

"He was accused twice since then of fathering a child; both had paternity tests and both came up negative. Nothing prior to Conway, or if there is, it's been really well hidden."

"Any chance you can get a copy of the trust?"

"What's it worth to you?" Pauline asked, her voice dropping into a soft, sexy tone.

"You already have it, don't you?"

"Almost. It's on its way. I'll let you know as soon as I get it. By the way, have you heard from the lab where the paternity test was done?"

"I called and left a message, but no one called back."

"I've got another name for you but no phone number, just an address."

"Let me guess: the address is in Tennessee?"

"Yes, but I'll text it to you so you have it. If you decide to go, let me know. I'm sure I could pull some strings to help you get what you need. I know my way around Nashville."

"No doubt. Thanks."

"Ta-ta," she said and hung up.

***

Sabre and JP finally had a night to themselves. They sat on the patio listening to the crickets chirp as the sun set. They had both agreed to have a few moments without discussing work. JP took her hand in his and raised it to his lips, kissing her lightly. When he let go, she traced his lips with her finger before bringing her hand back down. The sweet, romantic moment was interrupted when JP's phone beeped with a text message.

He fumbled through the simple process of retrieving his message. He still hated texting. His fingers hit wrong letters when he tried to type.

When he saw the photo of Pauline on his screen, he turned the phone just slightly. He didn't care that Sabre knew who it was from, but he hated that picture popping up. He had nothing to hide, but he still felt uncomfortable with that photo and he had no clue how to get rid of it. He decided he would go by and see Bob tomorrow and have him take it off.

The message read:

Pauline: *I have the copy of the Leveque Trust. Can I bring it by?*

JP: *Not tonight. Busy. Tomorrow morning?*

Pauline: *Sure. Want me to come by and wake you up?*

JP: *No. Can you meet for coffee? Jitter's?*

Pauline: *7:30?*

JP: *Yes.*

JP laid his phone down. "How did the McFerran court hearing go today?"

"I lost. Even Hekman won't order another paternity test unless I can show the first test was invalid."

"I'm sorry, Sabre. From what I learned today, it's even more crucial that you determine parentage."

"What did you learn?"

"Apparently Monroe's grandfather was worth a bucketload of money. When he died, Monroe received a hefty trust fund. That's what he was living on."

Sabre perked up. "So Conway may be entitled to an inheritance. But didn't Monroe have a will? I'm sure he didn't leave anything to Conway. But if he didn't have a will—"

"Slow down. Your mind is workin' faster than a New York minute. It's even better than that." He paused just to tease her.

"So tell me already," she said.

"Grandpa left Monroe an inheritance 'for life,' and then it was to pass on to his oldest living child."

Sabre perked up and leaned in toward JP. Immediately, she started thinking: *Did the inheritance" violate the rule against perpetuities? Are there any other children? How was she going to protect Conway's interests? Was Monroe really his father?*

"I see your wheels turning. What are you thinking?"

"I have so many questions. I need to see a copy of that trust, but I don't know how I could possibly do that."

"I'll have it for you today."

She reached over and kissed him on the lips. "You're the best."

"Boyfriend or PI?"

"Both." She frowned. "But none of this will matter if I can't get another paternity test. And that's not going to happen unless I can prove the first test was fraudulent."

"I'm working on that. I have another lead, but I may need to go to Nashville."

"Oh, I'd love to go to Nashville, especially with you." Sabre smiled.

"So let's go."

"No, I can't go. Not now. There's just too much going on in this case. And even if we can prove it's fraud, I would have to convince the court, get an order for paternity, and then figure out how to enforce it. You can bet the Bullards will fight it, and they have the money to do it. It could go on for years, and Conway could still come up the loser." Sabre sighed. "Do you really think you could learn something if you go?"

"Maybe. But it doesn't sound like it would do much good."

Sabre shook her head. "It's a start. Without that, we have nothing. I'll figure out the rest as I go. I can't let the boy down. If he's entitled to that inheritance, I'm the only one who can get it for him. It's my responsibility to protect his rights, and his right of inheritance is a big deal."

"Let me see what other information I can find today, and then we'll decide if you want me to go."

"Fair enough."

He stood up, took her hand, and pulled her up

toward him. "Now, are we done talking shop?"

"I am," Sabre said, as she leaned in and kissed him.

Chapter 32

Pauline was already at Jitter's when JP arrived, which was uncharacteristic of her. JP was sure she liked making a grand entrance.

"Good morning," JP said.

"I got you coffee. Leaded and black, right?"

"That's fine." JP appreciated the gesture but found himself thinking that Sabre would know he would be drinking half caff this late in the morning. It wasn't that he hadn't spent plenty of mornings with Pauline, way more than he had with Sabre, but Sabre was far more attentive to his needs. He almost chuckled when he realized he had no idea what Pauline ate or drank in the morning, but he knew exactly what Sabre would have.

Pauline pulled a file out of her bag that appeared to be about three inches thick. "Here's a copy of the trust from Thomas Leveque, maternal grandfather."

"Whoa, that trust is bigger than Texas."

"He had a large estate, but there's a lot of boiler plate language in there too. Your attorney will know what pages are pertinent. The bottom line is that if Monroe's the father, this kid is worth millions."

"Now all I have to do is prove that the test was tampered with."

"I have an appointment set up for you tomorrow morning with the lab tech."

"In person or on the phone?"

"In person."

"So I guess I have to go to Nashville today."

"It's all set up. And tomorrow night we're going to a fundraiser dinner at which Senator Bullard is the guest of honor."

"We?"

"Yes, of course, darling. You can't go without me. I've hitched us a ride with a wealthy friend on his private jet, and we'll leave soon." She looked at the time on her phone. "In exactly five hours and forty-two minutes," she calculated. "Can you be ready?"

JP thought about how he was going to explain this to Sabre and then remembered how important proving paternity was to her.

"I'll be ready, but I don't know about the fundraiser. I'm not real comfortable at fancy functions."

"You'll do just fine. I have a nice cover story for you that'll put you right at ease."

"Will I need a suit or tux or something for the dinner party?" JP cringed at the thought.

"Just bring your best hat and boots. Everything you'll need is already waiting for you at the hotel." She stood up. "See you this afternoon. All the information is in the front of that folder. Ta-ta."

***

The plane ride was unlike anything JP had experienced before. There were only six people on the plane besides the pilot: JP and Pauline; Evan, who appeared to be no more than thirty-five years old; Jaq, a young girl about twelve or thirteen, who referred to Evan as Dad; Alex, a brunette with little makeup and stylish, tailored clothes, who was soon identified as Evan's assistant; and a butler or steward, JP wasn't sure of his title or exact role. It didn't take long before JP knew the plane belonged to Evan, a techie billionaire.

JP sat in the plush leather seat trying to be social, but he had little to say after introductions were made. Pauline chatted freely with each of the passengers, especially Evan. As soon as JP was allowed, he picked up the drink the steward had served him and walked around the plane. It beat sitting. He walked past Jaq, who was sitting by herself and playing on her tablet.

"Are you from Texas?" Jaq asked.

"I was born there, but I live in San Diego now. Where do you live?"

"We have two homes, one in L.A. and one in Nashville, but we're building a new home in Sarasota, Florida."

"Which one do you like best?"

"I have more friends in Nashville, so I think I like living there the best. We have a lot of cowboys there too, like you, and lots of famous cowboy singers. Do you sing?"

"No, I'm afraid not. I'm just a regular cowboy."

JP sat down and chatted for a while with Jaq. She was a smart young girl, and if it weren't for the circle of friends she mentioned in casual conversation, one would never know she was raised in the lap of luxury. Suddenly, JP dreaded the dinner party he would be attending the next night. Here he was in this small group of elite people, and his best conversation was with a twelve-year-old. He was anxious to get to Nashville, get his work done, and get home.

***

They walked into The Hermitage Hotel across the street from the Legislative Plaza and the Tennessee State Museum. One glance around and JP saw nothing but dollar signs.

"Why don't you stay here, and I'll get a room at a Marriott. I'm sure there's one close by."

"Nonsense. I already have our rooms."

At least she said "rooms" plural, he thought.

"These were comped for me. I don't pay for hotel

rooms anymore. It's one of the perks of the job. Don't worry. You have your own room. Actually we have adjoining rooms. I'll leave my door open, and you can come in if you choose." She gave him a devilish smile.

JP sighed. It had been a while since he felt this uncomfortable around a woman, especially this woman. They had been friends for a long time, off and on, and he used to enjoy her company. But now it somehow felt like he was cheating. He wished he had been able to tell Sabre about Pauline going along before he left, but he didn't want to do it on the phone. He and Sabre had arranged to meet for lunch, but she got stuck in court and couldn't leave, so he didn't have a chance to tell her.

Pauline checked them both in, gave JP his key, and they took the elevator to their rooms. "Why don't we meet in the lobby in thirty minutes? We can get a bite to eat. There's a nice little Cajun place not far from here."

"That works for me."

***

Pauline and JP ate dinner, and then Pauline suggested they stop at the hotel bar for a drink.

"The first round is on me," JP said. "Then I'm hitting the sack."

JP had a beer, and Pauline had a mojito. They discussed their plan of attack for the next day. JP would meet with the lab tech alone and do whatever follow-up he had to do.

"I arranged a rental car for you. They'll deliver it here at eight o'clock. Just check with the concierge, and they'll bill it out for you." JP was fascinated by the way she operated. He would never have thought to do that. Instead he would have called the rental car place, arranged a way to get there, and rented the car.

"Thanks, that'll make it easier. And thanks for setting up an appointment with the lab tech."

"I'm glad I could help."

JP finished his beer and stood to leave. "Are you coming or staying?"

"That depends. Will I be going to your room or mine?"

"Yours," JP said without hesitation.

"Then I think I'll hang here a little longer. I'll see you tomorrow. Be sure you're back here in time to leave at five for the dinner."

JP had hoped the fundraiser had somehow been canceled.

Chapter 33

JP drove south on Highway 65, exited at Old Hickory Boulevard, and followed the instructions from *Siri* on his iPhone until he reached the parking lot. The lab appeared to share the building with a vision lab and a life insurance office. He checked the time. It was a little too early to call Sabre. He would wait until after his meeting, since he really had nothing to report yet and he didn't relish getting into the conversation about Pauline's presence.

JP entered the office marked AAA-DNA Testing Lab. A receptionist sitting on a tall stool behind a counter greeted him as he entered. The walls were covered with brightly colored DNA strands.

"My name is JP Torn. I'm here to see Chad Lambert."

"I'll call him," she said without a trace of a southern accent. She picked up the phone and paged the lab tech.

"You're not from around here, are you?"

"No, I'm from Orange County, California. I can't seem to get rid of the accent. Everyone around here teases me. I don't get it. They're the ones who talk funny."

Before she could say anything else, a round man with a small goatee and wearing Buddy Holly glasses and green scrubs walked into the room. He appeared to be around thirty-five or forty years old.

"I'm Chad Lambert." He didn't reach out his hand to shake JP's as JP expected. Instead, he handed him a surgical mask and some latex gloves.

"If you want to see the lab and how it works, you need to wear these."

"Sure." JP started to put the mask on.

"You can wait until we get to the lab."

They passed through the first door and stopped at the second door on the right. The 300-square-foot room contained a large desk, one file cabinet, and several stuffed leather chairs.

"This is where the intake is done, questions are answered, and decisions are made." They moved to the next room. "This is where we collect the specimen if they come directly to the lab for testing."

"And if they don't?"

"Then it's collected somewhere else, sent to us, and a careful chain of custody is established."

At the end of the hall was a small waiting room with about a dozen comfortable, straight-backed chairs. The seats and backs were covered in a soft, green bamboo fabric. Double doors to the left led to the lab. Chad scanned a card on a small box next to the door, and they stepped inside a cubicle about the size of a standard elevator. In front of them was another set of double doors. To their left was a single door.

"You can put those on now," Chad said, glancing down at the gloves and mask JP was holding. As JP slipped the mask over his head to cover his nose and mouth, he was glad he had left his hat in the car. When JP was ready, Chad scanned his card on the box near the single door on the left. It opened into a long hallway with a solid wall on the back. The front had a wall about three feet high, above which were five feet of glass that ran the length of the hallway, exposing the entire lab but keeping it separate from the hallway. They stepped inside.

The white and chrome lab had six people working at different stations, all wearing long-sleeve green scrubs, surgical masks, surgical or bouffant head covers, and latex gloves stretched over the ends of their sleeves.

"Do they always dress like that?" JP asked.

"We take every precaution to make sure our tests are not compromised. We do more than paternity testing here, and some of it requires every precaution."

"Is this the lab where you did Monroe Bullard's paternity test?"

"First, I have a couple of questions," Chad said. "Who are you working for?"

"I work for an attorney in San Diego who represents the subject of your paternity test."

"Conway McFerran?" Chad asked.

JP was surprised that he knew the name, but then realized he probably got it from the test. Since Conway was a minor, his name had not been released to the press.

"That's correct."

"And you work for Attorney Sabre Brown?"

"Yes." Again JP wondered how he knew that. Either this man had done his homework or Pauline must have provided the information.

"Then I can tell you. He had the test done here, and I was the one who did the procedure for it. And I did two more of them after that for other possible offspring of Monroe Bullard."

"Let me guess," JP said. "They all came up negative?"

"Yes, sir."

"And where was the blood drawn for Conway's test? Here? Or was it sent in?"

"Ms. McFerran first came with the baby, and we drew his blood as well as hers. About a half-hour later, Monroe and a male friend of his came in. That's when I drew Monroe's blood. We did the same procedure for the other two tests."

JP didn't really care about the other tests, but

Chad kept lumping them together, so he decided to inquire a little further. "Was there anything different about the three tests?"

Chad thought. "Not really. The mother and baby always came in first. Monroe always followed a half an hour or so later, and the same friend always came with him."

"Who paid for the tests?"

"They were always paid for with cash."

"And did you take a blood sample from his friend as well?" JP asked.

Chad hesitated. "Yes, I did, but I'll deny it to anyone else."

"Why are you telling me?"

"Because Mr. Bullard told me to."

Even though JP didn't expect that, he didn't show any sign of surprise. "Monroe Bullard?"

"Yes, sir."

"When?"

"A week or so ago."

"He was here?"

"No, he phoned me, but I recognized his voice. I know it was him." Chad took a couple of steps forward and then stopped. He pointed at a large chrome refrigeration system. "That's where we keep the specimens. There are different sections in the unit for different kinds of testing."

JP glanced inside and then said, "And Monroe told you that you could tell me about the paternity test?"

"Not you, per se. He told me that there was a court case occurring in San Diego that involved Conway McFerran and that paternity may be an issue. He told me that someone may come asking questions, and if they did, I should tell them the truth—but only if they were working with Attorney Sabre Brown on behalf of Conway."

"Did he say anything else? Perhaps any indication that someone had threatened him or anything?"

"No."

"Did you think at the time that Monroe knew he was going to die or was in danger?"

"No, not really. I just figured he was having second thoughts about what he had done. I didn't know what to think when I saw on the news that he had died."

JP watched Chad carefully as he spoke, trying to detect a sign that he might not be telling the truth. None appeared. "Did you even test Monroe's blood?"

"Yes, I was told to check paternity and if Monroe was the father then I was to use the friend's blood instead."

"And Monroe was the father?"

"Yes, it was the same each time he came in. And each time, they told me to discard Monroe's sample, destroy the test, and use the friend's blood."

"They?"

"Monroe and his mother, mostly his mother. She's the one who paid me to keep everything 'hush-hush.'" Chad sighed. "You've got to understand this isn't something I would ordinarily do, but I really needed the money. They knew that when they came to me."

"How did they know that? Did you know the Bullards before?"

Chad took a couple more steps forward and stopped. "I'm supposed to be showing you the lab, so let's keep walking and act as if you're interested in this place."

JP looked inside.

"No, I didn't know them before. I don't know how they knew, but they did. Somehow they found out that I had been trying to get extra money to buy a kidney for my grandmother who suffered from polycystic kidney disease. She was on the transplant list, but she was way too old to ever make it to the top of the list." He took a deep breath. "I guess it was no secret I was trying to raise money. I asked anyone who would listen."

"And you were trying to buy a kidney on the black market?"

"My grandmother raised me. As far as I was concerned, she was my mother. She was only seventy-five and could have lived another twenty years."

"Why didn't you just give her one of yours?" JP asked, thinking he was probably not compatible or something.

"I had already donated mine to my sister. She had the same disease."

"But you didn't have it?"

They continued to walk down the hallway, with Chad occasionally pointing at something in the lab. JP observed with feigned interest.

"No. At least it has never been detected. I run regular urine tests on myself, checking for proteinuria and gross or microscopic hematuria, pyruia, and bacteriuria." He waved his hand in the air as if dismissing that thought. "I guess that's too much information. Anyway, I've never shown any signs of PKD, as it's called."

"Were you able to buy the kidney?"

"No. I had a deal all set. I had even given them the money, but then someone came in with more cash and stole it out from under me. They wouldn't give me my money back, but they told me I would get the next one. Unfortunately, my grandmother died shortly after that."

"Did you get your money back?" JP knew the answer before he asked the question.

"No, and what was I going to do? If I turned them in, I would probably have gone to jail too."

"Were you paid more money when you ran two

more bogus tests for Monroe Bullard?"

"No. I was told, when I made the original deal, that there might be more tests in the future. She probably didn't want me to have the additional cash for fear I would disappear. I wouldn't have, though. I would never leave my sister. She and my nephew are all the family I have left."

They reached the end of the hallway and turned around. Chad walked faster than before.

"I don't suppose you still have the samples?"

"No. We routinely keep them for only six months; then they are destroyed. But we didn't even do that with these samples. I was instructed to destroy them as soon as the paperwork was done. That's why Monroe's friend needed to keep coming back."

"And the friend, do you know his name?"

"I never had a need to have it. In fact, I didn't want it, so I don't know his last name, but I did hear Monroe call him Marty if that helps."

When they reached the door, Chad said, "Make sure we are clear on all this. I will not testify or tell anyone else what I just told you, so if you have thoughts that this might help you in court, get rid of them. I will not," he emphasized the word "not," "help you prove paternity. I will lie, and I will protect myself no matter what the consequence."

Chapter 34

Frustrated that she wasn't able to obtain the order for a paternity test, Sabre kicked the idea over and over in her mind. She really hoped that JP was able to provide evidence that proved the first test was a fraud.

Suddenly, Sabre slapped the heel of her hand against her forehead. *Of course*, she thought. *There were other ways to show paternity*. She didn't need Monroe's DNA. She just needed someone in the family either to give her their DNA or someone with the authority to give her access to Monroe's. Why hadn't she thought of this before? They had all just assumed that the Bullards wouldn't be cooperative, but maybe they would. From all she had heard, she didn't think it likely that the mother would cooperate, but perhaps the senator would. She knew it was a long shot, but why not at least give it a try.

She looked online for the number for Senator Richard Bullard. She finally found a number to his office. After being placed on hold and transferred several times, explaining each time who she was and that she needed to speak to the senator himself, she reached his legal department. It had taken two more transfers before she reached the attorney who handled his personal matters.

"This is Carolyn House," the voice on the other end of the line said. Sabre guessed from the voice that she was probably in her fifties.

"I'm Attorney Sabre Brown. I represent a child, Conway McFerran, in a dependency matter in San Diego Superior Court, Juvenile Division. I'm sure you're aware that the late Monroe Bullard is the alleged father—"

The attorney interrupted Sabre before she could finish. "I don't believe he is the alleged father, at least not from a legal standpoint, since there has already been a test proving otherwise."

"I have not seen those test results, and the mother is still alleging that Monroe is the father."

"What is it you want from us?" Her voice was soft but matter of fact.

"I would like either the senator or his mother to submit to a DNA test. If there is no match, we will all go away."

"I'm afraid we cannot do that. I've already had this discussion with the family. First of all, there is no need to run another test. Senator Bullard is a very kind and cooperative, but busy, man. I'm sure he would embrace this young man if he were his nephew, but he is convinced that he is not. He has no reason to believe there was any issue with the first test."

"Conway's mother claims she was a virgin when she met Monroe and that she was never with anyone else until after the birth of Conway."

Carolyn sighed. "I've seen this mother on television. She really seems to be eating up the limelight. Do you suppose that might be the basis for her continued claims?"

"Possibly, but this would be a good way to make her stop."

"I have worked with the Bullard family for over ten years, and you could not find a more considerate man in politics than the senator. He would really like to be just left alone so he can do his job and grieve for his brother, so my answer is still no."

"And his mother?"

"His mother is doing what she thinks is in the best interest of her sons. She will not comply with your request. You can be certain of that."

"Thank you for your time, Ms. House."

Sabre returned to her task at hand, reading through the entire Thomas Monroe Leveque trust and skipping only the parts she knew to be boilerplate. Two hours later she had it narrowed down to a few simple notes:

T.M. Leveque left a cash sum of $500,000 to his only daughter. The remainder of his estate went to his two grandsons, Richard and Monroe, for "life." Each was to receive $25,000 per month for living expenses, plus money for their educations and any incidentals, which included a new car every three years. Upon the death of either Richard or Monroe, his half went to his firstborn, respectively. In each case, if he had no offspring, the estate would then be split between the other brother and their mother.

Sabre noticed a missed call from JP. There was no message, which wasn't unusual. He hated talking to machines. She returned the call but reached only his voice mail, and she left a message. "Please call when you can. It's crucial that we determine paternity. It appears that if Conway is Monroe's son, he is entitled to quite an inheritance."

She went back to studying the trust and researching the rule against perpetuities and other estate law to make certain there wasn't another way for the family to contest it. She couldn't find any problems with it, but she decided to take it to a colleague, Eddie Saunders, who spent about half his time practicing wills and estate law.

***

Twenty minutes later Sabre sat in Eddie's office across from her friend. They had been practicing at juvenile court together for over seven years. He was about fifty-five and had dark hair with some gray sprinkled throughout, mostly at the temples. Eddie had a thin face with a pleasant smile and a runner's body.

The trust was laid out before him on his desk. He held a pen in one hand and flipped through the pages with the other. He twirled the pen through his fingers with great agility as he read the document.

It took Eddie about fifteen minutes to go through the same document that had taken Sabre two hours, but he knew what he was looking for.

"It's pretty straightforward for such a huge estate. When did Thomas Leveque die?"

"Eighteen years ago. My client would have been in utero at the time."

"Which could explain the importance of why the paternity test was altered."

"I know. I thought it was because Mother Bullard was trying to protect her son's reputation so he could rise on the political ladder, but maybe it was all about the money."

"And she couldn't contest it because it has the clause in the trust prohibiting it. If she did, she would have been excluded completely."

"And now?" Sabre asked, as she watched Eddie roll the pen through his fingers and pass it with ease to the other hand where he did the same. "Can they contest it now?"

"Not really. Too much time has passed, and everything has already settled. Maybe they could show that the distribution from the grandfather's trust isn't valid because of recently discovered fraud or duress, but even that's a long shot. We're dealing with another state, so it's possible there could be some law in Tennessee that alters the outcome of this case, but I doubt it."

"I expect a fight from the Bullard family."

"When that much money is involved there's usually a fight, but the issue is going to be all about paternity. They already have proof that Monroe is not the father."

"We have to prove that he is." Sabre shook her head. "Piece of cake, right?"

***

Sabre returned to her office and prepared some cases for the next day's court hearings. She had spent so much time and energy on the McFerran case that she felt as if she had been neglecting her other cases.

Sabre glanced at her phone. Other than the missed call a few hours ago, she still hadn't heard back from JP, which was beginning to concern her. He was so good about checking in when he was out of town.

Just then her phone vibrated. Hoping it was JP, she grabbed the phone without looking at the caller.

"Hello."

"Hi, Sis," Ron said.

"Oh, it's you. What's up?"

"Don't sound so enthused to hear from me."

"Sorry, I always love hearing from you. I just thought it was JP. I haven't heard from him in a while, and I'm getting a little worried."

"Is he still out of town?"

"Yes, but enough about that. What can I do for my favorite brother?"

"I was wondering if you could find out what was in that last cache at Monroe's house. I'm really bored, and I'm curious to know what was in there."

"I'm going to try to call JP again right now. As soon as I talk to him, I'll see if he can get the info from Brad."

"Thanks, Sis. You're the best."

Sabre hung up and tried calling JP again.

"This is JP Torn. Please leave a message," the

deep voice said. Sabre loved to listen to his accent.

"I miss you, but I hope your trip is going well. I know your dislike for hotel living, so I'm sure you'd rather be coming home to me and staying in my nice, cushy, king-sized bed. That said, I really hope you've found the information we need to show that the first test was a fraud. In case there was any doubt how important it is that we prove paternity, the number is in the neighborhood of one hundred million dollars. That's what Conway would inherit if Monroe was the daddy."

Chapter 35

"**C**oors Light, please," JP told the bartender, as he tugged at his bolo tie. The black, braided, leather cord with sterling silver tips had a gold star on a silver clasp dangling from his neck. His black suit, white shirt, and tie made him feel strange, but at least he was able to wear his Stetson and his comfortable boots. And dressing like this was the least of it. He wasn't used to mingling with the one-percenters.

The bartender popped open the beer and poured it into a tall glass. JP wanted to tell him just to give him the bottle, but he decided it wasn't couth. When he reached in his pocket to pull out some money, the bartender shook his head.

"It's open bar."

When JP glanced around for a tip jar, the bartender shook his head. JP walked away and toward the crowd. He wondered why there weren't more people at the bar, especially since it was free. Then he noticed most of the guests were holding champagne glasses, and waiters were walking around the room with trays of them. He wondered what the attraction was to that bubbly drink that left his nose feeling funny. He had never cared much for champagne.

JP continued through the crowd, picking up bits and pieces of conversation. Most of it was about pending legislation or the price of gas or the Middle East crisis. He wondered why he let Pauline talk him into coming here. What could he possibly learn at this place? And what was taking her so long? Not that he wanted to hang out with her, either, but at least he wouldn't feel quite so awkward. When she had left him and told him to mingle, she'd said she had some business to take care of. JP didn't want to know what kind of business she had. He never quite understood how she made a living, but he knew she was paid handsomely for what she did. She was certainly "in the know."

JP spotted the guest of honor and his mother as they entered the room. He recognized them from Internet pictures and the recent television coverage. JP thought the noise level dropped a couple of decibels when they came in, but it wasn't long before it was back in full buzz mode. Like Conway, the senator stood about six foot two, was thin, and had a full head of light-brown hair. Although he was dressed in an expensive suit, he did not look debonair, but rather like a country boy in a suit. His mother, on the other hand, appeared refined. Her clothes were impeccable; her gray hair was perfectly coifed; and she carried herself with an air of superiority.

JP made his way toward the senator and his mother, who had stopped to talk with an older couple who were sitting about ten feet inside the doorway. He hadn't quite decided what he was going to do when he reached them. When he was closer, JP thought he saw a resemblance to Conway, not only in Richard's lanky body but also his face.

"JP Talbot." JP reached out his hand to shake the senator's. "Oil refineries, Texas and Louisiana mostly," he said, just like Pauline had instructed him to do.

"Nice to meet you," the senator said.

"I'm so sorry to hear about your brother, Senator Bullard."

The senator's eyebrows twitched, and the smile on his face was replaced with a look of pain. "Thank you," he said.

JP found his reaction to be sincere. Or perhaps, he thought, he was an excellent actor and had practiced earlier. JP stepped back and let other people greet the senator and share their condolences. At all times, Bullard seemed to have appropriate reactions to the comments. Monroe's mother, on the other hand, seemed more indifferent. Perhaps that was due to years of dealing with a debauched son. JP suddenly wondered if she wasn't the more sincere of the two. Richard Bullard was smooth and eloquent, and the smile came on his face at all the appropriate times. His actions all seemed so plastic.

JP was just giving serious thought to blowing off the dinner and going back to the hotel when Pauline approached him.

"I was just thinking about leaving," JP said.

"You can't leave yet. You need to talk to someone."

"I *have* been talking to someone, and I'm bored stiff. I don't understand half of what they're talking about, and I care even less."

"It's a childhood friend of Monroe's. They even went to the same university. He must know something about Monroe or the Bullards that would be helpful."

"Like who is Marty, maybe." JP suddenly was interested in what the man might have to say. "Where is he?"

"Over there," she nodded her head toward a thin man who stood about three or four inches above anyone else in the room.

"That tall, gangly guy near the window?"

"Yes, that's him. We'll wander over there and strike up a conversation, and then I'll leave and let you chat with him."

It didn't take long to reach the man. Pauline reached out her hand. "I'm Pauline Vasquez. This is JP Talbot."

"Huck Finn," the man said.

"Really?" JP asked before he could stop himself.

"Really." The man smiled.

"Sorry," JP said. "I didn't mean to be impolite."

"No worries. I get that all the time," Huck said. He turned to Pauline. "Do I know you?"

"I don't think so," Pauline said. JP knew she prided herself on remembering faces.

"What is it you do for work, Ms. Vasquez?"

"I'm a political analyst and special-interest representative."

"A lobbyist?"

She just gave him a sweet smile. "JP owns some oil refineries here in the south. And what about you, Huck? What do you do besides attending fundraisers for little children with serious illnesses?"

"That's about it." He winked at Pauline. "You can do that when you live off your daddy's trust fund."

JP liked this guy. He didn't know if the man was yanking their chain or if it was just his outlook on life, but either way he was a lot more fun to talk with than anyone else so far tonight. And his last comment left a great opening for JP.

"My friend Monroe Bullard was like that. Lived off his granddaddy's trust fund."

"Monroe was an expert at it."

"You knew him?"

"Practically all my life. We met in grade school, hung out some, and became real close in middle school. By the time we were in high school, we were inseparable. We almost got thrown out of USN— University School Nashville—on more than one occasion. But we survived and then went to Princeton together. It's a wonder we were admitted, but that's another story." A smirk passed over his lips. "Good old, Monroe. I haven't seen him for years, though. We drifted apart after college. He was headed down a serious political path, and to tell you the truth our political views were quite opposite one another."

"Have you seen him since you attended Princeton together?"

Pauline slipped away without saying anything. Huck didn't seem to notice or care. He said, "I saw him a couple of times after college, but it's been years. I spent a lot of time in Europe the last fifteen years. I didn't even know he had left Nashville until I saw it on the news."

"We just met a few years ago," JP said. "We had a mutual friend who introduced us. He loved to tell tales about 'the good old days' and some of his escapades. You were probably one of the friends he spoke about. There was another guy he mentioned a lot. What was his name?" JP rubbed his chin. "Marty, that's it. Did you know him?"

A waiter walked up with a tray of champagne glasses. "Would either of you care for more champagne?"

Huck set his empty glass on the tray and took another one. "Thanks," he said to the waiter and seemingly forgot the question JP had asked. "Have you been watching the news on Monroe's death?"

"Yes. It's a real shame."

"Did you see that crazy blonde in San Diego who's been stealing the limelight every time Monroe's death is on the news?"

"Yes, why?"

"I remember her." His eyes closed for a few seconds as if he were thinking back. "She was one gorgeous girl back then."

"Were they actually a couple, like she claims?"

"They dated for about six months, I think. I went out with them a few times, but I stopped because I didn't like the way he treated her."

191

"How was that?"

"He treated her like a kid. Well, hell, she was a kid, but that was no excuse. He shouldn't have been with someone that young. I told him she couldn't be more than sixteen, but he didn't care. That was the other thing I didn't like about Monroe—the way he mistreated women—but I guess I shouldn't be talking ill of the dead." He saw the senator moving in their direction. "Excuse me, I need to go say hello to Richard."

Chapter 36

Everyone was seated for dinner when Senator Richard Bullard was introduced and walked to the podium.

"Thank you all for coming here tonight to help raise money for this worthwhile cause. DREAM, as you all know, is a non-profit organization that has worked hard to provide services for children who are born with or have obtained deformities. I'm honored to do my small part to help them, and I thank each and every one of you for your generosity." JP wondered just how "generous" Pauline had been in obtaining the tickets. But knowing Pauline, he assumed they had been purchased by someone else.

The senator continued with his speech. After more syrupy words about DREAM, he switched gears. "I just want to take a few minutes to honor my brother who, as I'm sure you are all aware, passed away a few days ago. I know many of you here knew him and loved him just as I did. As you can imagine, our family is still in mourning, and we wouldn't have come here if it weren't for such a worthy cause. That said, I'm sure you will forgive us for leaving a little early. Please enjoy the evening."

One waiter for each table suddenly appeared with trays of salads and set them on the tables in front of the guests. Richard took his mother's arm, and they headed for the door.

"I think we should leave too," JP said softly. "I'm not sure how much longer I can handle this."

"You're not hungry?" Pauline asked.

"I'm good. I can get something at or near the hotel."

Pauline stood up. "Let's go."

They left the banquet room, and Pauline had an employee from the facility retrieve her coat. Near the front door, JP handed the valet his ticket for the rental car. The senator and his mother were just leaving the hotel through the lobby door. A minute or so later, JP and Pauline followed them out as a barrage of reporters greeted them. The cameras were all on Senator Bullard, and a news reporter stood right in front of him with a microphone in his hand.

"It was announced a little while ago that your brother was murdered. Do they have any suspects?"

"You probably know more than I do," Richard said. He took a few steps further, and another microphone was shoved in his face.

"What can you tell us about the woman who claims Monroe is the father of her child?"

"I've never met the woman. Now, please, my family and I would like to mourn my brother's death." Richard wrapped his arm around his mother and moved her through the crowd and into a car that had pulled up to pick them up.

Another driver brought JP's car up directly behind Bullard's. He exited the car, leaving the door open for JP, while another valet opened the door for Pauline. JP tipped the valets and drove off as soon as the senator's driver pulled away. He took a deep breath, glad to be finally getting away from the crowds and the media.

JP was anxious to get back to the hotel, have some quiet time to himself, and call Sabre. He had gained a lot of insight into the Bullard family, and he was certain the paternity test was not accurate, but he didn't have a way to prove it. Nevertheless, he wanted to hear her voice. He still felt guilty about not telling her that Pauline was with him, but he had decided to wait until he was home and tell her in person.

***

Sabre did some last-minute work on some cases for tomorrow's court hearings. She set the files aside on her coffee table and went into the kitchen to get a cup of hot lemon juice. She cut the lemon, squeezed the juice into her mug, and set it in the Keurig coffee maker to draw her hot water. Before the mug was full, her cell phone rang. She hurried into the living room to answer the call because it was the ringtone she had set for JP.

"Hi, kid," JP said.

"I was starting to wonder about you. Is everything okay?"

"It's been a busy day. I spoke with the lab technician who handled Monroe's paternity test, and he told me it wasn't Monroe's sample that was used."

"That's great," Sabre cut in.

"Not that great. He will not testify, sign an affidavit, or even tell that same story to anyone else. He made it very clear. I did, however, manage to get the first name of the man whose blood was used for the test. I'll keep following up on that, for what it's worth."

"Was it at least an unusual name? I'm hoping it wasn't Bill, Bob, or Jim."

"The name is Marty. I had a lead earlier, but it slipped away. Oh, and I met Senator Richard Bullard and his mother."

"Really? Where?"

"At a fundraiser." He paused for just a second. "Long story. I'll tell you all about it when I get home."

"When will that be?"

"Tomorrow, I hope. I don't think there is anything more I can do here now."

"Great. I miss you."

"It's been a long day. I'm going to bed. Can we get together tomorrow night?"

"I look forward to it."

Sabre picked up her hot drink, went into the living room, and sat down. She turned the television on to catch the news. Sabre watched the reports of a policeman who was shot in El Cajon, a burglary that went down in North Park, and two children who were found abandoned in a well in Lakeside. She'd had just about enough depressing news when she saw Monroe's picture flash on the screen. Some reporter was talking once again to Brandy McFerran.

"My son deserves to know who his father is," Brandy said in her acting tone, "but the court won't order another paternity test."

The reporter asked, "You said *another* test. Does that mean there has already been one?"

"Yes, right after my son was born, but the test was tampered with and so it came up negative."

"How do you know it was tampered with?"

"Because if he wasn't the father, it would have had to have been another case of the Immaculate Deception, or Perception, or whatever that is because I'd never slept with anyone else."

Before she could say anything else, the camera cut away to a scene in Nashville.

"Senator Richard Bullard and his mother were seen earlier this evening leaving a dinner where they were raising money for the nonprofit organization called DREAM. Senator Bullard has long been a supporter of this well-known organization that helps correct children's birth defects and other maladies."

The scene was that of the senator and his mother leaving a hotel and getting into their limo. Sabre caught sight of something else. She sat straight up and leaned forward, grabbing the remote and rewinding it. After freezing the frame right after the two came out of the hotel, she pushed "Forward" and then again when he put his arm around her and ushered her toward their car where valets waited with the doors open. Her stomach churned. She felt like her heart had dropped into her stomach.

"That's JP," she said aloud, "and that woman in the selfie."

All kinds of questions came to mind: *Why is she there? Why hadn't JP told her she was going to be there? What's going on?* She followed that with all the reasons she could think of as to why she needed to be there and how JP was just doing his job—a job she had hired him to do. She knew he didn't tell her about every contact he had, but somehow this one felt different.

Sabre slid her hand across her forehead, stopping to place it under her chin; her head suddenly felt too heavy to hold without help. She thought about calling JP and having him explain, but what was there for him to explain? He was working. She was a contact. She just happened to be a gorgeous, shapely contact. Sabre chastised herself for feeling jealous. It was an emotion she didn't like in others and refused to entertain herself.

The news continued to roll, but she didn't see any more of it. After about ten minutes of agonizing, she got up and went to bed. She expected it would be a long night.

Chapter 37

"You look horrible," Bob said, as Sabre walked into juvenile court. "Did you forget to sleep last night?"

"Lots of things on my mind," Sabre responded. "But I'm good now. I know what I need to do." As stressful as work was, there was nothing as bad as affairs of the heart to Sabre, except maybe health issues. She could deal with all the crazy things that came her way as an attorney as long as she put her own problems on the back burner. And that's exactly what she had decided to do. She would not say anything to JP about seeing him on national television with his arm around a beautiful woman. If he wanted to tell her, he would. In the meantime, she would just be careful not to fall too hard.

"That was cryptic. Care to explain?"

"Nope." Sabre picked up her files from the metal detector. "Are you ready to do the Gillespie case?"

"Let's go." They walked to Department Four while discussing the case at hand.

"I know what's wrong," Bob said. "You're missing JP, aren't you?"

Sabre smiled. "Yeah, that's it. He's coming home today, though." She immediately returned to the conversation about the Gillespie case.

They walked into the courtroom, greeted the clerk and the bailiff, and took a seat in the back. The judge wasn't on the bench yet.

"Did you see Brandy McFerran on the news last night?" Sabre asked.

"Ah, my 'movie star' client. She is about the worst actress I've ever seen."

Suddenly Sabre wished she hadn't asked because if he had seen Brandy, he had probably seen JP too. And she really didn't want to talk about that.

"Fortunately, I missed that one," Bob added. "Was she enlightening?"

"She did tell the world that there was already a test that excluded Monroe as the father, making her look like she's only interested in his inheritance."

He shook his head. "The woman does not know when to keep her mouth shut, that's for sure."

Sabre finished her morning calendar, had lunch with Bob, and returned to court for an afternoon trial. As usual, it was quieter in the afternoon. Instead of hundreds of people waiting for their hearings, there were probably less than fifty distributed throughout ten courtrooms. And since Bob wasn't there, it was even quieter.

Sabre sat on a bench in the corner near Department One waiting for her trial to commence. She felt the vibration of her phone ringing in her pocket. She pulled it out and looked at the face. It was JP. She took a deep breath and answered.

"Well, hello," she said with as much enthusiasm as she could muster.

"Hi, kid. I'm back in town and on my way home. Where are you?"

"I'm at court awaiting my afternoon trial."

"I need to go home, get some work done on another case, and type up your report. Can we get together for dinner?"

Sabre's first reaction was to say it wasn't a good night. It wasn't that she was angry with him; she was past that. Now she just wanted to protect her heart. But she couldn't resist the urge to spend time with him.

"Sure. Can you come by about seven?"

"That's good. Decide where you want to go."

"How about Filippi's in Little Italy?"

"That's good. I'll see you tonight."

"That's good. That's good," was all he seemed able to say. Sabre wondered what was wrong. She couldn't help but wonder if it had something to do with his "beautiful contact." Her thoughts were interrupted when the bailiff called her in to do her trial.

***

Conway McFerran jumped on his bike and started the three-mile trek from work to his foster home. It was a little later than usual and starting to get dark. He turned on his headlight that his foster father had given him and moved along the nearly abandoned street. The first part of the road home was used primarily by the people who lived in the scattering of homes that existed near there. Other than to go to the dairy, there was little reason to be on that road if you didn't live there.

Conway didn't mind the ride. In fact, he usually enjoyed it. This was his "alone" time. There were no kids around that he had to take care of and no adults he had to answer to. He was alone with his thoughts. Lately, those thoughts were about his father, Monroe Bullard. He had seen his mother on the news last night, and he heard her comment about a previous paternity test that proved Monroe wasn't his father. But Conway knew differently. He had heard that all his life, not directly from his mother, but while she was talking to others about her problems. He had come to believe it. He would never call his mother a liar, but he knew her to be very inventive with the world around her—like the "make-believe soldier" she had created as a father for him when he was younger. But this was different. She never let loose of the fact that Monroe was the only possible father. Perhaps he believed it because he didn't want to think of his mother having relations with a lot of men, but he was pretty certain there was more to it than that.

Conway turned west onto Willow Road, a two-lane road that led to the SR67, a state highway that started at I-8 in El Cajon and stretched to Ramona. Willow Road had the occasional car, but he knew the street would become busier the closer it neared the 67. As he biked further away from the dairy, Conway still only encountered two cars.

Glad that he had his headlight, even though it wasn't that bright, Conway picked up his pace in hopes he would be home before it got too dark. There were no lights along this road. In another half of a mile, he would pass a housing tract that would offer more lighting. He was pretty certain he would be in trouble from his foster father for not calling and getting a ride home. It was too late now for that; he had no phone, and he was halfway there.

Conway heard the engine of a pickup behind him. He glanced back and saw the headlights coming up Willow Road. He steered his bike off the road slightly to let the driver pass. The noise from the motor grew louder as the vehicle came closer. He looked back again to see how close it was. The pickup was almost upon him, and it seemed to be headed straight for his bike. He veered further off the road, but it wasn't far enough. Knocked from his bike, he felt himself fly through the air as he heard the sound of crunching metal. The air was knocked out of him as he hit the ground. Pain shot through his body and his head—and then nothing.

Chapter 38

JP arrived at Sabre's house at five minutes to seven. Late to JP meant not getting where he needed to be at least fifteen minutes early. She greeted him at the door with a kiss, but not with the same exuberance she normally would have shown after an absence. He wrote it off as just a bad day. Or maybe it was his own guilt that was eating at him. He had managed to avoid Pauline's advances, but he should have told Sabre that she had traveled with him. He knew he would not be happy if Sabre flew off in a private jet with a good-looking ex. Heck, it made his blood boil when another guy even looked at her wrong.

"How was your day?" JP asked.

"It was okay. Nothing earth-shattering." Sabre picked up her keys. "You still okay with Filippi's?"

"Sure."

When Sabre stepped toward JP, who was standing near the door, he took her hand and gently pulled her into his arms. She didn't resist. It's where she wanted to be. She didn't mean to appear distant. Her actions were not some sort of punishment. That's not the way she operated. Pulling back was just her way of protecting herself from heartbreak. Sabre knew she had serious trust issues when it came to men, and she was working hard to overcome them, but sometimes she kicked into automatic. And the worst part was that she had such a hard time talking through those feelings. It was so much easier just to shut down.

After a few moments of tenderness, JP said, "Ready?"

They talked about the McFerran case on the way to the restaurant. JP told her about Chad, the technician; about Monroe's friend, Huck Finn; and about meeting the senator and his mother.

"Was she as cold as everyone describes her?" Sabre asked.

"Colder than a mother-in-law's kiss."

Sabre snickered.

They were still talking about the event and the Bullards when they reached Filippi's. The restaurant was at the back of an old building that was once someone's home. They walked through the market to get to the café with the smell of cheese and Italian meats permeating Sabre's nostrils, making her hungrier. They passed the kitchen where cooks were tossing pizzas in the air and into the back room where red-checkered tablecloths covered the tables and Chianti bottles hung from nearly every inch of the ceiling.

Once seated, Sabre ordered a glass of wine. JP had a beer. They sat across from one another in the dimly lit room. JP reached out for her hands, which she gladly surrendered. It all seemed so romantic, until Sabre asked, "Did anything else of interest happen in Nashville?"

The moment she asked, she wished that she hadn't. This was not like her, and she felt like she was ruining the mood. She had decided that she didn't even want to know. That was his business. They had never talked about being exclusive. Maybe JP didn't want that.

"There is something you should know."

Sabre's phone vibrated on the table next to her. She glanced at the phone to see who the caller was. "I should take this. It's Conway's foster parents." She pulled her hand away and answered the phone.

"Hello," Sabre said. She listened for a few moments. "Thank you. I'll be right there."

"What is it?"

"Conway was hit on his bike coming home from work this evening. He's in the hospital."

JP stood up, reached in his wallet, pulled out a twenty-dollar bill, and tossed it on the table. "Let's go."

***

"What happened?" Sabre asked Mary Peabody, Conway's foster mother who was sitting in the waiting room at the hospital.

"Conway was hit by a vehicle on his way home from work. When he didn't come home, my husband, George, went to the dairy looking for him. Mr. De Jong told him that he had left on his bike just before dark. George drove slowly and methodically along Willow Road thinking maybe he'd had a flat or something. He spotted the bike first and then saw Conway lying in the dirt and weeds." She gulped, fighting back tears.

Rodger Peabody walked up carrying two cups of coffee. He handed one to his wife.

"You found Conway?" Sabre asked.

"Yes, he was unconscious. I called the paramedics right away, and they brought him here."

"Have you talked with the doctor yet?"

"No, we were told someone would be out shortly."

"Has his mother been notified?" Sabre asked.

"Yes, the social worker called her, and she and her boyfriend came right here."

Sabre looked around the room. "Where are they now?"

"I don't know. She made a phone call after we told her what happened, and then she got up and walked out."

"There she is," JP said, pointing to the television. He and Sabre walked closer to it so they could hear what she was saying.

"They tried to kill my boy," Brandy said in the most dramatic voice she had used yet. "Someone has to stop them."

"Who is them?" the news reporter asked.

"Why, Senator Bullard and his mother, of course. They want my son's inheritance."

Sabre's eyebrows lowered and pinched together. "She's in front of the hospital. June said she made a phone call and then left. Do you suppose that call was to the press?"

"Does a one-legged duck swim in a circle?" JP asked. "I'm wondering just how far that woman would go to get in front of a camera."

"You don't think she killed Monroe for the publicity, do you?"

"That, coupled with the inheritance, which I'm betting she knew about, might have been enough."

The outside door to the emergency room opened and a mustached man, who was about five feet ten and approximately forty-five or fifty years old, entered. He was wearing a light blue shirt and tie with a sports jacket.

"There's Greg," JP said. "I'll bet he's here about Conway."

Sabre and JP started to walk toward him. Detective Greg Nelson saw them and came in their direction.

"Is McFerran one of yours, Sabre?"

"Yes, he is."

"Do you know what happened?"

"Probably not any more than you know. We haven't been able to see him yet. All I know is that when he didn't come home from work, his foster father went looking for him and found him on the side of the road with a mangled bike."

"Why are you on this, Greg?" JP asked. "Does the department think this is more than a hit-and-run?"

"We got a call from the victim's mother saying that someone tried to kill her son. Actually, not just 'someone.' She accused a senator from Tennessee." Greg placed two fingers at the top of his tie and pulled it down as if to loosen it.

"Yeah, we saw her," JP said.

"Where did you see her?"

"She's right out in front of the hospital talking to a news reporter. We just saw her live on the news."

"We were also told that there's a possible murder of the senator's brother in Orange County that may be connected."

"Yes, Monroe Bullard is the alleged father of Conway McFerran."

"And I'm guessing you know a lot more about this than I do. Can you fill me in while we wait to see the victim?"

Sabre and JP sat down with the detective and reviewed everything they knew until they saw Conway's doctor approach the foster parents. They walked over to join them. The doctor had taken a seat across from the foster parents. JP, Sabre, and Greg stood near them.

"He has regained consciousness," the doctor said. "We didn't find any internal bleeding, but he does have a broken arm and a lot of bruising, so he's going to be sore for a while."

"Can he go home?" Mary Peabody asked.

"We'd like to keep him overnight for observation, but if all goes well, he can go home tomorrow. You can go in and see him now." The doctor stood to leave.

"Thank you, doctor," Sabre said. She introduced Detective Nelson to the foster parents. "I know you've been waiting a long time, but the detective needs to talk to Conway, and I would like to be in there with him. Do you mind waiting a few more minutes?"

"That's fine," George said. "We'll wait here."

***

After introducing Conway to the detective and asking some questions about how he was feeling, Sabre turned it over to Greg.

"Tell me exactly what you remember about the accident."

"I heard the engine, and I glanced back and saw the lights. I pulled off the road so it could pass. When the noise and the lights got closer, I looked back again, and it looked like it was heading right at me. The lights were up high like a truck or at least an SUV. I moved further onto the weeds, and that's when I felt it hit my bike and I went flying. It was actually kind of cool until I hit the ground."

"Did you see what kind of vehicle it was?"

"It was a pickup. I don't know what kind."

"Did you see what color it was?" Greg tugged at his tie.

"It was a light color, silver maybe. I didn't get a very good look at it. It all happened so fast."

"You said the pickup looked like it was coming straight at you. Was the road straight or was there a curve?"

"No, it was a straight shot, but it looked like he was coming off the road toward me. Maybe I just panicked. I'm not sure, but that's what it looked like to me. One thing for sure: he wasn't trying to avoid me. And I was well off the pavement when he hit me."

Chapter 39

Sabre had set a special hearing for Conway McFerran in front of Judge Hekman. In attendance were the social worker, Deputy County Counsel David Casey, Bob, and his client, Brandy.

"This hearing was set at your behest, Ms. Brown. What exactly are you requesting?"

"Your Honor, as you already know by the report the social worker provided the court, my client, Conway, was the victim of a hit-and-run accident. Fortunately, he survived with little more than a broken arm and numerous bruises. However, the police are investigating the circumstances of the accident. They have reason to believe someone did this intentionally, and it may be ruled as an attempted homicide."

Brandy could hardly contain herself. She sat there nodding her head in agreement. Several times Bob whispered in her ear to keep her from spouting off.

"But it has not yet been ruled as such. Is that correct, Ms. Brown?"

"Yes, that's correct, Your Honor."

"So what is it you want the court to do?"

"I'm concerned for my client's safety, and so is everyone else at this table. I believe, Your Honor, we are all in agreement with this request."

"Is that true?" the judge asked.

Both County Counsel and Bob said they were in agreement, and the social worker and Brandy were nodding their heads in the affirmative.

Sabre continued. "My investigation has turned up the technician who ran the paternity test on Conway and Monroe when Conway was an infant. He told my investigator that the test was not run on Monroe, but rather on another man, a friend of Monroe's."

"And you can produce the technician to testify to that?"

"No, Your Honor."

"Do you have his sworn testimony?"

"No, Your Honor. He refuses to come forward for fear of both the law and the Bullard family."

"Can you produce the man who donated his blood for Mr. Bullard? Or his sworn testimony?"

"No, Your Honor, but .... "

"Then why are we here? We just did this a few days ago, and I don't see any change of circumstances that would warrant a new order."

"The change of circumstances is the attempt on my client's life. Conway is in danger as long as Monroe is a possible father. If the court were to order a paternity test and it proves Monroe is not the father, there would be no reason for the Bullards or anyone connected to his estate to be concerned about my client's life."

"And if Monroe is the father, wouldn't that put him in more danger?"

"I don't think he could be in any more danger, but he could be in a lot less."

"Even if I were to make this order, we have no jurisdiction over this family, whom I'm quite certain are not willing to release his DNA."

"A request has already been made, Your Honor, and they've refused. But I've spoken to the detective in Orange County who is investigating Monroe's death, and he has DNA samples which he will only release with a court order."

"Not from this courtroom, Ms. Brown. As much as I would like to make that order, I can't circumvent the law to make that work. You bring me some real evidence to show that the first paternity test was a fraud, and I will gladly make that order." She looked at the other attorneys to see if they had any comments. No one spoke. "Request denied without prejudice."

***

Back in her office, Sabre had made several piles on her desk with the information on the McFerran case. The files with the social worker's and JP's reports were in one stack. Another held the trust and paternity test results that she had obtained from JP. To the right were the photos of Monroe and Brandy from years ago. On her computer screen, she had the photos taken from each geocache in the order they were obtained.

Ron, who had stopped by to see Sabre, was in the other room getting a soda from the refrigerator. He popped the tab as he walked back in.

Sabre swooped her hand from the computer screen and across her desk. "Somewhere in all this are the answers I need."

"What are the questions?" Ron asked.

"How to get that paternity test done and keep my client from getting killed."

"That's a pretty tall order," JP said, as he walked in the door.

"Hi, JP," Ron said.

"Hi, Ron."

Sabre gave him a half smile as JP handed her a file. "Here are the reports from the last couple of days." He reached in his pocket and took out a flash drive. "There are pictures on here of the box sitting on Monroe's coffee table and its contents. Brad believes it may or may not be the cache, and there's someone in his office trying to figure it out. The problem is they don't have a lot of time to put into it, and they're not convinced it's of any consequence anyway. When I volunteered your time, Ron, he was thrilled to hand it over."

"Thanks, I'll get right on it." Ron sat his laptop on the corner of Sabre's desk, opened it up, and plugged the flash drive into it.

"By the way," JP said, "Brandy's fingerprints were on the outside of the box, as well as on some of the contents."

"So she was inside Monroe's house after all."

"Or at least she had seen the box before. It's possible she handled the box elsewhere."

"But we already know that she was at the house the day Shafer, the construction guy, saw her, and he also saw her car there the morning Monroe was killed."

"Yes, but we don't know who was in the car that day."

Sabre continued to shuffle through the papers on her desk. JP kept glancing at her but avoiding eye contact.

"Okay, what's wrong with you two?" Ron asked. "Are you having a spat?"

"What are you talking about?" Sabre asked.

"The way you two are acting toward one another is colder than a gravedigger's shovel, or however you would say it," Ron said.

JP and Sabre both laughed.

"I think it's a well digger, not a gravedigger," JP said. "And the way I heard it, it wasn't his shovel but rather some part of his anatomy that gets pretty cold down in that hole, but your way will work too." JP looked at Sabre. "We're good, right?"

"Right," Sabre said. "Just all wrapped up in this case. I'm worried about Conway."

"After talking with Brad this afternoon, I think things are going to get a whole lot worse for them."

"Why?" Sabre's cell phone rang. "It's Bob." She put

211

him on speaker. "Hi, Bob. I'm here with JP and Ron. What's up?"

"Turn on the news," Bob said. "Channel 10. Brandy's on again."

"She's old news. We've seen it all before."

Ron pulled up the local news on his computer.

"Not this one. She was just arrested for the murder of Monroe Bullard."

Chapter 40

JP, Sabre, and Ron assembled around Ron's laptop computer, watching as Brandy McFerran was taken into police custody.

"Did you know they were going to arrest her?" Sabre asked JP with a slight edge in her voice.

"I had a hunch after my conversation with Brad this afternoon."

"And you didn't think to tell me? What else are you not telling me?"

"I was about to tell you when Bob called and told you to watch the news. Besides, I had no idea they were about to make an arrest, not this soon."

"But you did know they were going to charge her with Monroe's murder."

"No, Counselor," JP said, not raising his voice but with obvious indignation. "I knew she was a suspect. You knew that much too. I figured when her fingerprints were on the box that she had risen on the list."

Sabre picked up her cell phone and started walking toward the reception area.

"Where are you going?"

"I'm making some phone calls. Those kids are going to be devastated; I need to do some damage control."

"What the heck did you do?" Ron asked JP after Sabre left the room.

"I don't know."

"Did you cheat on her?" Ron asked. "You better not have cheated on her."

"Of course I didn't cheat on her. Besides, do you think she'd even be talking to me if I did that?"

"You have a point there."

"I think it's the way I've been acting toward her because I feel guilty about not telling her something that I should have. Or maybe she's just on edge over this case. I don't know what else it could be." JP shook his head. "Women."

Sabre came back into the room. "The foster parents are going to tell the children before they hear it from somewhere else." She slid her hand along JP's backside as she walked by. "Sorry, I know you wouldn't intentionally keep anything from me that made a difference on a case. I'm just so frustrated that I can't do more for these kids."

Ron rolled his eyes at JP, who scowled back at him.

"So come on guys, help me figure out a way to get that paternity test."

"I could have gotten you some of the senator's DNA the other night, but I'm guessing you want it obtained legally."

"Yes, something we can use in court would be nice."

"You're going to have to figure that out on your own. I have a geocache to find," Ron said, as he opened the flash drive and brought up each photo onto his screen.

JP stood at the corner of the desk so he could see both Sabre's and Ron's computers. Ron's screen had the blinged-out box that was on Monroe's coffee table. "Dang, that box is uglier than the south end of a northbound cow. And it sure was out of place in Monroe's house. Everything else in there looked like it was right out of a decorator's magazine."

"Here's another angle of it," Ron said. "The bottom of the box is marked, 'Made in Taiwan' and it has a Big Lots! sticker on it. This lovely box cost $4.99. What a bargain."

"It obviously doesn't fit in the room," JP said.

"But it could have been a keepsake," Sabre added. "The man was from Nashville and it has a jeweled cowboy on the box. Maybe someone he cared about gave it to him."

"That's it," Ron exclaimed. "It's not a jeweled cowboy. It's a rhinestone cowboy."

Sabre stood up and came around behind her brother. "Just like he or she did with the picture of George Clooney."

Ron added, "Only now the geocacher took it a step further. GC as in Glen Campbell, the Rhinestone Cowboy."

"All the geocache codes start with GC. I think you have something there, brother. What else do you have?"

"A photoshopped picture of Tennessee Ernie Ford and some other cowboy in a suit," Ron said. "Do you know who that is?"

"Beats me," Sabre said.

JP glanced at the picture. "It looks like Merle Travis to me."

"Who's Merle Travis?" Sabre asked.

"He's an old, country-western, singer-songwriter who died around the time you were born," JP said. "He wrote a lot of songs about coal miners."

"I've heard of him," Ron added. "I just didn't know what he looked like." He brought up another image. "Here's a photo of what looks like a tramp and a young girl. And the last one is a picture of Dolly Parton at a desk with a phone to her ear."

"Save those pics to your computer and let me take that flash drive home with me," Sabre said. "If I have time later, I'll play with them too."

Ron made a few clicks on the keyboard, ejected the flash drive, and gave it to Sabre. Then he closed up his laptop. "I'm hungry."

"We all have to eat. Do you want to join us for dinner?" Sabre asked.

Ron looked at Sabre and then at JP. "I think you two need some alone time. Besides, I told Mom I'd be home for dinner." Ron kissed Sabre on the cheek and left.

"We are going to eat, aren't we?" Sabre asked JP.

"You bet. Want to go to Filippi's and see if we can finish that date we started last night?"

"Sure, it's early. There won't be a line yet. Let me finish reading this report you wrote on your trip to Nashville, and then we'll go."

JP went to use the restroom, and when he returned, Sabre said, "The guy who gave blood for Monroe's paternity test was named Marty, right?"

"Right."

"And you couldn't get a last name?"

"No, I tried to get one from his friend, Huck Finn ... now there's a name for you. By the way, I checked it out. I thought he might be pulling my leg, but that's actually his name. Anyway, just as I was asking him about Marty, Huck spotted the senator and excused himself to go talk to him."

"Do you think it was a way to avoid answering your question?"

"Possibly, but I don't think so."

"What if Marty is not his first name?"

"Then I guess we have nothing," JP said.

"I dated a guy named Marty once. He was Italian."

"Your point?" JP asked before she could finish.

"His last name was Marticello. His first name was Augustine, but no one ever called him anything except Marty."

"The doctor," JP snapped. "Show me the photo of the death certificate."

Sabre brought it up on her screen. "There it is, Dr. Perry Lane Martin. Do you think he might be Marty?"

"I think it's worth checking out."

Chapter 41

After extensive research on Perry Lane Martin, aka Marty Martin, JP discovered several interesting facts. Perry was given the nickname, Marty, sometime before he started school, probably at birth. The son of Dr. Walter Martin, a surgeon, and his wife Georgianne, Marty was born in Kentucky but moved to Nashville when he was five years old. He attended the same grade school, middle school, and high school as Monroe Bullard. They both went to Princeton and then they seemed to have parted ways, at least geographically, when Marty went to UCLA Medical School.

After med school, Marty continued to reside in southern California, first in Glendale and then in the Orange County area. The last known address was in Laguna Beach, only a few miles from Monroe. His DMV records listed him as the owner of two cars, a Mercedes convertible that was less than two years old and a 1956 Porsche 356A.

Marty had both Twitter and Facebook pages. Most of his "friends" were women. No one was listed as family. There were photos from several trips, but nothing recently from Australia. JP downloaded and printed several pictures of him, studying them carefully in case he needed to pick him out of a crowd. He looked to be about five-foot-eight and had light brown hair with a receding hairline. In most of his photos, he wore a baseball cap.

The doctor maintained an office in Laguna Beach with several other plastic surgeons. JP called the office number listed online for Dr. Martin. The call went to his answering service, and JP was told the doctor was still in Australia and they didn't know when he would return. JP decided to visit the doctor's office in hopes he could gain a little more information.

***

The third floor of the building was used by a clinic with three plastic surgeons, all of whom appeared to specialize in breast augmentation. The lobby area of the doctor's office was decorated in expensive modern art on pastel walls. White, cushy leather chairs lined the walls. Atop the customized cabinet in the corner were a silver Starbucks Verismo 580 single-cup coffee and espresso maker with glass mugs and individual servings of Starbucks coffee. There was also a basket with hot chocolate and several baskets of pastries, chips, and energy bars. A small refrigerator with a clear glass door was also available for the patients. Inside, JP could see an assortment of sodas, juices, and bottled water.

The receptionist, an attractive, young, blonde woman, greeted JP. She appeared to have taken advantage of the doctor's specialty. Two very stylish women sat at opposite sides of the lobby walls. Neither of them was particularly attractive, but they both had an air of superiority about them. Perhaps it was the way they dressed or held themselves, or maybe it was the makeup they wore. Whatever it was, JP did not find them inviting or sexy. He much preferred a more natural woman. He tipped his cowboy hat and glanced at each one. One smiled. One snarled.

JP saw the receptionist smirk, and he winked at her. "Howdy, ma'am."

"Hello," she said, still smirking.

"My name is JP. I'm visiting here from Texas, and I'll only be in town a short while. I'm an old friend of

Marty's, excuse me, Dr. Martin. We went to high school together in Nashville. Is he in, by any chance?"

"No, I'm afraid he's out of the country."

"Let me guess … Australia."

"Yes. How did you know?"

"Because that's where he always says he's going. Has he ever brought you a boomerang or a didgeridoo from the outback? Or have you ever seen him with an Australian T-shirt?"

The receptionist tilted her head to one side and pursed her lips. "A didgeri-what?"

"It's a musical instrument that the Australian Aborigines make out of a long, wooden tube." JP raised his hands like he was playing the instrument. "You haven't, have you? Of course not, because he doesn't really go to Australia. He just plays hooky." JP lowered his voice to a whisper. "Do you know where he really is?"

The receptionist lowered her voice as well. "I heard he was in rehab."

"Again?" JP said. "Then I really need to see him. We have a mutual friend who died last weekend. We were all very close. I'm sure Marty is suffering. Is that when he went into rehab?"

"No, he's been gone for three or four weeks." She sighed. "Are you talking about Monroe Bullard?"

"Yes, did you know him?"

"I didn't really know him, but he would come in here to see Dr. Martin all the time. Or rather, he came in for about a month before Dr. Martin took leave. He was always flirting with me. He was a very nice-looking man, but way too old for me. I felt bad when I saw him on the news."

"Do you know what rehab facility Marty is in? I'm sure he could use some company about now."

The receptionist took a small piece of notepaper

from a fancy silver square that sat on her desk. She wrote down the name of the facility and the address and slipped it to JP.

"Good luck. Sorry about your friend."

"Me too," JP said. He tipped his hat at the woman who had scowled earlier, and walked out.

JP drove to the address on the paper, not knowing if he could even get in or obtain any information. He was shocked when he saw the facility. It looked more like a country club than a rehab center. Most rehab centers were in older buildings in cramped quarters with few amenities. This one had a tennis court, a golf course, an Olympic-sized pool, and lots of green grass and blooming plants.

I guess this is where people go who can actually afford the drugs they're using, JP thought. *More power to them. At least they're trying to get well.*

He opened the beautifully carved, cherrywood door and entered a lobby that would make the designers of the Wynn in Las Vegas envious. Even the front desk looked more like one in a hotel than a rehab center. The place even came with a concierge and valet parking.

JP made his way to the desk and asked for Dr. Perry Martin.

"What room?" the clerk asked.

"I don't know. I'm here from Nashville, and I haven't seen my friend in a really long time. His office sent me here."

"I can't give you his room number, sir. If you have the room number, I can ring his room."

"I'm sorry, I didn't get the room number, but if you look up his name and give him mine, I'm sure he will see me. My name is Huck Finn." The woman gave him a quizzical look. "I know it sounds made up, but it's not. That's my name. He'll know me."

"That's not the way we work here," she said.

"Look, we just had a mutual friend die, and I know Marty needs the company right now."

The woman typed something into the computer and without looking up said, "Sorry, he's not here."

"He's not staying here, or he has stepped out?"

"He's not a guest at this facility." Now she was looking at JP.

"Since when?"

"I don't know, sir. And I couldn't tell you if I did. All I know is that he is not a guest at this time at this facility."

"Thank you," JP walked back to his car and drove to the last known address for Dr. Perry Lane Martin in Laguna Beach.

It wasn't a huge house, but the location was flawless. It sat up just high enough to have a perfect view of the Pacific Ocean, which would explain the reason why windows surrounded three-quarters of the house. Someone had spent a great deal of time gardening, as every plant and bush was perfectly manicured. A flower garden bloomed from the steps of the front door all the way down the slight grade to the walkway. The backyard was fenced, so without snooping around, JP couldn't tell what was back there.

He rang the doorbell. No one answered it. He waited a minute and tried again. Still nothing. The curtains were open, and JP could see the front living area; there was no sign of life inside. He tried one more time before he walked back to his car.

JP was surprised he hadn't noticed it when he had parked because looming in the corner of the flower garden in the front yard was a FOR SALE sign. He jotted down the name and number of the realtor, placed a call to her, and drove away.

Chapter 42

Ron and Sabre sat in Sabre's living room, each with their laptop open and their eyes fixed on the photos from the Rhinestone Cowboy box. Brad had numbered the order in which they had been found in the box. They only hoped that was the order in which they were intended because, as it was, this appeared to be a daunting task.

They both pulled up the first picture, which was of Tennessee Ernie Ford and Merle Travis. It was obviously photoshopped.

"What do you think of when you hear the name Tennessee Ernie Ford?" Sabre asked.

"*I Love Lucy*," Ron said.

"What?"

"Remember how Mom used to watch the *I Love Lucy* reruns on TV? Tennessee Ernie Ford played Cousin Ernie. Other than that, I don't really know much more than his name and I recognize his photo. I guess the real question is: what do these two guys have to do with one another? They were put together on one photo for a reason."

Sabre Googled "What do Tennessee Ernie Ford and Merle Travis have in common?" She read what came up on her screen and then said, "Sixteen Tons."

"Sixteen tons of what?"

"They both sang the song, 'Sixteen Tons.' Merle Travis wrote and sang it, and then Tennessee Ernie Ford made it a big hit in the mid-fifties."

"Okay, let's try that." Ron opened up his account on www.geocaching.com, and in the search window he entered GC16. A geocache popped up in Oregon. "That's not it."

"Try GC16tons."

Ron tried it but found no file. They both continued to try several combinations with Ford's and Travis' initials but with no results. Each combination was added to an Excel sheet that Ron had created the last time he was trying to figure out the puzzles. "This way I can keep track of what we've tried because after a while we'll be going crazy wondering if we tried this or that."

"Good thinking, Bro," Sabre said. "The other photos must mean something too. Let's go with 16 and see what else we come up with."

"The next photo is a tramp and a young girl," Ron said. "What does that bring to mind?"

"Disney. You know, *Lady and the Tramp*."

"I don't even know what to do with that. Try the initials, maybe?" Ron tried them but came up empty. "Let's assume for a moment that Brandy is the killer. What do we know about her?"

"She's really into music and acting."

"So how about 'The Lady is a Tramp' by Frank Sinatra?"

Sabre tried the first letter of each word of the song title added onto GC16, but it didn't work. Then she tried GC16FS, Frank's initials, but that struck out as well.

"How about GC16OBE?"

"Why?"

"Ol' Blue Eyes."

"Of course, but it doesn't work either."

Ron then tried GC16BE, without the "ol." "I got a hit," he said. "But it's in British Columbia, Canada." He looked at the photo again. "Besides, that child is not a lady. It's a kid, and she looks as trampy as the man."

"Wait," Sabre said. "This isn't a tramp. Look at what's in his hand. It looks like a hard hat with a light on it."

"It's a coal miner with a little girl," Ron interjected. "'A Coal Miner's Daughter.'"

"Loretta Lynn. I think we may be onto something."

"Of course," Ron said, "it had to be a country singer."

"What's next?"

"Dolly Parton in an orange sweater and a telephone up to her ear."

They tried several codes with the letters and numbers they already had and Dolly's initials with and without her middle name, but none worked. They spent the next hour Googling Dolly Parton for her nickname, her birthdate, or anything that might work in the code.

Finally, Sabre said, "I'm done for now. I still have work to do, and I'm burned out on this."

Ron jotted down a code he'd been working on. "I'm going to list every possible combination I can come up with for each photo and then start plugging in the different codes and see if anything hits. It's going to take some time, though." He closed up his computer and stood up. "I'm out of here. I can do the rest from home."

He pecked Sabre on the cheek. "Bye, Sis."

***

JP drove to In-N-Out and ate a hamburger and fries while he waited for the realtor to arrive at Dr. Martin's house. He had nearly an hour before she would be there. After his lunch, he checked his emails on his phone. He wished he were more tech savvy so he could go on the Internet and get a little more information on the doctor's house. It could only help him to be more prepared, but he just recently learned how to check his emails, and that was a major task. *Sabre was very patiently trying to show this old dog new tricks*, he thought. He checked the time and drove back to the house. He only had to wait about five minutes before the realtor showed up.

"Mr. Nelson?" she said, when she exited her car.

"Yes, but please call me John." John Nelson was a name he often used when he didn't want to give his own. He had even made up some business cards with that name in case he needed them.

"John, I'm Yolanda Ulloa. Nice to meet you. As she led the way to the front door, she asked, "When are you looking to move?"

"As soon as I can. I have a home in Texas, but my business has brought me here to Orange County."

"And what business is that?"

"I've mostly been in oil and cattle ranching, but I'm also a venture capitalist."

Yolanda unlocked the lock box at the front door and removed the key. "Are you looking for something with a view?"

"Yes, ma'am. It would be nice to see the ocean. We don't get that in Texas, except way down south, but I'm closer to Dallas." JP waited for her to go inside first, and he followed. There were furnishings in the living room, but not a lot of personal items around. "Is the house vacant?"

"No, the owner is still living here. He just listed this a few days ago. The way it's priced, it won't stay on the market long."

"But he's not home right now?"

"No," she said, and then started in on her description of the house and all that it had to offer.

JP walked slowly through each room looking for any clue that might tell him something more about the good, or not-so-good, doctor. He would have liked to open drawers and look inside of them, but Yolanda was very close behind him. He had no clue what he was looking for; he just hoped he'd recognize it when he saw it.

When they reached the master bedroom, Yolanda opened the door to the closet to show him just how big it was.

"Whoa, ma'am. You're right. That closet is bigger'n a few apartments I inhabited back in the day." He walked inside the ten-by-twelve foot room with all its partitions, drawers, and shelves. There was a row of suits and another row of dress shirts. On the other side were the sportier clothes—collared shirts, T-shirts, and pants. There was a shoe rack in between that held about six pairs of dress shoes, five pairs of sneakers, some hiking boots, and some loafers and sandals. A suitcase and another small travel bag sat on the floor as if they were ready to be put away. JP picked them up and moved them slightly to the left.

"Just seeing what's behind there. You can never have too many shelves in a closet." The suitcase was light. JP guessed that Marty had been home long enough to put things away if that was the suitcase he took to the rehab center. When he moved the bag, he noticed each one had an identical luggage tag on it. It was a flat, round tag with a yin-yang shape on it. The left side was blue and resembled an ocean with trash in it. The right side was all green and had a park with trees, a bench, and trash. He had seen the logo somewhere recently, but he couldn't remember where. When Yolanda stepped out of the closet, JP took a quick snapshot with his phone's camera—another thing he was glad Sabre had taught him how to use.

They finished the tour of the house, and JP started for home. He was nearly to Oceanside when he remembered where he had seen that logo. Ron had one on the T-shirt he was wearing yesterday. He tried calling Ron but didn't get an answer, so he called

Sabre.

He told her about his visit to the rehab center and the doctor's house. "I saw a logo on his luggage that had a yin-yang type logo on it just like the one on the T-shirt Ron was wearing yesterday. Do you remember?"

"Yes, it's the CITO logo."

"What's CITO?"

"Cache In Trash Out. Marty is a geocacher."

Chapter 43

"I need to talk to Senator Bullard. Can your friend Pauline what's-her-name set that up for me?" Sabre said to JP on her cell phone.

JP hesitated for a moment.

"JP, are you there?"

"Yes, I'm here. Why do you want to see the senator?"

"I need to get through to him, to convince him to do the paternity test."

"Do you really think you can do that?"

"Only if I can see him without his mother. Everything I've read about him says he is a decent man. That he is caring, thoughtful, and truly wants to help people."

"That doesn't sound like a politician to me."

"His mother seems to be the politician. She's also the one controlling this paternity issue. According to Brandy, it was more about what Monroe's mother wanted than what he wanted. She was the one who paid off Brandy. Of course, back then, Brandy didn't know anything about the inheritance. She thought her motive was to avoid a scandal that would ruin his political career, but maybe that wasn't the only incentive."

"So how is that different now?"

"It's not, but it's not her I want to get through to; it's the senator. I'm hoping I can convince him to do the right thing."

JP hesitated again.

"Do you think your friend can get me an audience with the senator?"

"I don't know, but I'll see what I can do. I'll call you back."

JP didn't relish calling Pauline again. It was different when they were "friends with benefits," but now he had nothing to give in return. It's not like he paid her with his services, but he was usually available when she just wanted to let loose. Sometimes they would go for walks on the beach, have dinner, or just meet for drinks. Then he wouldn't see her again for months. He knew she wasn't in love with him or anything like that, but rejection on any level was hard to take. Nevertheless, he had to do this for Sabre.

"Hello, darling," Pauline said when she answered her phone. "This is a nice surprise."

"Hi, Pauline. I wanted to thank you for the trip to Nashville. It was time well spent."

"You already thanked me several times. What is it you really called for?"

"I need another favor," he said hesitantly.

"Name it."

"The attorney I work for, Sabre Brown—"

"The attorney you work for? You mean your girlfriend?"

Pauline was nothing if she wasn't blunt.

JP exhaled, "You know about her?"

"Of course I know, darling. It's my job to know these things. Look, we're good. I have no claims on you. That doesn't mean I don't miss what we had."

JP didn't respond. He wasn't sure what to say.

"What is it she needs?"

"She needs to speak with Senator Bullard alone. Can you make that happen?"

"That's a pretty tall order. Will it make your life easier?"

"It would, and it may go a long way toward helping Conway, who may have a target on his back." JP proceeded to tell her about Conway's hit-and-run. When she didn't respond, he guessed she probably knew about that too.

"Let me see what I can do," she said and hung up.

***

Approximately thirty minutes later, Pauline called back. "Every Sunday morning, if he's in Nashville, the senator goes for a long run in a park near his house. He's home this weekend, so Sabre could meet up with him in the park."

"That's tomorrow."

"Yes, next weekend he'll be in Washington D.C. so it has to be tomorrow, but before you panic, I've made arrangements."

"Of course you did. You're an angel."

"The plane is leaving in two hours, so Sabre can be in Nashville tonight. It's the same plane we took."

"I don't know how to thank you, Pauline."

"Of course you do." She paused. "I'm just kidding. I get it. There is one problem, though: She'll have to fly commercial coming home. The plane is going on to Florida tomorrow."

"We'll figure that out."

Pauline gave JP the name of the park and the route he would take. "It's always the same, and he always starts at six sharp, so I hope she's an early bird. Are you going with her?"

"I'm not sure yet."

"Just let me know so I can tell Evan how many passengers he'll have. Ta-ta."

JP called Sabre and told her what had just been arranged. "Do you want to go?"

"Absolutely. Let me see if I can get a return flight." Sabre was already in front of her computer. She

Googled flights from Nashville to San Diego.

"Can you get one for me too?" JP said. "I'd feel better if I went along."

"I'd like that, but it's not as if this is risky. I'm not going to see his mother, just the senator. And I thought you were on a stakeout at Marty's house. I'd feel better if you talked to him before he disappears again. He may be our only chance."

"That's where I am as we speak. With the traffic, I'm not even sure I could get back to San Diego in time to catch the flight."

"I got one," Sabre said, typing on her laptop. "There's a Delta flight tomorrow afternoon." *Click. Click.* "There, I'm on it. Now I need a hotel room and a car. Look, I'd better go. I need to line this up, throw a few things in a bag, and get to the airport."

"Sabre, are you okay?"

"I'm fine. And thank you for doing this. I could just kiss you."

"I wish you could."

"I'd better go. I'll see you tomorrow."

***

Sabre found her way to Landmark Aviation, a fixed-base operator, near the southeast end of the runway at Lindbergh Field where she had been instructed to go. She parked her car and walked into the building. A beautiful, dark-haired woman who Sabre recognized from the photo on JP's phone, approached her.

"You must be Sabre," she said in a welcoming voice.

"Yes, and you are Pauline?"

"I am, but I didn't mention to JP that I'm going. How did you know it was me?"

Sabre smiled. "I've seen your picture on JP's

phone."

Pauline skewed her lips to one side and then back again. "Sorry about that. It was not one of my finer moments." Pauline removed her ID from her bag and Sabre followed suit. They showed the woman at the desk their IDs, and a gentleman escorted them to the door and buzzed them out.

When they boarded the plane, a man dressed like a waiter in a fine restaurant greeted them at the door. Pauline said hello to him and then said, "Please be a dear and make me one of your special mojitos."

Sabre was in awe at the luxury. She had never seen anything quite like it, except on television. Pauline directed her to a seat and then sat down across from her. Everything was so plush, and the seats were so comfortable, quite unlike a commercial flight. She felt like a princess.

"I really appreciate your doing this for me."

"The truth is, Evan and I were going to Florida anyway. I just convinced him to make a stop in Nashville. He has a daughter who lives there, so it didn't take much convincing. And I was curious about you."

"About me?"

"Yes, it's a pleasure to meet the woman who could break that bronc."

It took Sabre a second to figure out just what Pauline was talking about.

"You mean JP." Sabre smiled. "I don't want to break him, just ride the range with him."

"Of course you don't, but you have tamed him, you know. He's sworn off the rest of the fillies in the stable."

Sabre wondered how long they were going to keep up this "barnyard" metaphor. "That's good to know."

The steward came by and brought Pauline her mojito. "What can I get for you, ma'am?"

"Just some water for now, thank you." When he left, Sabre said, "You seem to lead a very interesting life."

"I do," she said, pausing as if she were reflecting on it. "I travel a lot, hobnob with lots of famous people, and have one adventure after another, but I also work for and with a lot of people I don't much care for. You, on the other hand, get to save children every day."

"I try, but I don't always get to save them. More often than not, no one ends up happy on my cases. I may keep children from being abused, but I'm also taking them away from the only people they know as family—people they happen to love in spite of the pain they bring them."

"I guess there is no job that is perfect, and I have to admit that I really do enjoy mine most of the time."

They continued to discuss their respective professions until Pauline stood up and mingled with Evan and chatted with the steward. When she returned, she briefed Sabre on Senator Bullard's running habits. The topic of the conversation never returned to JP.

Chapter 44

JP took a nap for a couple of hours, got up and showered, made himself a couple of roast beef sandwiches and a thermos of coffee, and drove back to Marty's house to try and catch him as he came home. It was just getting dark, and no lights were on in the house. He took out the iPod Sabre had set up for him with all his favorite country songs and settled back for a long evening.

JP's car was parked on the same side of the street as the house. Two other cars were parked not far from his. Several other homes were located along the road, none of which were as close together as what he was used to in San Diego. They were older homes, but according to the realtor he had spoken with earlier, most had been remodeled. Across the street was an embankment about four feet high that dropped into the sand. The tide was high, so the waves from the ocean were slapping against it. The sound was relaxing. JP did all he could to keep from falling asleep, more from boredom than fatigue.

About four hours passed without any movement in or around the house. JP stepped out to stretch a little and walked to some bushes across the street and took a whiz. There were no lights on that side of the road, and the ocean looked black except for the moonlight shining on the whitecaps. He decided to go easier on the coffee, or he would be out of the car half the night. Just as he was going back to his car, his phone vibrated with an incoming call.

"I just wanted to let you know that I've settled into my hotel room for the night," Sabre said.

"Everything going okay?" JP asked.

"Yes, the flight was interesting. That's really some plane, but of course you've seen it. I'll tell you all about my flight tomorrow. I'm beat, and I have an early date tomorrow."

JP would have loved to stay on the phone and visit with her. He missed her and he was bored, but he knew she only had a few hours to sleep, so he said goodnight and went back to his watch.

A few more hours passed without any activity. JP was going stir crazy. He hated stakeouts. He ate half of his roast beef sandwich and drank some coffee. A few hours later he was about to give up. He had heard every song on his iPod at least three times. *I really need to have Sabre add more music. Or maybe I need to learn how to do it myself.*

Headlights appeared ahead. It was not a busy street, and the later it got the less activity he saw. At two o'clock in the morning, cars were averaging more than thirty minutes apart. JP sat up and readied his long-zoom camera, as he did with every other car that slowed down. The Mercedes convertible approached with its top down, in spite of the chilly fifty-degree temperature. JP set the camera to video mode.

Two people were in the car, the male driver and a female passenger. The couple was laughing, and the woman was making "whooping" sounds all the way down the street. JP continued filming as they turned into the driveway, barely missing the rock wall, and stopped just short of the detached garage. When the garage door wasn't open, JP wondered if it harbored the 1956 Porsche. He would love to see it.

The woman jumped out, threw her hands in the air, and swung around with her red hair circling her head, which made it difficult to take a good photo of her face. From what JP could see, she looked young, not jailbait young, but he would guess she was in her early twenties.

The driver, who was wearing a baseball cap, exited the car and staggered around to the woman. He appeared to be a few inches shorter than the redhead, although she was wearing some pretty high heels. She swung around again and knocked his hat off, revealing the man's head of light brown hair with a receding hairline. JP was certain it was Marty.

JP had planned to confront Marty when he came home, but the girl, and what appeared to be his intoxicated state, changed things. He didn't want to spook him and have him take off.

The couple reeled their way to the front door and went inside. JP could still hear the occasional "whoop" from the girl. JP waited until the noise subsided from inside and most of the lights were turned back off. Then he started up his car and drove away, frustrated with his lack of progress on the case, but thankful that there was one less drunk on the streets.

***

Five o'clock came very early for Sabre. That meant it was three o'clock at home. It was well after midnight when she finally fell asleep, and even though her alarm was set, she kept waking up and checking the time. She only had one chance to talk with the senator, and she feared oversleeping.

When the alarm went off, she hopped out of bed, brushed her teeth, brushed and braided her hair, and dressed, layering her clothes to try to keep warm. Then she drove to the park.

She arrived at 5:47, parked the car, and walked to the fountain where Pauline said the senator starts his run. "It is always the same route," she had said. "He always walks to the fountain, stretches his legs, and warms up his muscles a bit before he runs west around the small lake, past the baseball diamonds and the small train crossing, and back to the fountain." Sabre hoped today wasn't the day he changed his routine.

The outside temperature gauge in her car read forty-two degrees. Sabre pulled her skullcap down over her ears, donned her gloves, and stepped out of the car. The cold air hitting her face was both invigorating and intimidating. She wondered how far she would be able to run in this weather. At least it wasn't raining or snowing. She walked to a bench and commenced her stretching. Within a minute, Senator Bullard arrived and started his stretching, just as Pauline said he would. When the senator appeared to be finished, Sabre started her run west toward the lake. A few steps into it, she heard his footsteps close behind her. She let him catch up.

"Good morning, Senator," Sabre said.

"Good morning," he responded.

"Is it always this cold here?"

"Only for a few months. You're not from here?"

"No, just visiting."

"Yet you know who I am."

"Yes, you're the reason I'm here," Sabre said.

"That's nice. Have a good day." He picked up his pace, probably thinking she was some kind of crackpot. Sabre kept up. He was a good runner with long legs that gave him a good stride. Sabre had to work to keep up with him, but she pushed hard.

"I'm not some kind of nut. I needed to talk to you, and this is the only way I could reach you. I've tried several times to contact you by phone, but I always get directed to your legal department."

He slowed down. "Who are you?"

"My name is Attorney Sabre Brown. I represent Conway McFerran in a dependency case in San

238

Diego."

"The son of the crazy woman who killed my brother."

"First of all, she's not crazy, and second, I'm not so sure she killed your brother, but that's for the courts to decide. I represent her children, and all I want is what's best for them."

"What does that have to do with me?"

"Look, Senator, everything I've read about you paints you as a good, decent man. Either you have a great public relations manager who just makes you look good or you are, in fact, of sound, moral character. I'm thinking the latter." Sabre shivered. Her teeth were chattering, but she was on a roll and she didn't want to stop. "All I'm asking is that you do the right thing by this child—this young man, who could very likely be your nephew."

"There was a test done right after that baby was born. Monroe is not the father."

"I'm not certain that Monroe is the father, but one thing I am certain of is that the paternity test was not valid. Monroe's blood was never used for that test. His friend, Dr. Perry Lane Martin—I believe that's Marty to you—is the one who was tested."

The senator stopped. Sabre had to catch herself to keep from passing him.

"You think Marty took that test?"

"And the other two that followed on two other children."

When Senator Bullard furrowed his brow, Sabre realized he hadn't been privy to the other two tests.

"And why are you so certain that it was Marty and not Monroe?"

"Because we spoke to Chad Lambert, the technician who did the test. Your family paid him not to disclose what he did." Sabre wanted to say his *mother*, but she thought it wouldn't sting as much if she said *family*. "The technician was in desperate need of money. If we could get him to come forward and testify that the test was rigged, I could get another test ordered. There is plenty of Monroe's DNA around, but the technician won't do it. He fears being prosecuted himself, and he's afraid of what your family might do to him."

"So you want me to be tested?"

"Yes. Conway deserves to know if Monroe is his father, and he's entitled to his inheritance if he is."

"That's what this comes down to: his inheritance."

"No. Conway has wondered all his life about his father. He has heard conversations over the years that made him believe Monroe was his father. He has never had a father figure, someone to teach him right from wrong. We both know his mother is a little iffy, and yet Conway has turned into an incredible young man whom anyone would be proud to call son. He deserves his family and whatever else goes with it."

The senator frowned.

"If you take the test and it turns out negative, this will all go away."

"Until the next claim by the next woman seeking her fortune. I'm afraid I can't do it, Ms. Brown."

Sabre sighed. "Thank you for listening to me, Senator, and I want to offer you my condolences on the loss of your brother. I know how hard it would be for me to lose my only brother."

"Thank you. It's not easy."

"One more thing," Sabre said. "Did you know Conway was the victim of a hit-and-run a couple of days ago?"

"Is he alright?" Sabre could hear the sincere concern in his voice.

"He will be. He has a broken arm, lots of scrapes

and bruises, and his bike was demolished, leaving him without any means to get to work."

"And you think my family had something to do with that as well?"

"I don't know, but if you are so sure Monroe is not the father, a simple swab of your cheek could possibly save this young man's life from the next attempt."

"I'm sorry, Ms. Brown. Have a safe flight home."

The senator started to run at full speed. Sabre didn't try to keep up. He soon disappeared around the curve in the lake.

Chapter 45

Louie, JP's beagle, got a good lick across JP's face before JP could scoot him away. JP looked at the clock on his nightstand. It was nearly 8:00 a.m.

"I'm sorry, Louie. I'll bet you need to go out," he said, as he rolled out of bed and slipped his jeans on.

JP let Louie out in the backyard, made a pot of coffee, and showered while it brewed. He wondered how Sabre's meeting with the senator went. He didn't want to call her in case she went back to her room to catch up on her sleep. She still had a few hours before she would board her plane. He was hoping to have some good news for her about Dr. Martin when she got home. JP was frustrated because he hadn't been able to find much on this case that was of any help to Sabre, but if he could get the doctor to admit that he used his blood for the paternity test, it would surely be enough to have a new one ordered. He decided to drive back to Laguna Beach and try to confront the doctor.

***

It was nearly ten o'clock in the morning when JP turned onto the street that ran in front of Marty's house. When he saw Marty and the redhead coming out the front door, JP drove past and turned around in the first driveway where he couldn't be seen, which was four or five hundred feet away. By the time he came back to the house, Marty and the redhead were driving away.

JP followed the car as Marty made his way onto Coast Highway heading north. The beach area was already becoming crowded, so JP stayed close behind the Mercedes so he wouldn't lose him in the traffic and the many red lights. Marty turned right onto Broadway, and JP followed. When Marty pulled into Parking Lot 11 and stopped at the end of the parking area, JP drove on and made a right into Parking Lot 10, flipped around, and sat at the exit so he could turn either direction, depending on where Marty went.

JP was only about thirty yards from Marty, and he had a good view of the car. Marty never got out to open the girl's car door. The redhead stepped out and walked toward a white Kia in the corner of the lot. JP grabbed his camera, zoomed in, and took a picture of the license plate in case he needed it for later.

Marty pulled forward, exited the parking lot, and turned left toward Coast Highway. JP followed. They continued driving south until Marty arrived at a restaurant on the beach side of the highway called Coyote Grill. When Marty pulled in, JP dropped back, waiting for him to leave his car with the valet. Then JP did the same.

People were waiting inside and outside the restaurant for a table. JP approached the counter where a pad of paper awaited people signing in for a table. It had a column for the name, number in the party, and inside and outside seating. The last entry read: *Dr. Martin, 1, outside.* A quick search of the bar found the doctor sitting at a tall table. A waiter was taking his order.

JP waited until the waiter left and then joined him at the table.

"Hello. Dr. Martin, isn't it?" JP extended his hand.

The doctor shook it. "Yes, should I know you?"

"JP Torn. We have Monroe Bullard in common," JP said. "I know you've known him since childhood, me not quite so long. He always called you Marty, right?"

"That's right. Have we met before?" Dark circles

surrounded Marty's droopy eyes.

"No," JP said. "But you sure could be a big help clearing something up now that Monroe is gone."

"I could be a big help?" Marty asked.

"Yes, proving that Monroe is Conway's father."

Marty's face tightened, and he grimaced as he leaned forward. "Who's Conway?"

"Conway is Brandy McFerran's son. About seventeen years ago, your blood work was used instead of Monroe's when they ran the paternity test in a clinic in Nashville."

"What exactly are you saying?"

"I'm saying you stood in for Monroe. The technician drew your blood and used it for the test."

Marty sat back on his stool, took a deep breath, and said, "I don't know what you're talking about."

"And later, you came in again on two occasions, and two more tests on other children were done the same way."

"Produce the tests and I'll prove it wasn't me."

The waiter brought a Bloody Mary to the table for Marty and asked JP if he wanted anything. He declined.

"You already know they were destroyed."

"Then I guess we're done here." He picked up his Bloody Mary and stirred it with the celery stick.

"Look, we have a young man who not only needs to know who his father was but is likely entitled to a huge inheritance."

"I'm not going to admit to something I didn't do so the kid receives Monroe's money. Monroe was my best friend since we were in grade school. We just recently were able to spend time together again, and now he's gone. If Monroe wanted this kid to have the money, I'm sure he would have set that in motion. At the very least, he would have told me. I'm sorry for this young man, but I can't help you. Now, if you'll excuse me." Marty stood up, picked up his drink, and walked away.

***

JP was halfway home when Sabre called.

"I'm about to get on the plane. How did your stakeout go?"

"I'm afraid I struck out. Marty won't admit to anything. He's pretty smug about the whole thing since he knows there's nothing concrete to use against him. I tried appealing to his better side, but it didn't work."

"Same with the senator. He believes the first test was valid and there's no need for another one, nor does he want to open up that can of worms."

"I'm sorry, Sabre. I wish one of us would have been successful."

"Me too." Sabre took a deep breath. "Ron called me a little while ago. He's totally baffled with the latest cache as well. He has tried hundreds of combinations but can't come up with a cache that's close. He thinks it's the last picture, the one with Dolly Parton, that is messing him up. He doesn't know what else to use besides her initials. He tried BB for Big Boobs and DD for Double D's, but those combinations didn't work either."

"Leave it to Ron to come up with them."

"They're starting to board. I'd better go."

"What time do you get in?"

"Not until about ten o'clock. I'd like to see you, but it'll be late by the time I'm home and I have court tomorrow."

"I understand. We'll talk tomorrow. Goodnight."

Chapter 46

While waiting for Brandy's case to be called, Sabre and Bob sat in the back of the crowded courtroom where the felony arraignments took place.

"Do we really need to be here for this?" Bob whispered.

"I promised Conway I would be here and let him know what happened," Sabre said. "The other kids want to know too. And you need to be here because I didn't want to come alone."

"You know what's going to happen. She's going to plead 'Not Guilty,' and the court will set a date for the preliminary hearing. That's it. Why don't we just go, and you can call Conway in a little while and tell him that."

"Relax and watch the show; this judge is always entertaining."

Judge Link took the bench before Sabre could say any more. He had been handling misdemeanor and felony arraignments for as long as Sabre could remember. She had first come into contact with him while she was in law school. She'd appeared before him as an intern in the Criminal Clinic with her professor many times during her third year of law school. He had a great sense of humor, and he delighted in teasing the students and the new attorneys. She'll never forget her first case after she was sworn in. He embarrassed her so badly, and he had the packed room in stitches. To this day, Sabre was still a little nervous whenever she had to appear in front of Judge Link.

The clerk called the first case. A man in his fifties came to the podium with his attorney. The clerk read the charge, which was grand theft. "How do you plead?" the judge asked.

The man said, "Guilty, Your Honor."

"I need to hear in your words what you did."

"I went to a thrift store and stole some clothes and things for my children. I have nine children, Your Honor, and they needed clothes. I haven't been able to find work."

The judge turned to the ADA. "Really? A thrift store? How do you get 'grand theft' from a thrift store? Isn't that an oxymoron? Or did he wipe out the whole store?"

The new ADA stammered a little before regaining her composure. "The estimate from the store was over $400, Your Honor."

"How many trips did that take him? I can see it now. He's walking out of the store with a stack so high he can't see where he's going. Didn't anyone notice before he got to the 'grand theft' limit?"

"It was only one trip, Your Honor," the man's attorney said.

Still looking at the prosecutor, the judge said, "I can't accept that plea. Go make a decent misdemeanor plea agreement. Come back in twenty minutes."

"Yes, Your Honor," she said.

They started to walk out of the courtroom, and the judge said, "Someone steal that guy a television. It'll give him something to do besides make babies." The courtroom filled with laughter.

"The State vs. Brandy McFerran," the clerk called.

A deputy sheriff walked Brandy to the podium where her public defender waited.

The clerk read the charge of first-degree murder.

"How do you plead?"

Brandy stood tall, threw her head back, the back of her hand flew to her forehead, and in a slow, strong, southern accent she said, "I plead not guilty, Your Honor."

.The sound of chuckles rippled through the audience, and even Judge Link did all he could to keep from laughing. His eyes opened wide, and he clinched his lips shut. A few seconds later, when he had composed himself, he gave them a date for the preliminary hearing and denied bail in spite of the eloquent request by Brandy's attorney. As they were taking Brandy back to the holding tank, the judge said, "Someone tell Scarlett O'Hara that they lost the war."

***

JP sat with Detective Brad Williams at Jitter's Coffee Shop in La Mesa eating lunch.

"Thanks for meeting me here," Brad said.

"No problem," JP said. "You were at Brandy's arraignment this morning?"

"Yes. She pled 'Not Guilty.'" He threw his head back with the back of his hand against his forehead, mocking her over-acted southern drawl.

"Did she look around for the cameras?"

"She aimed it all at the judge, who found it very amusing." He hesitated. "I'm not surprised."

"What didn't surprise you? The bad acting? The Not Guilty plea?" JP looked at the concern on Brad's face. "Or are you having second thoughts about her guilt?"

"I know we're supposed to let go once we make our collar, but this one doesn't sit quite right with me."

"Why's that?"

"I wouldn't have arrested her with what we had, but there was so much pressure from the top brass because of his family."

"You don't think she did it?" JP took a bite of his

sandwich.

"I don't know. It's just that a lot of things don't make much sense. Like, why would you set up the geocaching treasure hunt, starting with a death certificate, kill the guy, and then let the trail lead back to you?"

"Maybe she's just not that smart."

"That's my problem. You would have to be pretty smart to set up something this elaborate. So if you're smart enough to do that, why wouldn't you be smart enough to cover your tracks?" He paused. "Why would you use your own birthday as one of the clues? And your own prescription bottle, even if you tore off part of the label?"

"I had trouble with that too."

"And then there's the fingerprints. You kill the guy and then leave your fingerprints all over the wine glasses and the ugly box on the table, but nowhere else."

"As if they were planted there?"

"That's right."

"Let me guess, you have other suspects?"

"I considered the kid, Conway, but I've since ruled him out. He was working at the time. Besides, what's his motive? He's so angry because his father rejected him that he kills him?"

JP's expression hardened, and he looked away from Brad for a second.

"What is it, JP?"

"There's lot of reasons why kids hate their parents. And sometimes they kill them."

"Did I hit a nerve?"

JP took a deep breath. "You're right. Monroe probably wouldn't speak to his kid if he met him in hell carrying a lump of ice in his hand, but Conway seems to have it all together. I really doubt that he killed

Monroe and certainly not because he felt rejected."

"I agree. He doesn't appear to be that kind of kid. That leaves the inheritance as the motive, which I'm convinced he didn't know about. Which is another thing: I'm not sure Brandy even knew about the money. And if she didn't, what motive would she have?"

"If not Brandy, who?" JP asked.

"Here's where it gets tricky. I hate to think a woman would kill her own son, but I like Mother Bullard for it. I discovered she's having a lot of financial problems. She lost a lot of money when the economy got bad, and she's been trying to claw her way back ever since. She needs megabucks to buy the senator a place in the next presidential race. On top of that, we know now that she fixed that paternity test, at least according to the technician you spoke with. That, coupled with the hit-and-run on Conway, makes it all very suspicious."

"But she needs to stop the paternity question, not kill Conway. His family could still contest the will even if he weren't around. And then the money would go to Conway's mother."

"I know. I thought about that, but maybe Mother Bullard thinks killing him will stop the process, and her father's money would go back to the family."

"But not to her?"

"No, but if it went back to the senator, they would still likely have the money for the campaign. But my captain doesn't want me opening that can of worms."

"I may have another suspect for you. His name is Dr. Perry Lane Martin, aka Marty. He's the one whose blood work was used for Monroe's paternity tests. He's some big-shot plastic surgeon in Laguna Beach who has a lot to lose if this all comes out. On top of that, I saw a tag on his luggage with a geocache logo on it."

"I'm not going to ask how you happened to see

that," Brad said.

"Don't worry. That one wasn't illegal."

"You think he's into geocaching?"

"Or he knows someone who is that could have done it for him."

"Thanks, I'll do a little snooping around."

JP pulled a notepad from his jacket, wrote a couple things on the paper, and handed it to Brad. "Here are the doctor's home and office addresses, the make and model of his cars, and I have his license plate number in my car if that will save you a little time."

"Thanks," Brad said and stuck it in his pocket.

"You'd better eat. Your food's getting cold."

Brad picked up his chicken sandwich and started to eat. After a couple of bites, he laid it down. "Have you heard any more about Conway's hit-and-run?"

"I spoke with Nelson this morning. So far, he has nothing new."

Brad took another bite of his sandwich, set it down, and shook his head. "I don't know, but there's just something missing in this case."

Brad's phone beeped, "Excuse me, I need to take this. It's my partner." He answered his phone. "Hello." He listened. "Just a second, Eric, I'm going to put you on speaker so JP can hear you."

"Chad Lambert, the technician at the lab where Monroe did his paternity tests, was killed last night," Eric said.

"Murdered?" Brad asked.

"It looks like an accident, but the cause hasn't been determined yet. Nashville PD seems reluctant to call it anything else."

"Do they know about the rigged paternity test and how much money is involved here?"

"They do now. I told them everything," Eric said. "They may be calling you, JP. I gave them your contact

information."
    "No problem. I'll help if I can."

Chapter 47

Sabre was sitting in the back of Department Six, waiting to do the last case on her morning calendar, when her cell phone vibrated in her pocket. She recognized the area code but not the number; the call was from someone in Nashville. She walked out of the courtroom and took the call.

"Hello, is this Attorney Sabre Brown?" the male voice said.

"Yes, who is this?"

"Senator Richard Bullard."

Sabre perked up, more than a little bit surprised at the caller.

"What can I do for you, Senator?" Sabre asked, afraid to hope that he had changed his mind about the test.

"It's what I can do for you. I'm willing to be tested. It's time this family stepped up."

"Thank you. Thank you." Sabre paused. "How do you want to do this?" Suddenly, Sabre thought that it might be a trick—that they would pay some lab to take the sample, only it, once again, wouldn't be the right sample. She wasn't going to allow that to happen again.

"I'm in Los Angeles right now. If you can set the test up for late this afternoon, I'll show up. You pick the facility, get the child and his mother there, and give me the time and place. You can call on this number."

Sabre was relieved. "The mother is in custody. I don't know if I can get her produced that soon, but if I can't we can probably have a sample taken and sent over. There's also another test known as Y-STR, Y-Short Tandem Repeats that is based on the Y chromosome. The Y chromosome is passed unchanged down the male line, so as long as both parties are male, the test is accurate. We don't need the mother for that one, although it may take a little longer to get the results back. You can ask more about it at the lab if you like." Sabre realized she was rambling and stopped talking.

"I'm sure you want what's best for your client, so I'm good with whatever you choose as long as it holds up in court. If you can get the boy there, I would like to meet him. All I ask is that you call me directly and let me know what the results are before anything gets leaked to the press."

"I can do that," Sabre said, hoping she could have the results before Brandy went to the media. It helped having her in jail.

"I'll see you this afternoon."

Sabre walked to the far end of the hallway to find Bob, who was doing a case in Department One. She waited, not so patiently, for the judge to finish the case. She accosted Bob before he could get out the door.

"The senator called. He's willing to do the paternity test."

"No kidding? My client will be thrilled to hear that."

"Mine too," Sabre said. "Here's the problem: The senator is going to be here this afternoon. I have to find a lab, make arrangements to get my client there, and yours if possible, or get a sample from your client with a good chain of custody. Can you help?"

"Call Regina Collicott. She'll know which lab is the fastest and the best. Then tell me what I need to do."

"I just saw her. She's still here. I'll track her down, and then I'll meet you in front of Department Six."

Sabre left and walked down the hallway looking for Regina, checking each courtroom as she passed. When she reached the metal detector, she glanced outside and spotted her leaving. She dashed outside and called to her.

"Are you leaving?" Sabre asked.

"Yes, do you need something?"

"I need a paternity testing clinic that will work with me on short notice."

"How short?"

"I need to get in this afternoon."

Regina opened her purse, took out a business card, and handed it to Sabre. "Southern California DNA Collections & Lab. Call them. Tell them I sent you and that you need the appointment today. I'm sure they'll accommodate you. I send them a lot of business."

"Thanks, Regina." Sabre glanced at the card to see the address. It wasn't too far from Conway's foster home, which simplified things. "I represent the child in this test, and I can get him there. The uncle has agreed to be there, but the mother is in custody. I've never tried to get a paternity test done with a parent in custody before. Do we need a court order?"

"Is the mother willing to do the test?"

"Absolutely."

"She doesn't have to go to the lab, which is a good thing because getting her there wouldn't be easy. Just have her attorney draw up an order for the sample. I'll email you an example as soon as I get back to the office. You'll know what you have to do from there." Regina pulled a pack of cigarettes and her lighter out of her purse. "I've got to go. Call if you need anything else."

***

Bob went with Sabre to her office where they opened the email with the sample order Regina had sent them. Sabre had called the testing facility on the way and scheduled an appointment for 3:30 that afternoon. She also learned the procedure for getting the swab from Brandy while she was in custody. Then she called Senator Bullard and gave him the appointment time and the address for the facility.

"I'll type up these orders. We need one for Las Colinas to allow the technician in to take the swab, and I need one so Conway can be tested," Sabre said. "Why don't you call the social worker and tell her what's going on. Oh, and call Deputy County Counsel Casey; tell him so he can confer with his client, and see if he is going to be in court this afternoon. Otherwise, we'll have to go to his office and get a declaration signed. You can use David's office if you want." Sabre pointed toward the office across the hall. "He won't be back today."

Sabre started to work, pulling the details she needed from her files and typing up the orders. Then she completed the declaration to be signed by County Counsel, Bob, and her stating that they were all in agreement in their request for the paternity test.

Bob returned to Sabre's office. "Casey will be there this afternoon. The social worker is on board, and she's going to call Casey and let him know. As soon as you have those done, we can go see Judge Hekman."

Sabre finished typing the orders, made five copies of each, and they drove back to court. Everyone signed the declarations, and Sabre gave them to the clerk, explaining the urgency. Things were finally looking up—until the clerk came back and said Judge Hekman wanted a hearing on it and she would be out shortly.

"Of course she does," Sabre murmured.

The clerk chuckled.

"Oops, did I say that out loud?"

Sabre checked the time. She had one hour and forty-five minutes to have the hearing, make sure transportation for Conway was provided, and get to the lab to meet the senator. They waited another ten minutes before the judge took the bench.

"This is a special hearing on the McFerran case for a request to have a paternity test done on Conway McFerran. Is that correct, Ms. Brown?"

"That's correct, Your Honor. All parties are in agreement with the request. As you know from the paperwork, we are asking for an order to test Conway McFerran and for the department to get him to the facility this afternoon at three thirty. We also need an order so Las Colinas will comply with the technician and allow a buccal swab to be taken from Brandy McFerran, Conway's mother."

"Is that correct, Mr. Clark?"

"Yes, Your Honor."

"Mr. Casey, on behalf of the department?"

"Yes, Your Honor, we're in agreement."

"So ordered," Judge Hekman said.

Sabre whispered to Bob, "So why didn't she just sign the orders? What did we need the hearing for?"

"Because I wanted it on the record, Ms. Brown," Hekman retorted.

Sabre grimaced and then smiled. "Thank you, Your Honor."

Sabre and Bob packed up and hurried out of the courthouse.

***

They reached the lab at 3:15. Conway arrived shortly after that with the social worker.

"Is Senator Bullard here yet?" the social worker asked.

"No, not yet. But we don't have to wait for him; Conway can be tested whenever they're ready for him."

At 3:45 the senator still wasn't there and Conway had not yet been called. When Sabre inquired, she was told they were short two technicians and extremely backed up, but they had called someone else in and Conway would be tested soon. Meanwhile, Bob provided the court order to the receptionist, who said there would be someone going to the jail within the hour.

Conway became restless and asked if he could go outside and get some fresh air.

"Of course," Sabre said.

Another fifteen minutes passed, and the social worker said, "I need to go. Could you give Conway a ride home?"

"Of course. I hope we're not here for nothing. I wonder if I should call Senator Bullard and find out what happened."

"I would," Bob said. "At this rate, they'll have my client's DNA before they get yours."

Sabre waited another ten minutes before she called the senator. It went straight to voice mail.

"Dang! I'll bet he's changed his mind," Sabre said.

"He's probably stuck in traffic or something."

"And he couldn't call?"

"Maybe not."

"He's not coming, is he?" Sabre wrung her hands together. "I knew this was too good to be true."

"Relax," Bob said. "He could still make it. The lab doesn't close until six."

Sabre stood. "I'm going to check on Conway."

When she reached the door, she saw Conway standing next to the senator. Conway was only an inch or so shorter than Bullard. They both had the same light brown, unruly hair. Sabre hadn't realized when she saw the senator yesterday morning how much he resembled Conway. She could hear bits and pieces of their conversation. They seemed to be swapping war stories about work.

Sabre walked back in and sat down next to Bob. "He's here," she said.

"The senator?"

"Yes, he's talking to Conway. I decided to let them have a little time together. If he has half a heart, it won't take him long to fall in love with that kid."

Twenty minutes later Senator Bullard was called in for his buccal swab with numerous apologies for making him wait. When he came out, Conway went in.

"What changed your mind?" Sabre asked Senator Bullard.

"I'd like to think you got through to my good nature, but it wasn't until I heard that the lab technician, Chad Lambert, had died. I wouldn't have even known about him if you hadn't told me." He took a deep breath. "It made me question a lot of things. One of those is making sure I do the right thing by my brother. And as you so aptly put it, it will either end this whole fiasco or it will give me a nephew—something I've always wanted but never expected to have."

Chapter 48

JP decided to make another visit to see Dr. Martin. As he drove up the street toward his house, he could see the doctor's Mercedes parked in the driveway. The spot where JP had parked a few nights ago was taken by a dark-colored sedan, and a man was sitting in the driver's seat. JP knew the house next to Marty's was vacant, and since there were plenty of other spots he could have parked, he was either watching Marty's house or he stopped to admire the ocean. The latter didn't seem likely since it was too dark for much of a view.

JP drove past the car, around the curve, and parked where neither Marty nor the man in the parked car could see him. He dropped his binoculars in his coat pocket, got out, crossed the street, and made his way down to the beach. Walking along the street would have made him too visible, so the beach was the only way back where he wouldn't be seen. The tide was higher than he would've liked, and he had to dash back toward the embankment when the first wave came in. Even so, the back of his boot and pant leg got wet.

JP waited and watched for the next wave, calculating how much time he had to make it to the spot where he could see Marty's house. The embankment protruded, making it closer to the water, and stayed that way for about twenty feet before it turned back inward toward the road. JP had to avoid the higher water or his feet would get soaked. As soon as the tide started out, JP dashed around the rocks and up toward the road. He knew his boots were wet, but the dampness hadn't started to soak through to his feet.

JP climbed up the side of the embankment directly in front of Marty's house, keeping low so he wouldn't be seen. The man was still sitting in the car watching Marty's house. He was positioned just slightly to JP's right.

JP took out his cell phone and called Brad.

"You're calling awfully late. What is it?" Brad said when he answered the phone.

"Do you have someone watching Dr. Martin's house?" JP spoke softly.

"No, why?"

"I'm here at his house, and I'm not alone. There's a car parked in front of his house with a man sitting in the driver's seat. He appears to be solo."

"I'll be right there. Without traffic I'm about fifteen minutes away."

JP made himself as comfortable as he could, with his upper body lying on the ground behind some bushes and the rest of his body on the side of the embankment. His feet were planted on a ledge. He couldn't go any closer without being seen, but he could see the man in the car. He could also see any activity inside the front interior of the house through the large windows that stretched the full length of the home. He took out his binoculars and peered through them at the man in the car, but it was too dark to see his face.

Eight minutes had passed without any movement from either the stranger or Marty. JP wondered if Brad would hit traffic and if he did, how long it would take for him to arrive.

Marty stepped into view in the upstairs bedroom window wearing a towel wrapped around his waist. From the looks of his wet hair, JP assumed he had just taken a shower. As he walked further into the bedroom, he became more visible.

The car door opened, and the stranger stepped out. JP noted that the dome light did not come on in the car when he opened the door, but he could see the man stood about five-foot-ten, had an average build with a slight paunch, and had white or very blond hair with a matching beard and mustache. The man held a cell phone in his hand. He appeared to text a short message and then dropped his phone into his pocket.

"Crap," JP said, as the man leaned against the side of his car, positioning a high-powered rifle on top of it, and pointing it at Marty. JP had to do something. He couldn't just let someone kill the doctor. He slid his hand slowly along the ground until he found a loose rock. He picked it up and flung it toward the bushes in front of Marty's property and to the left of the man near the car.

The man swung around with his rifle pointed at the bushes and then dropped down behind the side of the open car door. He stepped back, closing the door but not letting it latch. Then he remained crouched down and worked his way around the car. For several seconds JP lost sight of him until he came out on the other side at the front of the car, still creeping along with his rifle aimed at the bushes where the rock had fallen.

JP glanced up at the house, but he could not see Marty. He hoped he would stay out of sight, at least until Brad arrived. He hit the button on his phone to check the time; eleven minutes had passed. The man with the rifle had reached the area where the rock had hit and stopped, most likely blaming the noise on a rodent. The man moved up the walkway a little ways and crouched down behind some juniper bushes, which protruded about three feet above the ground—

almost directly in front of JP. Given the man's proximity, the best JP would be able to do was to get off one shot, and then he would have to drop down the embankment or he would be an easy target, even in the dark. He needed to cross the street and get better cover. Marty still had not reappeared and Brad hadn't arrived. JP was afraid to let the gunman out of his sight.

Inside his pocket, JP felt his phone vibrate with an incoming text message.

Brad: *We came up the back street, parked before the curve, and we're walking toward the doctor's house. Will he be able to see us?*

JP: *Stay close to rock wall and keep down. He's close enough to house that he won't be able to see you until you pass his car. I'll text you if he moves down. He has a high-powered rifle.*

Brad: *OK*

JP: *Who's with you?*

Brad: *Eric*

JP: *His car door is not closed tightly. Light won't come on. You may want to get his keys if they're in there.*

Brad: *OK.*

Within less than a minute, and with the help of his Bushnell's, JP saw Brad and his partner creeping toward the house. As they reached the car, Brad stayed to the right and Eric came around to the driver's side. He slowly opened the door and removed the keys. Then he made his way to the end of the car, gun drawn, and pointed in the direction of the gunman.

JP could no longer see the sniper, but he crept to his left in an attempt to get a better view. Just then Marty appeared in the bedroom window. The gunman raised his rifle. Brad yelled, "Stop! Police!" The sniper fired and the bedroom window shattered. Another gun fired; JP wasn't sure if it was Brad's or Eric's. Then he saw Eric move forward and drop down by the rock wall. The gunman shot again toward the spot where Brad had just been. JP aimed at him, but he didn't shoot for fear the bullet might hit Eric. It was difficult to see what was happening, but suddenly Eric moved forward and the gunman sprang up from behind a juniper bush, and in what looked like some kind of Ninja move, the man kicked the gun from Eric's hand, threw his arm around his throat, and dragged him like a shield the few steps to his car. Brad did not surface. JP still didn't make his presence known. Instead, he dialed 9-1-1 and gave them the address. "I think a cop has been shot."

When the gunman opened his car door and discovered his keys were gone, he backed up across the street and toward the embankment, still holding Eric in front of him with his left hand. In his right was the rifle lying against Eric's back with the tip of the barrel at the base of his head.

JP quietly moved down the rocks and onto the beach, moving just around a rock where he couldn't be seen. When the gunman reached the lowest part of the embankment, he shoved Eric into the street, and he jumped onto the beach and headed toward JP. As soon as he made the corner, JP flung out his leg, tripping him, and then jumped on top of him, pinning his face in the wet sand. The rifle slid across the sand. The gunman's hand flew up in the air while holding his cell phone. As he started to fling it into the ocean, JP grabbed his wrist and with his knee stuck in the man's back, JP wrenched the phone from his hand. By the time JP had him pinned, Eric had reached them. He cuffed him, not taking any precautions to be gentle.

"Check on Brad," Eric said. "I think he was shot."

Sirens could be heard not far away as JP climbed back up the embankment and dashed across the street. He found Brad lying on the ground, his head against the rock wall. JP shined his flashlight from his phone on him. Blood stained the wall around his head and his shoulder. Suddenly bright headlights appeared and three black and whites screeched to a halt.

"Over here," JP yelled. Several officers ran to JP and Brad. JP pointed to Brad. "That is Detective Bradford Williams. He's been shot."

An officer pointed a gun at JP. "Step back, sir," he said.

JP kept his hands out in front of him, stood up, and moved away from his friend. "I'm JP Torn, a private investigator. I was on the force with Brad in San Diego. We have a common interest in a case. His partner, Eric Ridenour, is across the street on the beach with the perp. He may need help." JP pointed at Marty's house and added, "And the man in that house may have been hit as well." Several officers dispersed in both directions as the paramedics pulled up, followed by four more police cars, lighting the block up like a festival.

The paramedics went to work on Brad while the officer continued to question JP. "Are you armed?" he asked.

"Yes. It's in my shoulder holster. You can take it out. It hasn't been fired."

Another cop pulled JP's jacket back and removed his gun. Then he patted him down for other weapons. Satisfied that he had no other weapons, the officer lowered his gun.

"What were you doing here?" the first officer asked.

"I was watching the man who lives in that house, Dr. Martin. When I arrived, I saw the perpetrator sitting in his car. I called Brad because the man looked suspicious, and we had reason to believe someone might be trying to kill the doctor."

"How did Brad get shot?"

JP was explaining what had gone down when Eric approached and clarified JP's role.

"Where's the shooter?" JP asked Eric.

"He's locked in the car. He's in good hands."

Brad moaned as the paramedics put him on the stretcher. "Brad, can you hear me?" Eric asked.

Brad tried to reach his right hand to his left shoulder, but one of the medics stopped him. "Hurts," Brad mumbled.

JP and Eric stayed with Brad until the paramedics put him in the ambulance. Then they walked toward the house to check on Marty. He was seated downstairs in the living room with a female officer, shaken up but intact. The gunman had missed him.

Chapter 49

"This is driving me crazy!" Ron said as he stared at the computer, switching from one photo to another. "I've tried every combination of codes I can come up with, and nothing works."

"And you still think the problem is with the Dolly Parton photo?" Sabre asked.

"I think so."

"So let's concentrate on that one."

They sat in Sabre's office with the picture blown up on the screen. "Why is she on the phone?" Sabre asked. "That must have some significance."

Bob walked in just as Sabre spoke. "Because that photo is right out of the movie *Nine to Five*."

"And how would you know that?" Ron asked. "You watching chick flicks now?"

"It's Marilee's favorite. She watches it all the time. I just watch Dolly's boobs. So we each get something out of it."

"You're sinful," Sabre said. "Try it, Ron."

"Already on it." He punched in the code GC16LL95. "Nope, it doesn't work. I thought we had it this time."

"I don't know what to tell you, but that's definitely right out of that movie," Bob said. "I recognize the sweater."

Ron started Googling the movie, reading everything that he could find on it that might work. Sabre did the same.

"Her name in the movie was Doralee Rhodes," Sabre said. "Try her initials, DR."

He typed in the code, pushed Search, and the screen read "*404—File Not Found*." "Nope, not it."

"DR is doctor; try MD," Sabre suggested. "I know it's a stretch, but we're dealing with a sick mind here."

"Not it."

"Our geocacher has used dates before; try the release date for the film. It's December 19, 1980."

Ron did more searches. "It's not 80." He paused while he put in the next code. "It's not 198."

"Try 19," Sabre suggested.

"Nope, not that."

"How about 12 for December?"

"Nope, that's not it."

"Try the number 3," Bob said. They both looked at Bob with furrowed brows. "It's about three working women."

They continued to research the movie and the song while Bob walked around the desk singing the lyrics."

"You know that whole song?" Ron asked. "That's just totally weird."

"He knows the lyrics to a lot of songs and a whole lot of other useless information," Sabre interjected. "It's scary what's in that head."

"Besides, I told you, Marilee watches the movie all the time. I can't tell you the number of times I've sat through it."

They all spent another half hour on the code together, and then Bob left. Sabre and Ron tried a few more things but got nowhere.

"I'm done for the night. I'm hungry, and I'm tired. I need to go home."

***

Ron ate dinner with his mother and then parked himself in front of the computer and resumed trying to figure out the code. He gave up about midnight and went to bed. He tossed and turned, dreaming of codes, caches, and scenes alternating between Bob running through the hills and dancing in the office singing *Nine to Five*. About three o'clock Ron woke up. He tried to shake the images of Bob from his brain, but the song still swirled around in his head. Then it hit him. He jumped up, grabbed his computer, and put in his attempt to crack the code. Bingo!

He wanted to call Sabre, but it was too early. He turned the television on, surfing the channels to find something that would either keep his attention or put him to sleep. He settled on an old episode of *Perry Mason*. Another episode of Mason and half a *Twilight Zone* later, Ron couldn't stand it any longer. He had to call Sabre.

The sound from the phone woke Sabre with a start. The only light in the room came from the face of her phone. She reached for it, observing the picture of Ron.

"What's the matter? Is it Mom?"

"No. It's 9-2-5."

"What?"

"The code isn't 9-5. It's 9-2-5. I'm sorry to wake you up, but I've been up for hours and I couldn't stand it any longer. I'm going to check it out. Do you want to come with me?"

Sabre sat back on the bed and stretched her shoulders as she did.

"Now? Are you crazy? It's still dark."

"It won't be by the time we get there."

"I may as well; I'm already awake." She yawned. "Where is it?"

"It's close to you, near Tecolote Canyon."

"All right, come on over. I'll have time to go before I go to court."

"Do you have coffee?"

"Yes, I have coffee."

Sabre took a shower and got ready for work. Instead of a suit, she put on jeans, a long-sleeved shirt, and her sneakers. Then she went downstairs and made herself a cup of hot lemon water and made Ron's coffee while she waited for him. It was less than five minutes when he rang her doorbell.

"Good morning, Sis."

"So you say." She hugged him. She wondered if other families were as affectionate as hers. She and her brother always hugged when they saw each other, no matter how long it had been since their last encounter. Their father was like that as well when he was alive—their mother not so much. Sabre clung to her brother even more since he returned after being gone for seven years. She was so afraid she might lose him again.

"Is my coffee ready?"

"There's coffee ready for you and a mug you can take with us."

Ron grabbed his coffee and they left.

***

The coordinates for the cache were well into the trail in Tecolote Canyon and led to a clump of bushes. Ron removed two pairs of work gloves from his backpack and handed one to Sabre. He always carried extra latex and work gloves with him in his geocache pack. Normally they would wear the latex gloves, but some of the bushes were sharp and would have torn the latex. They each started pushing the dense bushes back, looking for any kind of container they could find.

Sabre found an empty beer can, picked it up, and placed it in the plastic bag they brought with them to carry out the trash they found. Both Sabre and Ron were invested in the CITO program that www.geocaching.com promoted—Cache In Trash Out. Anything to help save the earth.

They searched bush after bush without finding the cache.

"Are you sure we're at the right coordinates?" Sabre asked.

Ron checked the numbers again. "We're getting a little off track. We need to move that way a little," Ron said, nodding his head in a southwest direction.

"If we don't find it soon, I'm going to have to leave, and you'll have to come back and finish on your own."

Just beyond the clump of bushes were three old trees with gnarly roots that surrounded a small pond of water. The trail ran alongside the trees and then into a forested area. They searched all around the trees, the edge of the water and the rocks near it, but found nothing.

"Maybe it fell into the water," Sabre said.

"Maybe. I can go get one of those basket things with the long handles that people use to clean the leaves out of their swimming pools. What are those called?"

"I don't know, pool-sweeper things."

"Yeah, one of those. I can sweep the pond and see if it fell in, but it should be closer to those bushes."

Sabre checked the time. "I have to go."

"Okay, I'll take you home, and I'll come back and keep looking. It has to be here somewhere."

Chapter 50

"Hey, Sobs, there's someone looking for you at the Information desk," Bob told Sabre, as he approached her in Department Four.

"Who is it?" Sabre asked.

"I don't know. She's young, maybe twenty."

"Did you talk to her?"

"No. Patricia—you know, Leahy's squeeze—told me to tell you."

"I'll go as soon as we finish this case."

"You're submitting on the social worker's recommendations, right?"

"Yes."

"Then go talk to her. Patricia said the girl is pretty anxious to see you. I'll handle this if you're not back. We're all in agreement here. What could go wrong?"

"Famous last words." Sabre handed him her file and walked out.

Patricia spotted Sabre as she walked toward the Information counter. She held up her hand and waved her over.

"Sabre, this is Holly Hodges." She turned to the petite blonde standing at the counter. "Holly, this is Attorney Sabre Brown."

"Thanks, Patricia."

"What can I do for you, Holly?"

"Can I talk to you somewhere private?"

"Sure, follow me."

Sabre worked her way through the crowd and up the stairs. They sat down on a couple of chairs that backed up against the three-foot wall that looked down into the lobby.

Holly was holding a cloth bag. She kept twisting the handle around in a nervous motion.

"Are you okay?" Sabre asked.

"I think so."

"Are you in trouble?"

"No, it's nothing like that. It's just that ... I found something that I think was meant for you."

"Okay."

Holly opened the bag and pulled out a box identical to the Rhinestone Cowboy box that was found on Monroe's coffee table the day he died.

As soon as Sabre saw it, she said, "Wait. Don't touch it any more. I'll be right back."

Sabre jumped up and dashed down the hall into the clerk's office where she retrieved a pair of latex gloves. Then she returned to Holly, put the gloves on, and took the box from her.

"We've touched it a lot of times."

"Who's we?"

"My boyfriend, Jeff, and I."

"Where did you get it?" Sabre asked.

"We were hiking in Tecolote Canyon, and we stopped to eat a snack. I sat down on a fallen tree, and I saw something shiny off in the bushes."

"Was there a pool of water near some trees?"

"Yes," she said, looking surprised that Sabre might know that.

"When did you find it?"

"Yesterday afternoon, but it was after the courts closed, so I waited until this morning."

"And why did you bring it to me?"

"Because of the note inside."

Sabre opened the box. There was a folded piece of paper lying on top. "Is this the order everything was in when you found it?"

"Yes, there are just two things and the note was on

273

top."

Sabre picked up the paper. Underneath it was a photo of George Carlin. She left it there and opened the note. It read:

I am Monroe William Bullard, and I am dead.

This cache is meant for Attorney Sabre Brown. Most days she can be found at San Diego Juvenile Court, 2851 Meadow Lark Drive, San Diego, CA. It is paramount that she gets this cache. If you found this box by accident and your name is NOT Attorney Sabre Brown, you will not be able to decipher the code for the next cache, which will reveal my real killer.

Sabre's face lost a little color.

"Are you okay?" Holly asked.

Sabre took a deep breath. "Yes, I'm fine."

"Is this for real?"

"I'm afraid it is."

"Jeff and I thought it was a hoax, but then I Googled 'Monroe William Bullard' and found out he had been murdered. I was going to take it to the police, but since you were an attorney, I thought I should bring it to you."

Sabre reached out and placed her hand on Holly's. "You did the right thing. And I will see that the detective handling the case gets this."

"What does the photo mean?"

"I think the photo of George Carlin stands for 'GC,' which in turns stands for 'Geo Cache.'"

Holly looked puzzled, but Sabre didn't want to explain it all right now. Instead, she picked up the picture of George Carlin and turned it over. On the back of the photo, in red marker, was written: *Your birth month, the third letter in your license plate, the last two numbers you can figure out because you've been there before.*

***

As soon as Holly left, Sabre called Ron. "Where are you?" she asked.

"I'm still in the canyon looking for the cache."

"You can stop. It's been found." She explained about Holly and the contents of the cache, reading him the note and the words on the photo.

"So there's another one?"

"Yes, and it sounds like they were planted by Monroe."

"This is getting weirder and weirder."

Sabre's phone beeped. "Hold on, Ron." Sabre switched over to the incoming call. "This is Attorney Sabre Brown."

"Hello, this is Darlene from Southern California DNA Collections & Lab. We have the test results on the McFerran minor. We're closed from noon until one. But if you'd like to come in this afternoon, anytime after one, you can pick up a copy of the results, or I can fax them over at the end of the day."

"I'll be there at one," Sabre said. She clicked back to Ron.

"I have to go to the paternity lab shortly. The test results are in. I'll call you when I'm done, and we can figure this out."

***

On her way to see Conway, Sabre called Senator Richard Bullard to inform him of the test results she had just obtained from the lab and that she had also told the lab to fax him a copy of the results.

Conway was sitting in his room doing homework. His left arm in a cast rested on the desk. Fortunately, he was right-handed, so at least he could write.

"Are you doing okay?" Sabre asked.

"I'd rather be working. Mr. De Jong said he could

have me do some things, even with just one arm, but I can't leave the house by myself until they figure out who hit me. Do you think someone is trying to kill me?"

"I don't know, Conway, but until we know for sure, we just need to keep you safe."

Sabre sat down on the bed across from Conway's desk. There were a few seconds of silence before Sabre spoke. "We have the test results."

Conway looked up. His face was pale. "Sometimes I think I don't want to know who my father is. Then I can just make him into anything I want. He can be that soldier my mother always told me about—the one she made up. Or sometimes when I was a kid, I'd tell myself he was a famous astronaut who would fly me to the moon, or maybe he was a big Texas rancher and we would ride horses together. But I haven't done that since I was little."

Conway was very mature for his seventeen years and was a delight to converse with, but this was unusual for him. Sabre let him ramble until he was ready to hear the results.

Finally he asked, "Was Monroe my father?"

Sabre nodded affirmatively. "Yes." Sabre watched his face change expressions. She saw his furrowed brow change to confusion, and then he seemed to let it all go. His face relaxed and his color returned.

"The senator seemed real nice. He likes to hunt and fish, and his job seems real interesting. I've often thought I would like to be a politician. I wonder if I was, if I could make a difference."

"I'm sure you could, Conway. You are a very kind and considerate young man. I expect you'll grow to be a productive, compassionate adult."

"What happens now? I don't have to change my name or anything, do I?"

"No, your legal name is McFerran. That does not

change. Now my job is to make sure you get the inheritance you are entitled to."

"Yeah, that cop said something about there being an inheritance. Did Monroe leave me money?"

"Actually, your great-grandfather—Monroe's grandfather—did. It was in his trust that a rather significant amount of money went to Monroe's firstborn. That would be you."

"Is that why he didn't want to claim me?"

"I'm not sure what was in Monroe's mind, but I think it came more from other members of the family than it did from your father."

"The senator?"

"No, I don't think he knew anything about it. He seems like a decent man."

Conway gulped. "There's something else I wanted to talk to you about."

"Anything. What is it?"

"It doesn't look like Mom is going to get us back now that she's in jail."

"She hasn't been convicted yet, Conway, and she claims she's innocent. It's possible she could be acquitted."

"Even so, from what the social worker said, it might be awhile. So I was thinking: I'm going to be eighteen next month. Doesn't that make me an adult?" He stood up, perhaps to make himself seem grown-up.

"Yes, it does."

"So couldn't I take care of my sisters and my brother?"

"But you're still in high school. And I thought you planned to go to college."

He paced around the room. "I was thinking that if I finished high school—that's only a few months away—then I could work full time at the dairy. Mr. De Jong said he'd hire me full on. I could take care of them. My sisters and brother listen to me—well, most of the time, anyway."

"And what about college? I thought you wanted to study law."

"I do, but if I worked, I could see that the kids got to go, and maybe I'd go when they were all done."

"That's a big sacrifice. And what about the kids while you are working? Who's going to watch them?"

"Ms. Brown, we really want to be together again as a family." He hesitated and then started again. "I don't know how much money I'd get, if I get any, from Monroe, but maybe it would be enough to hire someone to help. Do you think we could do it then?"

"I don't know how long it's going to take to get that inheritance or how big a battle it will be, but let me see what I can do."

Chapter 51

George Carlin stared back at Sabre and Ron as they held the photo Holly had brought them from the cache. On the back of the photo in red marker was written: *Your birth month, the third letter in your license plate, the last two numbers you can figure out because you've been there before.*

"This should be easy," Ron said. "George Carlin is the GC. Your birth month is ten. What is the third letter of your license plate?"

"W," Sabre said.

"So we have GC10W. It's apparently a cache you have already been to, so let's look at all the codes we've deciphered so far."

"I don't know if I have them all."

To recreate the codes, Sabre and Ron rifled through the scraps of paper they had been working with, the notes they had on the computer, and the photos that were taken of the caches. They made a list of every code they had deciphered, but none of them started with GC10W.

"This is really taxing my brain," Sabre said. They went back through the list, making sure they didn't miss one. "We got the cache code off of the death certificate, the prescription bottle, the brandy bottle, Brandy's birthday, and the Rhinestone Cowboy. What's missing?"

Ron rubbed his forehead. "I don't know. And I don't know how he pegged you to do this in the first place, but it's starting to make sense. Once he got you started, he could set up a cache, plant the code for you to find from the cache before, and then take it out as soon as you found it. He must have been following you around, though, for the first couple of caches. Otherwise, how would he have made sure it was you who found them?"

"Or maybe he was following JP and me the first time and quickly planted the cache in place of the one that was supposed to be there." Sabre looked up from her computer. "You know, there was a man near the cache. That could have been Monroe."

"Do you remember what he looked like?"

"I hardly saw him. He was just passing by JP when I found the cache and called to JP. I think JP said hello to him. I only saw the man from behind. I do remember he was wearing a baseball cap, and he was several inches shorter than JP. And now that I think of it, there was a man in a baseball cap at the ball field where Jennifer and I found the cache with the note that said to 'look more carefully.'"

"If Monroe followed you the first time, he could have switched the real cache for his. That would have started the ball rolling. But he probably had to do it again because he couldn't be certain that you had figured out the first cache. After that, all he had to do was plant his caches and then remove them from the Internet as soon as you found them. The last two he couldn't take out of the system, but he had to make sure that they got to you. There was no issue with the cache in his house because no geocacher could find it. The risk, of course, would be that the police solved the puzzle and found the next cache. Although, with your name on the note, they probably would have come to you anyway."

"And that's why he had to create the cache that Holly found. In case the cache fell into the wrong hands, it would eventually get back to me."

"And it did. So where is this cache? Where you've been before," Ron said. "He doesn't actually say it was a cache where you've been before."

Sabre threw both hands up in the air. "Duh! It *is* a cache where I've been before." Sabre opened her geocaching account and checked her logs. "That's it. It's the one where the death certificate was. That's the only one we haven't eliminated. We were looking at all the codes we deciphered, but we missed the first one—the cache with the death certificate. How did we do that?"

"Because we didn't have to figure that one out. I didn't have that one written down, so I didn't even think about it. I think our brains are fried."

"Or as JP would say, 'The porch light's on, but nobody's home.'"

Sabre's cell phone blared out a Leonard Cohen song. "Hello, Bob," Sabre said, answering the phone.

"Are you watching the news?"

"No."

"You know, you should watch the news more often. You can learn a lot."

"It's all too depressing. Besides, if there is anything worth seeing, you'll call and tell me."

"Turn on Channel 10. After the commercials they are going to be interviewing Senator Bullard."

Sabre picked up her remote, powered up, and found Channel 10. The GEICO Camel appeared, speaking to a very annoyed desk-jockey, "Mike, Mike, Mike, Mike, Mike, guess what day it is."

Following the commercial, the news reporter commented about an interview with Senator Richard Bullard. The scene switched to Nashville. The senator was at a podium with ten or fifteen news reporters in what was obviously a planned press appearance.

"As you know, I recently lost my only brother. There has been a lot of controversy about his death and his murder is under investigation, so there is little I can comment about."

"Is it true Monroe has a son?" a news reporter asked.

"Yes, it is true. He is a fine young man, and I hope I'll have the chance to get to know him."

"Brandy McFerran, the young man's mother, is in custody for your brother's murder. Do you think she did it?"

"I don't know. I trust the police and the courts will figure it out."

"Chad Lambert, a technician for the lab where paternity tests were initially run, has recently died in a car accident. Do you think Brandy McFerran killed him too, or are there other suspects?"

"As far as I know, that was an accident. I don't know anything else about that young man's death."

"Have you officially dropped out of the presidency race?" another news reporter called out.

"I will not be continuing in the race for the presidency."

The same reporter asked, "Is there any truth to the rumor that you are leaving the Senate as well?"

"The voters have asked me to serve as their senator from this fine state of Tennessee, and I will finish my term unless they tell me differently."

"What are your plans after that?"

"I expect I'll do some fishing." The senator walked away from the podium.

Sabre had no sooner turned off the television when JP called.

"I just spoke with Greg Nelson. They arrested the man who hit Conway."

"Does he have any connection to the Bullards?" Sabre asked.

"None that we can find. He's only eighteen years old. He's a senior in high school."

"What's his story?"

"I don't know. I'm going there now to watch the interview with Greg Nelson. The kid's pickup is smashed on the front fender, the paint matches, and he was in the area at the time. That's about all I know."

***

JP stood behind the glass at the San Diego Sheriff's Substation in El Cajon while his friend Greg Nelson interviewed Mitchell Graham. The young man looked terrified, but he had not requested an attorney.

After some preliminary questions that established he was driving on Wilcox Road that night, Greg said, "Tell me what happened."

"It was my birthday and my parents were out of town, so I went to my friend's house that afternoon to celebrate. Both of his parents were at work. We had some beers, and then we found a bottle of tequila in the cupboard and had a few shots. I wasn't feeling very well and I was pretty dizzy, but it was only a few miles to my house, so I thought it would be okay to drive."

"So you drove home?"

"Yes, it was getting dark, and I didn't see anyone on the street. There were no other cars around, and I think I might have dozed off or something because I felt the pickup go off the road. The pavement got real rough, and it woke me up."

"And that's when you hit the young man on the bicycle?"

"I never saw anyone or the bicycle, but when I hit something I woke up and swerved back onto the road. I thought it was a post or something, so I just kept going."

"When did you realize it wasn't just a post you hit?"

"Not until you told me what happened. I swear I

didn't know I had hurt someone."

"Do you know Conway McFerran?"

"No."

"He goes to the same high school as you."

"It's a big school. We must not have any classes together."

"Do you know anyone with the last name of Bullard?"

"No, I don't think so."

"We know you didn't act alone. We know that someone else is behind this. Did someone force you to run that kid off the road?"

"No."

"What you need to do, son, is tell us who put you up to this, and we can help you."

"I don't know what you're talking about. I got drunk. I screwed up."

After some time and pressure from Greg along the same lines, Mitchell didn't change his story. "I didn't mean to hurt anyone." He started to cry. "I didn't do it on purpose."

Greg got the name of the friend at the house where he had been drinking and had Mitchell write out his statement. Then he rejoined JP.

"I think he's telling the truth," Greg said, "but I'll check out the friend. He made no effort to fix or even hide his truck. We've checked his background, and we can't find any connection to the Bullards."

Chapter 52

Mission Hospital in Laguna Beach was situated on a hill with breathtaking views of the Pacific Ocean. JP wondered how the hospital managed to procure such a fine piece of real estate. He knew the hospital was known for having a great trauma center, but he soon discovered from the signs on the wall that it was also a facility that treated chemical dependency, eating disorders, and psychiatric conditions.

JP found Brad lying in his hospital bed. He was tethered to an IV pole, had bandages around his head and shoulder, and an oxygen cannula coming out of his nose. His eyes were closed, so JP walked softly to his bed.

"I'm awake," Brad said, opening his eyes. "Thanks for coming by."

"You gave us a scare," JP said. "Nice to see you're winning the war."

"I'll be released in a few days, get some time off to recover, and then I'll have some light duty. It's all good."

"When you ride the bulls, you're bound to get trampled once in a while."

"I feel like I was trampled." Brad gave a slight chuckle. "Have you talked to Eric today?"

"No, the last I heard they had identified the gunman, but he wasn't talking."

"Still isn't, but we know he's a hired gun and we like him for killing Chad Lambert, the technician."

"Did the Nashville police rule that a murder?"

"No, and they likely won't," Brad said. "Did they ever call you to ask you any questions?"

"Nope. I haven't heard a word from them."

"Hey, smooth move getting the gunman's cell phone. We were also able to confiscate his computer and a few other digital devices from his home in Tennessee. They were all sent to the Orange County Regional Computer Forensics Lab."

"That's the FBI lab, right?"

"Yes."

"I remember they were just starting those when I left the force. How is that, working with the feds?"

"It's a great program. All the major law enforcement agencies in the area have a representative in the lab, and they all work together. They have a lot of super cool equipment. If I weren't so darn old, I would like that gig."

"I can't see you leaving the streets."

"I only have those thoughts when the bullets get too close. I'm sure I'll get over it." Brad shifted his body, trying to get comfortable. "Anyway, they found a couple of phone calls to the senator's mother."

"So he probably took out Chad Lambert too."

"Most likely, but I don't think they'll prove that one unless they can get the hit man to talk, and no one's holding their breath for that. He'd be foolish to confess, since the most we have him on now is attempted murder. I'm guessing our DA is not going to be too willing to make a deal with the hit man in order to solve a case in Tennessee that isn't even considered a murder."

"Do you think he also killed Monroe?"

"Probably, but I'm not sure how we're going to prove it. And if he did, that means Monroe's mother ordered *that* hit as well."

"That woman makes a hornet look cuddly." JP shook his head. "Are you going to keep investigating?"

"You know how this works. Both crimes have a suspect in custody. The department isn't going to let us use too many resources and time on this case, and Nashville PD certainly isn't going to. As far as they're concerned, the only crime committed in their city is fraud on a paternity test."

"And since Monroe and the tech are both dead, and the good Dr. Perry 'Marty' Martin is here, they aren't going to give that too much time or effort. They'd need some hard evidence that the mother was involved."

"I doubt if Marty will talk unless he's arrested. He already has his lawyer on board. We don't have jurisdiction over that case, so there isn't much we can do."

"Besides, Marty may not even know about the mother's involvement."

"That's possible."

"Monroe's mother is going to walk on this, isn't she?"

"Probably."

Chapter 53

"The first cache, the one with the death certificate, was right over there," Sabre pointed to a patch of eucalyptus trees. "It was up in a tree."

"Which tree?" Ron asked.

"That one, I think." She looked up into the tree. "No, it's that one. It was easy to climb. There it is! I see it." She grabbed the bottom branch with her latex-covered hands and pulled herself up into the tree. Then she took hold of the next branch and reached around to a pocket where the branch connected to the tree and pulled out a grayish-brown cylinder exactly like the one that had held the death certificate. "I've got it."

Sabre tossed the container down to Ron and climbed down.

"I hope this isn't another code. I'm pretty much done with this."

"Oh, I don't know. It's been the best treasure hunt I've been on in years."

"You need a job." Sabre smiled.

Ron handed the cylinder back to Sabre. She opened the lid and pulled out the scroll. The top page was an identical note to the one that was in the cache the young hikers had found.

Sabre read it:

I am Monroe William Bullard, and I am dead.

This cache is meant for Attorney Sabre Brown. Most days she can be found at San Diego Juvenile Court, 2851 Meadow Lark Drive, San Diego, CA 92123. It is paramount that she gets this cache. If you found this by accident or your name is NOT Attorney Sabre Brown, please take it to her. She will know what to do with it as it reveals my real killer.

It was followed by five very legible, handwritten pages:

Hello Sabre Brown,

This is Monroe Bullard writing to you from the great beyond. We never had the pleasure of actually meeting, but I've seen you and I appreciate your natural beauty. Had we been able to meet under different circumstances, I think we could have had something special. I know this must sound strange to you because I would bet this is the first time you have been flirted with by a dead guy. Enough of that.

I want to apologize for using you as my catalyst to pull this grand hoax on the people who have wronged me, but I have to admit, you were perfect at it. For those things you haven't yet figured out, I'll list them here. Please forgive me if you already know all this.

Conway McFerran: He is my biological son. I'm sure of that. My mother made me rig the paternity test by using someone else's blood work. I blame my mother, but I didn't exactly fight her on it, although it is very difficult to say no to my mother. I was young and didn't want the burden of caring for a child. The older I became, the more I realized what a lousy father I would make. Consequently, each "slip" after that was followed by the same kind of rigged paternity test. And then there is the inheritance. It doesn't matter much to me because I have use of it until I die, but my mother could never see it leaving our family. So, here is what I offer you: if you haven't been able to prove that I am Conway's father, I hereby give you permission to use any DNA collected by the police or any reliable medical facility to prove paternity.

Senator Richard Bullard: He is my dear younger brother. Richard doesn't make for a good politician because he's way too honest and has a kind heart much like that of our father's. However, our mother, his campaign manager, makes up for all of Richard's scruples. She has none! And she has, and will continue to do, whatever it takes to make Richard the president of the United States. I'm hoping my death, combined with this letter, will be enough to put an end to his career. Maybe then he can be the writer he always wanted to be. I don't do this to punish Richard, but rather as an act of kindness to get him out from under our mother's thumb. He has never known about the fraud that was perpetrated on Conway or my other children, nor does he know most of what else our mother has done to further his political career. If he did, he would not go forward.

Richard has always shown his love for me, even when I screwed up, which I did plenty. Although I miss the respect and admiration he had for me as a child, I know he's continued to care about me even in these later years when no one else in the family has. I expect that Richard has already volunteered to take the paternity test, and if he did, I'm certain he will embrace Conway as his nephew. If he has not taken the test, please tell him that I would like him to do so. Please don't mistake this as an act of kindness on my behalf, for I am not a kind person. Frankly, it's just another way to even the score with my mother.

Mother Dearest: Ah, the beautiful, cold, calculating woman who made Joan Crawford look like Mother Teresa. She emotionally abused my father on a daily basis. She pressured him into running for mayor of Nashville, and I'm sure he was relieved when he lost. She didn't let up, though, and she nearly killed him when he lost the race for governor. She wanted more than anything to be a "First Lady." She drove my father to work long hours so he wouldn't have to come home to her. I blame her for the little time I was able to share with him. Our mother physically abused us when we *didn't show proper manners, sent us to private school to isolate us from the lower classes as soon as she could, and started us down the political path in pre-school. She stole my childhood from me. She lies and cheats to get what she wants and does not hesitate to show her disappointment whenever we demonstrate a behavior more like our father's than hers.*

I'm hoping my mother is a suspect in my murder. I do regret missing it, though, if she's taken off in handcuffs and put in jail with the "low-lifes" she so detests. But I'm sure if she were a suspect, she would pay someone off to keep her out of jail. And although I wouldn't mind if she spent the rest of her life in prison for my murder, she is not the killer.

Brandy McFerran: Yes, I had sex with her when she was only fifteen. I was twenty-three. She loved the lifestyle I could give her, although I don't think she was really into me that much. Mostly, she was interested in the connections I could make for her to become the next Queen of Country Music. The problem is that she just wasn't that good of a singer. My mother paid her off to keep her from ruining my political career. But it was too late. It was already ruined. When my mother realized that, she placed all her efforts into grooming Richard for the job. Brandy was a stupid kid, but even more inane as an adult. She made the mistake of coming back recently and asking for more money or connections to the acting world. She said all she needed was one break and she could prove herself. I told her to go ahead and tell whomever she wanted that I am Conway's father. They wouldn't be able to prove it anyway. When she told me she was a geocacher, it gave me all sorts of ideas. I invited her to my house under the pretense of introducing her to Steven Spielberg. She proved to be just as naive as she was at fifteen, but she was kind enough to leave lots of fingerprints and DNA behind, as well as her prescription bottle. Hopefully, the police found those. I expect she is the prime suspect in my murder, but they will probably soon realize she's just not smart enough to pull this off. No, Brandy isn't the killer either.

So who has killed me? Maybe the police have already figured it out, but in case they haven't, here it is:

I have cancer—a cancer that will kill me soon no matter what I do. I doubt if my mother knows. She long ago stopped caring about my health or even what I am doing, as long as I'm not embarrassing the family. I don't want to spend my last days in chemo, in pain, or watching my body and mind deteriorate. Instead, I wanted to do something fun, something where I could use my mind, get revenge on a few people who irritated me in life, and really stick it to my mother.

I am writing this note in long hand so my handwriting can be analyzed in case you need further proof. If the police want to check, they will find my fingerprints on this note and this last cache. If the cops have checked the history on my laptop, they will already have discovered my research on cyanide poisoning and the Tylenol Terrorist. Please excuse my lack of originality, but I haven't had time to come up with anything more creative. The cancer is starting to drain me, so I've put all of my energy into the geocache hunt. I have to admit I've had a lot of fun doing it, and after all, it's all about me.

Anyone who knows me knows I have always been selfish. I was a selfish child and an even more selfish man. I have to give credit for that to Mother Dearest, and this is my last selfish act—suicide.

Monroe William Bullard

***

"Hi, kid," JP said when Sabre called.

"Ron and I just found the last cache," Sabre said. "You're not going to believe this." Sabre went on to explain the contents of the letter.

"So the whole thing was some big, crazy game to amuse himself?" Sabre could hear the irritation in JP's voice. "And he used you as a pawn, that—" He stopped short of expressing his anger in any profane words. Silence filled the phone.

"Are you okay?"

"I just hate how he used you. It makes me so mad I could chew up nails and spit out a barbed wire fence."

Sabre smiled to herself. "It's all over now."

"He just put you through so much. And I'm mad at myself for not being able to figure it out."

"You can't blame yourself. We were all duped," Sabre said. "Hey, I have to go meet Eric and give him the cache. I took pictures of it so you can see the letter."

"What time will you be back?"

"I should be home by seven thirty. If you're not too tired, I'd like to see you. We've had such a hard time finishing a date lately."

"I'm never too tired for you, kid. I'll pick up some pizzas at Pieology and meet you at your house at seven thirty."

"Wheat dough, ricotta cheese, and lots of veggies."

"And extra sauce. I know what you like."

***

They finished the pizzas, and Sabre leaned back into JP's arms on the sofa.

"It's nice to be home, but I'm beat." She looked up at JP. "Can you stay?"

He kissed her softly. "I can, but I need to tell you something first. I think we need to clear the air."

"No, we don't." She kissed him this time, stopping his words. She knew what was coming, and she didn't want to get into the whole Pauline thing. She didn't want to have to explain her feelings either. She didn't want to have to apologize for her own behavior the last few days. She knew she could trust him, and that's what she would do from now on, or at least she would try.

"Yes, we do. I should have told you before, but Pauline went with me when I went to Nashville."

"I know. I saw you on the news."

"On the news?"

"Yes, when you left the charity event for Senator Bullard. The media were there asking him questions about Monroe. You and Pauline were getting into a car."

Sabre stood up and reached for his hand, nodding her head toward the stairs that led to the bedroom. JP stood and followed her up.

"Nothing happened, you know."

"I know."

They reached the top of the stairs, turned right, and went into her bedroom.

"But I should have told you."

"Yeah. You should have." She closed the door behind them.

Chapter 54

Two Months Later...

Sabre sat on the bench outside of Department Four with Conway McFerran, who was pacing next to her. She marveled at how much Conway had matured in the last few months. He was no longer a kid.

"When did you get your cast off?"

"About ten days ago. I'm still doing some physical therapy, but it's getting stronger." Conway stood in front of Sabre and shifted from one foot to the other.

"Why don't you have a seat?" Sabre said.

Conway sat down. He clasped his hands together, intertwined his fingers, and moved them back and forth. "Do you really think it will go alright?"

"I'm sure it will. We have everything in place."

"Do you think she'll let you speak for me?"

"I think so, but if she doesn't, you'll do just fine. Just remember to stand when you talk to her and always say, 'Your Honor.'" Sabre smiled in an attempt to put him at ease, although she never knew for sure what Judge Hekman would do. She was a wild card, and although Sabre expected the judge to order the placement with Conway, she wasn't sure what else she might do. "Have you talked to the senator lately?"

"He called me this morning and apologized for not being able to be here for the hearing. It seems weird having an uncle. I've never had any other family besides my mom and my brothers and sisters."

"You never knew your grandmother?"

"I guess she was around some when I was a baby, but I don't remember her."

Sabre remembered from the case file that Brandy never knew who her father was and that her mother had overdosed on methamphetamines when Conway was about five years old. Richard Bullard and his family were the first extended family he had. Some of Conway's siblings had paternal grandparents or aunts and uncles, but none of them were in California.

The bailiff, Mike McCormick, came into the hallway and called the McFerran case. When Sabre saw the look on Conway's face, she said, "Just take deep breaths. It's all going to work out."

Sabre sat at the table next to Conway. On their right sat Bob and his client, Brandy. On their left were the social worker and Deputy County Counsel, Dave Casey.

"In re Conway McFerran," the court clerk called the case.

Sabre stood up. "Your Honor, as you know this is a 388 motion filed on behalf of my client, Conway McFerran. Since he is no longer a minor, we're asking that his petition be dismissed."

"Any objection?" the judge asked.

"No objection," the County Counsel and Bob both said.

"So ordered," Hekman said. "Ms. Brown, you are relieved as counsel.

"Thank you, Your Honor. I have also assisted Conway in his request for placement of the children with him, which we have filed with the court. I would ask that the court allow me to continue to represent him for this hearing only. The requests we are making are in the best interest of the other minors."

"Based on the request by Conway to have custody of his siblings, I think this is a small task for him to handle. Should I grant his request, what lies ahead will be much harder. You may remain here and represent the interests of the other children. I take it your position is that these children should be placed with their brother, is that correct?"

"Yes, Your Honor."

The judge looked at Conway. "Tell me, Conway, what have you done in the past to help raise your siblings?"

"I—" he started to say and then stopped and stood up. He continued, "I help them with their homework, and I ... I get them off to school when my mom isn't up. Sometimes she stays up late and can't get up early enough. I'm up anyway so I get their lunches and get them to school. I make sure they get to bed at night so they won't be too tired for school. If they get skinned up, they usually come to me to clean them up and put bandages on because Mom doesn't like blood ... uh ... Your Honor."

The judge frowned at Brandy. "And what does your mom do?"

"She buys clothes for the girls, Your Honor," he snapped back. "And she almost always cooks dinner at night. Dolly helps her a lot now that she's older."

"And you, do you cook?"

"Mostly breakfast, but I'll cook all their meals if you think I should." Again there was a pause before he added, "Your Honor."

"How are you going to go to school if you are taking care of your siblings?"

"I graduate from high school next week, Your Honor." He sighed. Sabre wondered if it was because he was relieved he remembered to use the judge's title or that high school was almost over.

"So you don't plan to go to college?"

"Yes, I do, Your Honor. I have been accepted into the University of San Diego. I will start in the fall, but I'll make sure my schedule works so that I can get the kids off to school."

The judge put her fingertips to her lips and nodded her head. "I'd rather see you get an education and have a somewhat normal college life."

"I plan to get a degree, and I want to go on to law school. I hope to be a politician like my uncle some day. If you'll let my brothers and sisters live with me, I will see that they all get good educations. I have plenty of money now, and I want to use it to give them and my mother a good home."

"Have you already received the money?"

"I have received some of it, Your Honor. I bought a five-bedroom home in a good part of town, and I bought a new car. It's a Honda Odyssey van."

"Did you pick out the car?"

"Yes." Pause. "Your Honor."

"Why did you pick that car instead of a sports car or something?"

"Because I need a car that seats seven people so we can all go places together. And the gas mileage is better than an SUV."

"You have a lot of money now. Have you taken any steps to make sure you don't just waste it?"

"Ms. Brown found a legal firm to set up a trust for me and a firm to help with investments, as well. Also, my uncle, the senator, is helping me too. They both put in a lot of safeguards so the money will be protected. I will receive enough to live on and to cover my education and when we need something, like when Travis is ready to go to college, we'll just need to apply for it."

"Conway, this is a huge responsibility you are asking for. Why would you want to do this?"

"I only have one family. They consist of my mother, who tries to do the best she can, and my four siblings. I know our mother stumbles sometimes, but we all love her. And I know she loves us. All we've ever had is each other, and our mother has made sure that we respect our family and put it above all else. We've never had much money or nice clothes or fancy cars. Sometimes we didn't have a lot to eat, but we've always had each other, and I hate that our family is torn apart now. It's hard on all the kids, especially Reba. She tries to act tough, but she's not really. I think I'm the best placement for my brothers and sisters, and if you will let my mother live with us, I promise you I will follow all your rules, Your Honor."

The judge turned to Brandy. "That's a fine young man you have raised. With all your bad choices, and I have seen plenty, you have done something right or he wouldn't be who he is today. For that I commend you." She paused. "On the other hand, if I allow you to stay with your children under Conway's care, you have to follow the rules as well. Do you think you can do that?"

"Yes, ma'am," Brandy said. "I sure can."

Bob stood up. "Your Honor, my client has been in parenting classes since she was released from custody six weeks ago. She has been cleared of all criminal charges, she is in therapy to deal with her co-dependency issues and whatever else she needs, and she has been looking for work."

"Acting work?"

"No, Your Honor. She's looking for restaurant work, office work, or anything she can find that will provide her income."

"I have a better idea," Judge Hekman said. "Before I make my orders, I'd like to hear from County Counsel. I see the social worker is recommending placement with Conway with the mother living in the home. Is that still your recommendation?"

"Yes, Your Honor," Casey said. "We think that is the best placement for the children, and as long as the mother continues in her programs, we would like to see her living with them. She understands that she cannot have any man living with her."

"Is that clear?" the judge asked Brandy.

"Yes, ma'am. I'm no longer with Doug. One of the things I'm working on in therapy is to make better choices about the men in my life."

When the judged paused, Deputy County Counsel spoke up. "We also have an affidavit from Senator Richard Bullard that we would like to file with the court. He's stating that if the court is willing to place the children with Conway, he will help in any way that he can." Casey stood up and brought the affidavit along with copies to the court clerk, who stamped them and handed a copy to the judge.

"Have you had any contact with the senator?" Hekman asked Conway.

"Yes, we talk on the phone about once a week, and he has invited me to go there for a visit this summer if I can. Of course, I wouldn't leave my brothers and sisters if they're placed with me."

"I'm glad to hear that. The senator seems to be a good man." The judge looked at County Counsel. "I know the grandmother was arrested for her part in the paternity test fraud. What is her status?"

"She took a plea, received one year probation, and fifty hours of community service."

The judge rolled her eyes. Sabre covered her mouth to keep anyone from seeing her smirk at the judge's inability to hide her feelings. Bob winked at Sabre but kept a straight face.

"Conway, you are an exceptional young man," Hekman said. "I would like to see you go off to college somewhere and study to your heart's content, maybe see what it is like to be an eighteen-year-old single man instead of a father of four." Conway looked at

Sabre with wide, fearful eyes; his shoulders slumped. The judge continued. "But I truly believe that would break your heart and you wouldn't be able to enjoy your life. I also think you are what is best for these children. So I'm going to place the children with you in your new home." Conway's whole face lit up. "I want you to have some help with the children so you can go to school. You could hire a nanny; I'm sure the funds for that would be approved. But instead, I am going to allow your mother to live in your home and take care of the children. That can be her job and you can give her room and board, and you can pay her what would amount to an allowance. I don't want it to be extravagant, so I'm going to ask the attorneys on this case to name a reasonable amount to cover her necessities and give her a little spending money. Does that work for you, Ms. McFerran?" She looked at Brandy when she asked.

"Yes, ma'am," Brandy said.

The judge glanced at Conway and then focused on Brandy. "You will cook all the meals and you will see that the children get to school every day on time. You will help them with their homework when you can and only enlist Conway's help when you do not understand the material." Brandy shook her head in agreement as the judge spoke. "And you will not bring any man home to your house to meet your children until you have dated him for at least four months, and he will not stay the night as long as this case is open. Do you understand and accept those conditions?"

"Yes, ma'am," Brandy said.

"So ordered," the judge said. She looked directly at Conway. "I hate to put you in a position to police your mother, but I get the feeling this is not a first for you. If she does not follow the orders, you'll need to report to the social worker. I think your mom has learned her lesson, but if she hasn't and you allow her misconduct, you could lose the children. Do you understand?"

Conway was still beaming. He couldn't contain his glee. "Yes, ma'am. I mean, Your Honor."

"Ms. Brown will be a good source for you since she will still be representing the children. I know she'll be dropping in often to check on them. The social worker will also be making regular visits. In six months, we'll have a review hearing, and if your mother has done what is required, custody may be returned to her. If she has not, we may need to consider some other permanent plan. That would most likely be with you as long as you follow the court's orders." The judge looked at the social worker. "Please try to make some arrangement for the children so Conway can go spend a little time with his newly found uncle. He needs to get to know his family."

"Will do, Your Honor," County Counsel responded for the social worker.

The court clerk set a review hearing date and they all left the courtroom.

"Hekman came through this time, didn't she?" Bob said to Sabre.

"She sure did. I was a little nervous there at first."

Conway asked, "When can my brother and sisters come home?"

"Right now," Sabre said. "The social worker has already made the arrangements. She prepared the foster parents just in case. You can go help your mother get her things from where she's been living, and the social worker will take Travis and the girls home in about an hour."

Conway put his arm around his mother's shoulder, still wearing his big grin. "Come on, Mom, let's go home."

About the Author

Teresa Burrell has dedicated her life to helping children and their families. Her first career was spent teaching elementary school in the San Bernardino City School District. As an attorney, Ms. Burrell has spent countless hours working pro bono in the family court system. For twelve years she practiced law in San Diego Superior Court, Juvenile Division. She continues to advocate children's issues and write novels, many of which are inspired by actual legal cases.

Teresa Burrell is available at www.teresaburrell.com
Keep in touch with her on Facebook at
www.facebook.com/theadvocateseries

What did you think of
THE ADVOCATE'S GEOCACHE?
Please send an email to Teresa and let her know.
She can be reached at:
teresa@teresaburrell.com